As Mike Manning grieves ov
lover, NY police officer Ken F
socialite Mildred Hamilton who ~~........~~ ~~..~~ ~~.....~~ ~~...~~
husband and his girlfriend. Drawn into a double murder on
a snowy New Year's Eve takes Mike from a Fifth Avenue
penthouse to a gay strip bar, a ride on a corporate jet and,
finally, to two humpy preppies who do their best to change
Mike's grief into unabashed passion. Many private lives go
public before Mike uncovers THE MASK OF NARCISSUS
to reveal the face of a murderer.

MLR PRESS AUTHORS

Featuring a roll call of some of the best writers of gay erotica and mysteries today!

Derek Adams	Z. Allora	Maura Anderson
Victor J. Banis	Jeanne Barrack	Laura Baumbach
Ally Blue	J.P. Bowie	Barry Brennessel
Michael Breyette	Nowell Briscoe	Jade Buchanan
James Buchanan	Charlie Cochrane	Karenna Colcroft
Jamie Craig	Kirby Crow	Ethan Day
Diana DeRicci	Jason Edding	Theo Fenraven
Angela Fiddler	S.J. Frost	Kimberly Gardner
Michael Gouda	Roland Graeme	Storm Grant
Amber Green	LB Gregg	Kaje Harper
Jan Irving	David Juhren	Thomas Kearnes
Kiernan Kelly	M. King	Matthew Lang
J.L. Langley	Josh Lanyon	Vincent Lardo
Anna Lee	Elizabeth Lister	Clare London
William Maltese	Z.A. Maxfield	Timothy McGivney
Lloyd A. Meeker	Patric Michael	AKM Miles
Reiko Morgan	Jet Mykles	William Neale
Cherie Noel	Willa Okati	Neil S. Plakcy
Jordan Castillo Price	Luisa Prieto	Rick R. Reed
A.M. Riley	AJ Rose	Rob Rosen
George Seaton	Jardonn Smith	Caro Soles
JoAnne Soper-Cook	DH Starr	Richard Stevenson
Liz Strange	Marshall Thornton	Lex Valentine
Maggie Veness	Haley Walsh	Missy Welsh
Stevie Woods	Lance Zarimba	Mark Zubro

Check out titles, both available and forthcoming, at
www.mlrpress.com

THE MASK OF NARCISSUS

VINCENT LARDO

mlrpress

www.mlrpress.com

Published by
MLR Press, LLC
3052 Gaines Waterport Rd.
Albion, NY 14411

Visit ManLoveRomance Press, LLC on the Internet:
www.mlrpress.com

Cover Art by Deana C. Jamroz
Editing by Neil Plakcy

Print format ISBN# 978-1-60820-529-5
ebook format ISBN#978-1-60820-530-1

Issued 2011

spelling test.

"NARCISSISM."

 his mind wondered. finally,

it was smugly shaped to the English language.

intuition. no small wonder.

some and not many years later,

looking at his own hand

[the growing lines and elegant muscles]

he would imagine the only touch that might move him.

—JStill

New York is a late town and on New Year's Eve it becomes an even later town. At 7 p.m. on this December 31st, upper Fifth Avenue, except for a scattering of smartly dressed people leaving and entering cabs and limousines, was deserted. It would remain deserted because the rich, as a rule, do not like crowds.

"Have a nice evening, Mr. Manning." The driver turned to look at his passenger, flagging down the cab's digital meter as he spoke. Having verbally been presented with the celebrity's equivalent of the Nobel prize — recognition — Mike Manning responded in kind by waving away the offered change for his five dollar bill. The meter read two dollars and eighty cents. Both were hard core New Yorkers and as such knew by instinct the etiquette necessary for survival in their natural habitat. Give and take…the object being to take a lot more than you give. In this particular instance the cab driver was the momentary winner. However, before the evening was over a dozen hack drivers would be told that Mike Manning was a sport. In two days the fact would be common knowledge to every hack driver in the city and any of their passengers who cared to listen and take the hint. It's the kind of goodwill publicity that is unobtainable from the media at any price, but Mike Manning had just purchased it for two dollars and twenty cents. Mike had lost the first round but would ultimately win the game. Mike Manning usually did. A strong wind blew from the west and carried with it the particular odors of the zoo across the street as well as a chill factor that was close to zero. Mike pulled the collar of his camel-hair coat tightly about his neck as he walked under the canopy which stretched from the curb to the building it graced. The ancient keeper of the door, warm and snug behind his insulated glass post, saw him approach and opened the door just in time for Mike to enter the lobby without breaking his cadence.

"Good evening, Mr. Manning." Mike flashed the old man his most insincere smile. The corners of his mouth jerked upward and his eyes squinted in myopic fashion. A moment later the old man was gazing at the back of a camel-hair coat draped over the frame of a tall, muscular body. Mike had not been deliberately rude. He knew that a simple, "How are you Joe?" would bring forth a detailed account of the old man's diseased lungs and his need, stymied by a lack of cash, to move to a warmer climate. As he retreated Mike was keenly aware of the old man's eyes boring into the back of his neck.

Counsel: "Did Mr. Manning visit the Burke residence often?"

Joe: "I wouldn't say (cough) often."

Counsel: "But often enough for you to recognize him."

Joe: "Yes, (cough) sir."

Counsel: "And did he pay a call on Mrs. Burke on the evening of December 31st at approximately seven p.m.?"

Joe: "Yes, sir, he did."

Counsel: "And did you notice anything unusual about Mr. Manning on that particular occasion?"

Joe: "Well, sir (cough) I would say he was somewhat abrupt."

Counsel: "Abrupt?"

Joe: "Yes, sir (cough) we usually pass the time of day, Mr. Manning and me, but that evening Mr. Manning was (cough) abrupt."

The elevator door stood open but the attendant was conspicuously absent. As Mike entered the car he remembered that the cooperative had elected to forego the luxury of twenty-four hour attended elevator service in favor of one shift, from 10 p.m. to 6 a.m., the official working hours of most New York thieves. Even the rich were feeling the pinch of inflation.

Mike pressed the button marked seventeen. The elevator door closed and the lift began to rise. It was really very simple. When the elevator stopped Mike exited and walked a straight line to the only door on the seventeenth floor. Opening it he entered a large, marble-floored foyer, sparsely but elegantly furnished and mirrored from floor to ceiling. Ignoring the infinite number of Mike Mannings which now accompanied him he crossed the marble floor and, turning left, stepped into a room the size of which a family of four would be content to call home.

Mike's eyes moved down the length of the room and came to rest on Mrs. Stephen Burke, née Mildred Hamilton. Milly, seated in the corner of a couch especially built for the vast space it occupied and under a sixteen-foot-high ceiling, looked like a miniature representation of an adult female. She was framed by a picture window which presented a scene as black and forlorn as the park it overlooked. Even the lighted apartment buildings on Central Park West resembled a slightly blurred rendition of a pen and ink sketch on this dark, winter night.

The room, with its mahogany fireplace, dark wood-beamed ceiling and huge pieces of ugly, Empire furniture, reflected as much warmth and charm as a baronial castle. Milly was wearing a simple black dress, the kind Mike Manning never tired of describing as a simple black dress. Her eyes were red and swollen. In one hand she held a rock glass filled with Scotch and no rocks. Her other hand held a cigarette.

As Mike walked into the room he was tempted to ask, "Where's the body?" but under the circumstances the quip would be in very bad taste, indeed. Instead he opened with,

"Drinking is not going to help." Then he glanced at an ashtray filled with the remains of at least a pack of filtered cigarettes and added,

"Neither is smoking." Milly watched him approach. The hand holding the cigarette shook and a long, white shell of ash fell onto the plush carpet.

"I don't need a lecture," Milly responded.

"You don't need more Scotch, either." Mike took the glass from Milly's hand and put it on the coffee table which fronted the couch.

"Where?" he asked, making a deliberate effort to place a question mark after the one word.

"I'm glad you're here, Mike," she said, trying to sound

relieved and failing miserably. Mike acknowledged this with an almost imperceptible nod of his head. Then she whispered, "In the bedroom." Mike turned and retraced his steps, passing the foyer with its mirrored walls, down a long hall until he came to a closed door on his left.

Without hesitation, he opened the door and entered the master bedroom suite. The room was large enough to hold two king-size beds and an array of American antique furniture of museum quality. The room's prime colors were blue and white... cheerful colors which could not cheer the two bodies that lay sprawled between the twin beds.

Mike moved into the room for a closer look. Before taking over the society column of the New York *Ledger* from a deposed Count who knew all the right people but none of the right words to describe their antics, he had been a first-rate crime reporter for the same newspaper. Mike had tackled that job in the same manner with which he approached everything in life: a determined will to succeed. Corpses — whole, mutilated and in various stages of decay — were not a new sight to the *Ledger's* society editor.

He looked at the two bodies in the blue and white room with a callous detachment his crime reporting days had taught him. His story, without emotion or opinion, began to form in his mind as the critical eye of the reporter took in every detail of what lay before him. Stephen Burke was lying on his back, stark naked, parallel to the beds.

Most men would have looked ridiculous, even obscene, to be exposed thusly in death. Stephen Burke looked beautiful. The longish blond hair, always in a state of studied disarray, fell like corn-silk across his forehead. The face, with its perfect complexion, square jaw and high cheekbones, looked tranquil in repose and there was even a hint of a smile on the thin lips. The eyes, had they been open, would have revealed a dazzling shade of blue; a perfect match for the room's color scheme and, Mike had always suspected, not by coincidence.

The shoulders were broad, the chest full and masculine and

covered with down a shade or two darker than the white-blond hair on the head. The smooth, tanned skin was broken only by the small red hole which appeared directly over the area of Stephen Burke's heart. Mike was surprised that so little blood flowed from the fatal wound.

Next, the flat, hard stomach and then Stephen Burke's most celebrated attribute met Mike's eyes. The degree of celebrity it was accorded depended, to be sure, on what end of the give-and take line the rater was currently on. However, true cognoscenti had long ago awarded it an eleven on a scale of one to ten.

The sturdy, masculine legs were a familiar sight to Mike. He had seen them often in tennis shorts, bathing trunks and beneath the hem of a variety of cashmere dressing robes. This reminder of Stephen Burke's wardrobe caused Mike to quickly survey the bedroom. Where were Burke's clothes? There was not one personal article of male clothing visible in the room. But there was a pile of female attire stacked at the foot of the bed furthest from where Mike stood.

Their owner lay at a perfect right angle to the body of Stephen Burke, her head almost touching his waist and forming with him the letter T. For together?...tragedy?...Mike discarded the idea almost as soon as it occurred.

The lady was more modestly attired in a pair of yellow bikini panties. Mike was ready to wager his typewriter that the hair under the bikini was darker than the blond, curly hair on the lady's head. She was a pretty girl, not more than twenty, with a narrow waist and full breasts which rose proudly from her now stilled chest. The nipples were dark and pointed.

Her face, upside-down from Mike's point of view, was cute rather than beautiful. The hole over her left eyebrow didn't help her cause. Blood had turned her forehead and nose a brownish red. On impulse Mike walked across the room to the bed which held the girl's clothing. With one finger he pushed back the collar of a white blouse and read the label. If the lady was a hooker she belonged to the sisterhood's upper echelons.

Mike looked at the body, now right-side up, again. The girl

looked more Vassar than Eighth Avenue. He took a deep breath and started for the door. On the other bed, in the center of the blue satin spread, he saw the gun. How like Milly, tossing it like a hair brush or magazine she had no further use for. There had always been a maid to pick up after Mildred Hamilton Lakewood Burke. Well, not this time, Milly…not this time.

Mike took off his coat as he re-entered the baronial living room. Under it he wore a blue blazer over a white turtleneck sweater. His grey flannel trousers completed the picture *GQ* would have been proud to run on its cover. Manning was six foot one, with a full head of brown hair, green eyes and the kind of regular, clean-cut features that made it possible for him to work his way through the Columbia School of Journalism as a male model. The agency that employed him had begged him to stay in the business, but once he got his degree Mike wisely left the fickle modeling world for a job as cub reporter for the *Ledger* and had never regretted this decision. There's a time for everything and the smart crowd knows when the time for moving on has arrived.

He still did some modeling, but now it was strictly for endorsements. Cigarettes, liquor, sports cars and anything else fancied by those who liked to spend and had the cash to do so. It was a fast, easy buck and Mike Manning liked to live fast, easy and expensively. All things considered it worked .. and what worked was good in Manning's book.

He dropped his coat on the couch and reached for the drink he had taken from Milly Burke. Milly stared at him as he swallowed the liquor and Mike wondered if the new widow was drunk or in a state of shock.

"Did you call the police?" he asked.

"No."

"Why the hell not?"

"I didn't know what to tell them."

"You didn't know what to tell them?" Mike almost shouted. "Milly, I can't see how one could make an ambiguous statement about what's in the bedroom."

A faint smile appeared on Milly's face. It was the first sign of animation she had displayed since Mike's arrival.

"Are you all right?" he asked.

"Yes," she answered, "now that you're here." The expression on her face reflected neither humility nor embarrassment. It was a simple statement of fact.

"Why did you do it, Milly?"

"You saw the scene in the bedroom and you have to ask why?"

"Stephen Burke *in flagrante?* I've seen that scene a thousand times and so have you."

"But never in our home." Milly sounded adamant. Mike again reached for the glass of Scotch and sipped as he thought. Was this going to be the line of defense? The wandering husband piling up straw after straw until finally the straw that broke the wife's sanity? Not very good but, God knows, he had heard worse.

"And with a friend of the family," Milly added, speaking so softly that Mike, lost in his own thoughts, almost missed it. He put down the glass and picked up a cigarette.

"Who is she, Milly?"

"A friend of Kevin's."

"Kevin! Christ…where is he?"

"At a party."

"This early?"

Milly shook her head as she spoke. "He went out early and then was going on from there. I don't understand the very young, Mike, and have given up trying."

"The police aren't going to ask for a philosophical accounting of your relationship with your son, Milly. They're going to want the facts."

"May I have a cigarette?" she asked.

"Go ahead, they're yours." Her hand seemed much steadier as she lit the cigarette.

"There's a party tonight…here in the city, I suppose. Kevin drove out to the Island to pick up a friend…Brad, I think…yes, Bradley Turner…he was going to have dinner with Brad and then drive in for the party." She looked at Mike as if silently asking if he were satisfied.

"Were you home all day?" Mike continued, ignoring the look and its implication.

"No, I went out to do some shopping around four this afternoon."

"When did you get back?"

"Six … I think."

"Kevin?"

"He was gone when I got back."

"So…

" Mike nodded toward the bedroom.

"Susan Kennedy," Milly answered the unspoken question. "She's a friend of Kevin's. I don't know where they met."

"So Susan must have arrived between the time Kevin left and you arrived."

"I would imagine…yes."

"Tell me exactly what you did from the minute you entered the apartment."

"Well," Milly began slowly,

"I didn't think there was anyone here…"

"Where's your housekeeper?" Mike interrupted.

"Betty is off for the holiday. She's gone to her daughter's in New Jersey, I suppose. That's where she usually goes."

"Go on," Mike prompted.

"I put some packages down in here, hung up my coat in the hall closet and…and then I heard sounds coming from there." She pointed in the general direction of the bedroom without looking that way.

"I was afraid. I told you I didn't think there was anyone at home. I started for the bedroom and then I remembered the gun. We keep it in that drawer." She nodded at a refectory table which flanked the wall at the opposite end of the long room.

"Why?" Mike asked.

"Why did I take the gun?"

"No…why do you keep one in the house?"

"For protection, I guess…I don't know, Mike. We've had it for years."

"Okay…go on."

"I took the gun from the drawer and went to investigate." She spoke very rapidly now. "I opened the bedroom door and there they were. I lost my head and fired. That's it, Mike." One between the eyes and one directly into the heart. Not bad for someone who had just lost her head. Mike wondered what Milly would be like on a firing range when she had her wits about her. He began to pace the width of the room.

"It doesn't make sense, Milly."

"It's what happened."

"What was she doing here…on New Year's Eve? Kevin obviously didn't invite her, and did Steve think you were gone for the day or did he know you had just gone to do some shopping?"

"I told him where I was going," she answered.

"So why did he take what's-her-name into the bedroom for a quick screw knowing that you would return any minute?"

"You know Steve," she replied.

"Knew, Milly, knew…he's dead. And I knew him very well. He was as sharp as a fox and twice as cunning. He would never pull a stunt like that."

"Well he did…and I did…and if you don't believe it go back into the bedroom and have another look." Milly's voice was a pitch below total hysteria.

"I'm sorry, Milly. I didn't mean to badger you but the police will. And they won't stop if you get hysterical."

"But why? There's nothing for them to prove or disprove. I did it and that's that."

"That's not that," Mike answered, shaking his head.

"There's going to be a trial and at a trial all the facts are going to be laid out for a jury of your peers and those facts have to add up. What you just told me does not add up to the two bodies on the bedroom floor."

"Do you want me to lie?"

"God, no…the truth sounds bad enough. And where the hell are Steve's clothes?"

Milly raised her eyebrows.

"His clothes, Milly, there's not a sign of them in the bedroom."

"I don't know. He took them off, naturally. One usually does."

"One usually does, yes, but one does not usually put them all away in closet and drawer, including socks and underpants. Your husband was casual with his affairs but that would be carrying nonchalance to the point of comedy."

"I don't know," Milly repeated. "I wasn't there for the warm-up."

Mike crushed his cigarette in the overflowing ashtray.

"Why did she come here on New Year's Eve? Did she know Steve?"

"She might have met him. Yes, I guess she had. And I told you I don't know what she was doing here."

Mike shrugged his broad shoulders and helped himself to more Scotch. "Let's take it from the top. A friend of your son's calls on New Year's Eve, unannounced, is greeted by your son's stepfather, in the nude I guess, and ten minutes later friend and daddy prepare for a toss in the hay." He looked at Milly and she stared back, her lips drawn in a straight line. Mike shrugged again, sighed and continued.

"Was she having an affair with Steve? They seemed to have

gotten down to the nitty-gritty in record time."

"Steve was a fast worker."

"Not that fast, Milly not that fast. Were they having an affair?"

"I don't know."

"Would Kevin know?"

"Ask Kevin."

"I won't, but the police will."

"Kevin has nothing to do with this." Milly's voice rose an octave.

"And what did you think…what did you feel when you saw them. Did you just raise the gun and bang, bang? You're not the type, Milly. My God, what were you thinking?"

"I was thinking I had had it." Her voice continued its upward climb. "I was thinking I had goddamned well fucking had it, that's what I was thinking." And then she broke down. Her head fell into her hands and she began to sob, long heavy sobs that echoed sorrow and anger, frustration and despair, sobs which told more clearly why two bodies lay on the bedroom floor of a fourteen-room apartment high over fashionable Fifth Avenue than had her precise answers to Mike Manning's questions.

"I'm sorry," Mike whispered. Milly shook her head and answered without looking up.

"It's not you…it's not you." When she raised her face to reveal again the red, swollen eyes, her cheeks were bone dry. There had been no tears left to shed. "I just wanted it to be over and done with…and now it is."

Wanted what to be over and done with…the marriage? Divorce is certainly simpler than murder. And, if one could measure such things, one murder is simpler than two.

"Why the girl?" Mike spoke this final thought aloud.

"Why not?" Milly let out a short, hysterical laugh.

"I don't know, Mike…I was crazy, that's why. Temporary insanity, isn't that what it's called?" Mike looked at the Tiffany clock on the mahogany mantle. It was almost seven-thirty.

"What time did it happen?"

"Six…six thirty…"

"Over an hour and the police haven't been notified. I'm going to have to call them, Milly."

The woman nodded.

Mike reached for another cigarette and thought aloud. "I'm worried."

"About what?"

"Everything…what she was doing here…Steve's clothes… you…everything, Milly."

"Would it make you and the police happy if I went in there and dumped his entire wardrobe all over the damn room?"

"Christ, no. Don't touch a thing."

"Mike, if I had staged it all the facts would mesh. But I didn't and they don't. I don't know where his clothes are or why she came here. It happened just as I told you it did."

She's right, Mike thought. The perfect set-up or alibi is always suspect. Reality contains neither perfection not logic. Perhaps that was the point that was worrying Mike. Milly's story was too perfect because it was complete with imperfections. He recalled how quickly and accurately she had described the entire shoddy scene. Had she rehearsed it? Of course…she had almost an hour to think of nothing else before Mike's arrival. This last thought moved him directly to the telephone.

"Get me the 19th precinct, this is an emergency…if I wanted nine-one-one I would have dialed nine-one-one…no, I don't want an ambulance, just connect me with the 19th precinct, please. This is Mike Manning. I'm at the home of Mr. and Mrs.…of Mrs. Stephen Burke, 830 Fifth Avenue. There's been an accident. Could you send a couple of men here at once…if I wanted nine-one-one I would have dialed nine-one-one…no, I don't want an ambulance, it's too late for that…look, sergeant, there's been an accident and two people are dead of unnatural causes, now would you please get someone here as quickly as possible."

Mike put down the phone and turned to Milly Burke.

"Go ahead, Mike."

"I feel like a damn fool."

"Why? It's your job. Go ahead, I'll try not to listen." She stood up and headed for the liquor cabinet, certain Mike wouldn't criticize her a moment after she had been so gracious to him. Mike picked up the phone and dialed again. When the connection went through he spoke into the mouthpiece with the assurance of one who knows exactly what he wants and how to get it.

"Harry?...Mike...get your pencil and pad, take down everything I say and don't interrupt...there's no time. Ready?" Mike's opening line contained, in one sentence, the gospel of journalism...Who, What, Where, When.

"Stephen...that's S-T-E-P-H-E-N...Burke was shot to death in the bedroom of his posh Fifth Avenue apartment at six p.m. on New Year's Eve. Lying next to Burke's nude body was a second victim of this crime of passion; beautiful, blond socialite Susan Kennedy. Ms. Kennedy was clad in a pair of yellow bikini panties. Mrs. Stephen Burke, née Mildred Hamilton and formerly married to Kevin Lakewood, has confessed to the double murder.

"Burke, born Steven...that's S-T-E-V-E-N...Burkowski in Astoria, Queens made headlines in...check the date, Harry... when he eloped with heiress Mildred Hamilton Lakewood. Milly Hamilton, only child of the late millionaire Russell Hamilton, made her debut in New York society in...check the date, Harry... and a year later married the socially prominent sportsman, Kevin Lakewood. They had one child, Kevin junior, and Milly was widowed in...check the date, Harry...when Kevin Lakewood died of a heart attack at the young age of thirty-eight.

"It has often been rumored, and the story persists, that Burkowski was chauffeur to Mildred Hamilton Lakewood. In fact, Burkowski was employed by a limousine service based in Long Island City. In this capacity he often chauffeured Mrs. Lakewood but was never on her personal payroll.

"Shortly before eloping with Milly, Burkowski changed the spelling of his first name and shortened his second name to become Stephen Burke. The couple moved in a society peopled by the rich, the famous, the beautiful, the Ins of the moment... take out Ins, Harry, and put in celebrated. This lifestyle was maintained because of Burke's ambitions and not Milly's desire. Add, it has long been thought, to that last sentence, Harry.

"The extraordinarily handsome Burke was the quintessential playboy whom wife and stepson were never able to domesticate. Stephen Burke had an eye for the ladies and the ladies never seemed to tire of Stephen Burke. One could say the circumstances of his death accurately summarize the story of his life...

"That's it for the early edition. I'll send you a more detailed version for the later editions and, Harry, tell them to kill the front page photo of Times Square at midnight and dig up one of Burke in a bathing suit. That should be easy to come by...I told you, Harry, no questions...of course it's an exclusive, the police don't even know about it yet."

"You do your job very well," Milly said when Mike put down the phone.

"That doesn't make doing it any easier."

"But it had to be done and I'd rather you did it than some hack or sob sister."

"Oh, my little exclusive is just the beginning, Milly. This is going to be bigger than your elopement."

"Murder wins out over love."

"It usually does. It's so much more permanent." Milly smiled and held out her hand. He moved toward her and took the offered hand in his.

"I wish I could say I was sorry, Milly, but I'm not. I hated the bastard."

"That makes it unanimous."

She moved closer to him and his arms encircled her ; her small body pressed tightly against his.

"It could have been different, Mike."

"Yeah," he grinned over her head, "that could be me on the bedroom floor."

"Never, Mike, never…we would have made it work."

"I doubt it, Milly," he sighed, "it's easy to think it would after the fact."

"When this is over…"

The house phone rudely interrupted their conversation with a loud, persistent buzz.

"Over? Christ, Milly, it's just beginning."

2

She pressed a piece of paper into his hand. "My lawyer's name and phone number. Call him and tell him what's happened."

Mike glanced at the small sheet of lined pad paper and wasn't surprised to see the name of one of New York's most prominent and most social attorneys.

"Saxman…and on New Year's Eve…that's not going to be easy, Milly."

"I know you can do it." She spoke with great urgency, as if mentally racing her words against the elevator they both knew had already begun its ascent from the lobby.

"And Kevin…"

"What about Kevin?" Mike joined in the race.

"Find him and keep him with you until we know what's going to happen to me. The *paparazzi* will have this building surrounded night and day and I don't want them to get at him. He might say something…do something foolish. He's so young, Mike."

"We can't keep him under wraps forever."

"Just for now, Mike. Please, for me."

"How do I find him?"

"Call the Turners…they live in Sands Point on the Island. They might know where the party is tonight. Please, Mike, for me…"

And then all hell broke loose. It began as Mike hurried through the mirrored foyer and vowed to himself that he would not become personally involved with the death of Stephen Burke. The harder Milly tried to drag him into the unfolding drama the tighter he would cling to his spectator's front row seat. He had been called in as a friend of the family and would fulfill Milly's two requests…but that was all. From this point on he was a working reporter, on the scene to observe and report, objectively and dispassionately, on behalf of his readers. Feeling noble he opened the front door and saw his resolution evaporate even before the New Year had officially begun.

"You," Detective Inspector Andrew Brandt grunted and somehow managed to express more dislike than surprise in that single pronoun. Mike felt himself being yanked from his comfortable front row seat and shoved onto the center of the stage. He immediately assumed the role of butler and with a courtly mock bow pointed the way to the scene of the crime. Brandt, his face still glowing from the cold and his blond hair all but covering his vivid blue eyes, looked like an angry Norse God. He dug his hands into the pockets of the tweed coat that hung from his broad shoulders and grunted again as he marched past Mike.

The Inspector was followed by a patrolman in uniform who smiled a weak apology at the country's most celebrated newsman and then blushed as Mike responded with a reassuring wink. The patrolman almost tripped over himself as he hurried to keep up with his chief. A few minutes later Brandt came into the living room, glanced at Milly and without asking permission picked up the phone and dialed. He mumbled into the mouthpiece, hung up and started toward the woman sitting on the long couch.

"You don't have to say anything," Mike cautioned before Brandt had a chance to speak.

"Are you her lawyer?" Brandt asked.

"I'm her friend."

"You don't know the meaning of the word." Mike took a step forward, hesitated, and then retreated by turning his back on Brandt.

"I have nothing to say, officer," Milly whispered. Nestled once again in the corner of the couch and looking up at the two tall men who flanked her, Milly Burke looked more diminutive than ever. Her auburn hair, cut short and loosely curled, had suddenly lost its body and now hung limply about her pretty face. She had long been considered one of the most attractive matrons in New

York society and could easily pass for a decade younger than her forty-odd years. But in the past few hours she appeared to have added ten years to her true age. There were deep shadows under her brown eyes, her pale cheeks looked hollow and her mouth was drawn tightly in an unattractive downward curve.

"I prefer to wait for my lawyer," Milly added in a louder tone.

"Saxman," Mike said, his back still to Brandt. "You better get out your heavy artillery."

Ignoring Mike the detective said to Milly Burke, "I wasn't going to question you, Mrs. Burke. I know better than that. A doctor will be arriving with my men and if you need anything I'm sure he'll oblige."

"Thank you, officer." And a few minutes later the apartment was swarming with men, the promised doctor and one policewoman who dutifully took her place next to the new widow. Mike had seen the scene many times before and even noticed a few familiar faces among the group that moved with a remarkable efficiency between the big, baronial living room and the master bedroom suite.

Photographers, print men, a bright young man wearing rimless glasses who recited, by rote, Milly Burke her rights and even a stenographer, complete with pencil and pad and fur hat now pushed far back on his balding head. The latter approached Mike along with a plain clothes man who looked like a prize fighter and went by the unlikely name of Cookie. "You got a statement for us, Mr. Manning?"

"I usually ask that question, Cookie."

Cookie ran a finger under his big, broken nose and wiped it on the sleeve of his top coat.

"Just like old times," Mike mumbled.

"Beg your pardon, Mr. Manning."

"Nothing, Cookie, just reminiscing. You were saying?"

"I need a statement," Cookie repeated. Mike looked at the steno and nodded. The man nodded back and Mike told his story as it happened from the time he received Milly's phone call to the moment Detective Inspector Brandt entered the apartment. "Got it?" The steno saluted Mike with his pencil.

"You know all the answers, Mr. Manning," Cookie said with an admiring glance at Mike.

"The answers don't mean dick, Cookie. It's the questions that count."

"What's that supposed to mean?"

"Think about it for a while," Mike responded as he handed the policeman a clean handkerchief, then made his way across the crowded room. Cookie, somewhat startled, looked at the handkerchief as if it contained all the right questions. A group of men, including Brandt, surrounded Milly Burke and Mike knew it would be impossible to speak to her. Instead, he found a small opening among the heavily coated masculine backs and catching Milly's eye he gave her a reassuring nod. She managed a brave smile and for one brief moment her eyes sparkled and then dimmed as she was once again drawn into her inquisitors' web. The policewoman stood rigidly next to the accused, her facial expression about as compassionate as a stone wall. Mike's heart went out to Mildred Burke.

"You want something?" Brandt asked.

"Just your permission to leave. Cookie has my statement."

"You've got it…along with my advice to stay out of this."

"Fuck you," Mike mouthed the words but they couldn't be clearer if he had spoken them aloud. Brandt smiled as he pushed the blond hair from his forehead.

"I can always get a rise out of you, Manning." The double entendre was implicit, not accidental, and was accentuated by the man's grinning face. Bastards are supposed to be ugly, not handsome, Mike thought as he forcefully broke their eye-to-eye contact and went in search of his top coat. He could hear Brandt laughing as he retreated.

The policeman who had arrived with Brandt was on duty in

the mirrored foyer. "Are you supposed to keep people in or out?" Mike quipped as he headed for the door.

"Both, I guess," the officer shrugged.

"Well, I'm on my way out."

"I wouldn't stop you, Mr. Manning."

Mike paused, his hand on the door knob. "You wouldn't stop me from doing what?"

The patrolman's face turned scarlet. "From…from doing… anything…I guess."

Mike laughed as he asked, "What's your name?"

"Sadowsky. Harold Sadowsky. S-A-D-O-W-S-K-Y. You gonna mention me, Mr. Manning?"

"You never know, Harold S-A-D-O-W-S-K-Y. You never know."

In the lobby Joe rushed toward him as soon as he stepped out of the elevator. "Mr. Manning…Jesus Christ…What's going on?…I…"

Mike marched passed the doorman without a backward glance. "I haven't got time now, Joe."

Joe followed him, coughing and waving his arms in the air. "But Mr. Manning…"

"Not now, Joe."

"But Mr. Manning…you gotta…" A cold blast of air carrying a spray of fine sleet greeted him as he opened the lobby door. The temperature must have fallen ten degrees in the past hour. A patrol car stood in front of the elegant building, the red light on its roof revolving to catch the icy rain which fell in white, criss-crossed streaks under its eerie glow. There were two uniformed men in the car. The one on the passenger side looked like Kenny.

Mike turned the collar of his camel-hair coat up and tucked his chin into his chest as he headed south on Fifth Avenue. Before he walked a block his hair was coated with a white glaze.

"Fuck Brandt," he muttered, the words escaping his lips in

white puffs of icy air. He stepped off the curb, a car horn blasted and his tan coat was painted with slush.

"Screw you, too," he shouted at two red tail lights. The cop in the patrol car didn't look like Kenny. It was Brandt's unrelenting vendetta and his own vivid imagination that had turned a face he could hardly see into one he could remember all too well. And it was only just beginning.

Mike could feel it as keenly as he felt the cold wind coloring his ears a numbing crimson. He would see Kenny every time he turned a corner, every time he flipped through the pages of a magazine and every night when he rested his head against his pillow. First the nagging doubt...then the guilt. The guilt he thought he had finally exorcised months ago. But Brandt wouldn't let it rest. Why? Because Brandt was right? No...Mike was not ready to concede to that.

A group of merrymakers got out of a cab in front of the Pierre and before the doorman could commandeer it Mike leaped into the back seat and gave the driver his address in the east Fifties. The car began to make its slow way down Fifth Avenue as Mike closed his eyes and rested his head against the leather upholstery. Why did Brandt's taunts sting like a well-aimed arrow? If Right was Might then Andrew Brandt was under the comforting wings of justice. So where did that leave Mike Manning...and what difference did it make? It left Kenny dead and that was all that mattered.

Before the burning sensation behind his eyes could erupt he was jostled back to the present by the cab driver's sudden exclamation..."Say...ain't you Mike Manning?"

Mike's apartment building was one of those rare gems of unpretentious graciousness which made every possible effort not to draw attention to itself and succeeded admirably. The lobby was small, the marble floor clean and the brass accents shined to a welcoming warmth. The elevator was big and mercifully unadorned. It was a fortress of the upper-middle class, that fast diminishing New York breed whose struggle to survive in midtown Manhattan is constantly being challenged by the very rich and the very poor.

His apartment was spacious and furnished to comfort, not impress. Nothing matched but everything blended. It was neat enough to be presentable and untidy enough to look happily lived in. It was, in short, a true reflection of its owner. The first thing he did was look at his watch. It was nine forty-five. Less than three hours ago he didn't know Stephen Burke had been murdered and had forgotten that Andrew Brandt even existed. He got out of his clothes and took a hot shower. He even shampooed his hair and thought, with a grin, of Lady Macbeth.

"All the perfumes of Arabia will not sweeten this little hand…"

Stark naked, he went into his small kitchen and put two ice cubes into a rock glass. These he covered with Jack Daniels, downed half the brew and again drowned the ice with liquor.

"What Lady Macbeth needed was bourbon, not perfume." He began to pat dry his body, that near-perfect masculine form which was a direct result of inherited genes and not daily visits to a gym. Mike Manning loathed exercise. His chest and belly were firm but smooth with only a fine line of hair running down from his navel and spreading into a small forest which surrounded the proud arc of his manhood.

As he wrapped himself in a comfortable robe he headed for the telephone. As expected, no one answered Samuel Saxman's phone ; not even an answering machine. Mike flipped through his file and dialed the number next to the name Stuart Symington. *The* Stuart Symington, whose grandfather had started a small discount store in upstate New York which he then parlayed into a chain of shops all over the state. Today Symington stores circled the globe and Stuart and his widow mother were the sole beneficiaries of granddaddy's thoughtfulness.

Stuart and Mike were old sparring partners. Their association went back to the days when Mike was a student and working for the model agency. Stuart had called his company's ad agency and told them to hire the model in the jean ad on page 32 of *Sports*

Illustrated for a Symington Co. photo layout. When Mike arrived at the Symington's Park Avenue duplex the first thing he did was ask where the photographer was. Stuart showed him a bed and Mike walked out the door. Symington Inc. was billed for the two hour minimum at a hundred fifty dollars an hour…and paid.

Stuart was still trying to collect his three hundred bucks' worth. Stuart Symington had managed to position himself as the last of the red-hot playboys and rumors concerning his life and loves were always making the rounds…from gay bars to board rooms to Park Avenue salons. Some were funny, others bordered on the macabre.

One had it that Stuart had a passion for policemen and that many of New York's finest, if they fitted the bill, moonlighted in the bed Mike Manning had turned his back on. Another told of an aspiring young actor who caught Stuart's eye and was invited for a weekend of fun and games at the Symington's Palm Beach mansion. Stuart returned on Monday morning…the other followed three days later in a pine box.

The official verdict was accidental death due to a drug overdose. The boy's friends swore the only thing he was on was an occasional glass of white wine. Stuart swore the boy was alive and well when he left him in Florida. There was an investigation of sorts but nothing ever came of it. Mike, whose work was nothing but rumor, reserved judgment but leaned toward giving Stuart the benefit of the doubt. Given the evidence, this was not easy.

"Stu? Mike Manning…I need a favor."

"From me? Nobody is that hard-up."

"I'm trying to track down Sam Saxman. Any ideas?"

"Why do you need a lawyer…and don't tell me to read all about it in that rag of yours."

"Personal business, Stu."

"We have some unfinished personal business."

"You have the mind of an elephant."

"And if I don't start dieting I'm going to have an ass like one. Why do you want Sam?"

"I told you, it's personal. Do you know where he is, or don't you?"

"Trish Naughton's. Aren't you going?"

"My invitation said eleven."

"So did mine. But that's just for us peasants. There's a sit-down dinner for the noblesse at eight. At eleven they bring in the clowns to amuse. For a gossip columnist you don't show me shit."

Ignoring the last comment Mike said, "Thanks, Stu. I owe you one."

"No, dear heart, you owe me three hundred."

"Oh, shit…"

Mike disconnected the line with one finger. He found the Naughton's number and dialed again. The butler answered and said that Mrs. Naughton was 'at table' and could not be disturbed.

"This is Mike Manning…disturb her." A good butler is like a breathing edition of the Social Register. He knows who to cut and who to butter. Mike Manning was in the latter category and Trish Naughton's butler was a good one. A minute later the lady was on the line.

"Yes, he's here, Mike, but why at this hour and on New Year's Eve?"

"Trish, take a deep breath. Stephen Burke is dead and Milly put him in that lamentable condition." What the hell, Mike thought, it would be all over the city in a couple of hours. The news was met with a marked silence.

"Trish? Are you still there?" And then he remembered. Trish Naughton had been one of Burke's many conquests and for all Mike knew the affair was still going on. Could she really have liked that bastard?

"Are you serious, Mike?"

"I'm afraid so, Trish."

"My God...hold on, I'll get Sam. How is Milly?"

"As well as can be expected under the circumstances." While he waited for Sam Saxman to come to the phone, Mike glanced out his window. The sleet had changed to a heavy snow and Kevin Lakewood was someplace out there. Funny, it was the first time he had thought of...

"Is she crazy, Mike?" The tension in Samuel Saxman's voice meant nothing. He always sounded like an actor portraying Clarence Darrow.

"Afraid not, Sam. Did Trish make a grand announcement to all assembled?"

"Let's say she played it for all it's worth. Her party will be a stunning success, isn't that what you usually say? Where's Milly?"

"The 19th. Can you get right over there?"

"I'm on my way."

"Thanks, Sam. She's counting on you."

"She should have listened to me when I told her to dump the fucker the day after she married him. The bastard is all cock and no heart...you know what I mean, Mike?"

"Was, Sam...not is...Stephen Burke is dead."

The Turners of Sands Point were listed with information. A slightly drunk Mr. Turner picked up on the first ring. The noise in the background told him the Turners were getting it on for New Year's Eve.

"Hold on, I'll get my wife." And then, lower, but still audible, "A friend of Brad's pretending to be Mike Manning. Who knows what he wants...you talk to him."

"Mrs. Turner? This is Mike Manning...yes, really, Mike Manning. I have to get in touch with Kevin Lakewood...it's very urgent or I wouldn't be bothering you...I understand he's with your son and I was hoping you might know where the party is they're attending tonight."

"Kevin told me you were a friend of his mother's. How exciting. Is anything wrong, Mr. Manning?"

"Nothing that would concern you…or your son. Do you know where the boys are, Mrs. Turner?"

"As a matter of fact, I do. Victoria Yates' daughter is giving the party tonight. I went to school with Victoria you know and…"

"What's the address, Mrs. Turner?" She gave him an address in the east Seventies and Mike hung up with a polite but firm thank you.

He sat at his typewriter and pounded out a detailed story of Stephen Burke's death. It contained all the facts, an element of the 'sob sister' genre of journalism and promised that better and more exciting news would follow. Harold Sadowsky would see his name in print on the first day of the new year.

Mike Manning was very good at his job. He called the *Ledger* and told them to send a messenger for the copy. Looking out the window again he noted that the storm was worsening. Getting a cab would be next to impossible. He called a car service he often used and was told that anything was possible for Mr. Manning.

He decided on a tux because he didn't want to arrive at the Yates' party and stand out like a sore thumb. What he had to do was move in quickly and get Kevin Lakewood out as quietly as possible. A black chesterfield coat with velvet collar and a white silk scarf completed the image of urban sophistication.

He left his copy for the *Ledger* with the doorman in the lobby and stepped outside. The snow was blinding, but not blinding enough to hide the ten-year-old Chevy Impala the service had sent for him. But it had wheels, and that's what he had ordered.

3

When Mike Manning had taken over the society page of the *Ledger* some ten years earlier it was a tired, seldom read section of an otherwise popular newspaper. In a year he turned it into the most widely read syndicated column in America. He did this by giving society what society is always in need of...a shot of new blood. Mike's society included everyone and everything that was newsworthy. Show business, big business and politics ; the worlds of fashion, publishing and medicine ; murderers, heroes and embezzlers ; all found their way into MIKE MANNING'S NEW YORK.

Taking Kipling's advice to heart, Mike Manning walked with kings but never lost the common touch. He was read in Park Avenue drawing rooms and in kitchens in Des Moines ; on the subway and in the back of limousines; in the oval office and at deli lunch counters. When he wrote his tongue was usually in his cheek but his fists were always poised in defense of the defenseless. He was loved, hated, feared and respected. He was everything a good journalist should be.

His success had not come easily. A couple of lucky breaks had gotten him through the first few bewildering weeks in a job thrust upon him because no one else wanted it ; writing the society column for the *Ledger* had once been considered tantamount to writing your own obit. But soon his own considerable ability, charm and natural instinct for separating the newsworthy from the newshounds catapulted him to the top in a profession crowded with formidable competition.

One of those lucky breaks had come in the person of Mildred Hamilton Lakewood. He had caught her eye at a big, strictly-for-the- press fundraising ball and she had befriended the new society editor on the spot. With Milly as guide and patroness he gained entry into homes and attended social events the press had only heretofore reported upon via second hand accounts of not-too-trustworthy informers: that group of social climbers who would trade anything for a mention in the columns.

Mike may have gotten in through the back door but he was soon lionized by all the right hostesses and hosts as his own person and not Milly's escort. Still, the handsome reporter and the then-new widow remained an item in all the columns but Mike Manning's. At the start, their relationship was one of mutual fulfillment. Milly enjoyed showing the cub all the right paths through a jungle she had been born and raised in. The cub was very appreciative. They were good friends and a recent widow is supposed to wait a respectable period of time before she sets her sights for a new mate. Milly considered six months respectable and a year nothing less than Victorian. She began to hint, broadly, that her needs consisted of more than social functions, political intrigue and brotherly kisses on the cheek.

"Did I ever promise you more of a relationship than we now have?" Mike questioned when he felt he could no longer avoid the issue.

"Promise? What a strange choice of word. You make it sound as if our friendship is based on some unwritten contract or pact."

"It's based on love and mutual respect, I hope, but it's you who want to cement it with a contract." She smiled her appreciation of his quick wit.

"You do know how to turn a phrase, Mr. Manning…and the tables. Okay…is it another woman?"

"Let's just say it's…other interests."

"You're not talking about your work."

"No, Milly, I'm not talking about my work." She looked at him for a long time and he stared back, unblinking.

"You had me fooled, Mike."

"Oh, but I didn't try to fool you, Milly. I don't try to fool anyone. I'm up front, all the way."

"But I thought ."

"You thought in terms of a stereotype," he cut her short.

"You see we come in all shapes and sizes and demeanors. Behind many a ribbon counter you'll find a stud and on an impressive number of football fields you'll find…"

"What you're telling me is you're no different than anyone else."

"You said it, Milly…and don't ever forget it."

Their friendship remained intact. If anything, they became closer than ever. The air had been cleared…the tension relaxed. But a few months later Mildred Hamilton Lakewood eloped with Stephen Burke.

Mike's thoughts wandered in as many directions as the old car which skidded sideways more often than it moved in a straight line up First Avenue. Would Stephen Burke — and Susan Kennedy, whoever she was — now be celebrating the arrival of the new year if he had compromised his principles and married the lady? And how easy it would have been to do so. He knew dozens of men in politics and the business world who led that sort of double life. In show business their number was legion. They presented an image of married respectability and relegated their passion to something you do in the dark and try to forget in the morning.

This, though convenient, was not Mike's style. He found it an effrontery to both worlds and a degradation of the self. He had stuck by what he believed to be right and now Milly Burke had murdered her husband and a pretty, innocent young woman. He had talked Kenny into upholding the same principle and Kenny was dead. At what point does the struggle for self-respect become a malignant disease?

The address Mrs. Turner had given him was a townhouse between Park and Madison Avenues. Every window of the four-story building was ablaze with light and not even the heavy snowfall could dim the roar coming from within.

He pressed the door buzzer and no one responded, probably because no one could hear the buzz. He opened the door and walked in. The big kitchen on his left was empty and the room beyond was dark. He followed the sound of the noise up a flight of narrow stairs flanking the right wall and entered bedlam.

The front room of the parlor floor was bursting with young people, all in a state of frenzied motion. The boys, for the most part, were dressed in black tie, the girls adorned in everything from formal gowns to sequin-encrusted jeans. The stereo was tuned to a deafening pitch but this didn't seem to bother one meditative lad who strummed a guitar and obviously marched to the sound of a drummer only he could hear. The air was so thick with the smell of pot one could have been busted for breathing.

The back room, separated by an open archway, looked like a mirror image of the front...with one exception. It contained Kevin Lakewood. Peering over the wiggling bodies and bobbing heads Mike spotted the boy leaning against the marble fireplace, a champagne glass poised lightly in one hand.

He had not seen Kevin Lakewood for several years but had no trouble recognizing Milly's son. Kevin had his mother's auburn hair which covered his head in an array of soft waves and was cut in no particular fashion. He had his father's straight, small nose, full lips and clean-cut features. The fact that he was standing alone amid the chaos enhanced a countenance which quietly stated that Kevin Lakewood was very much his own man.

Mike began to push his way toward his mark. No one paid the slightest attention to the uninvited guest until his shoving was interpreted as dancing and half way across the room he found himself surrounded by a boy and girl who rotated their groins at his front and rear in a most exciting manner. He responded in kind and the three of them moved across the crowded floor at a rapid and unobstructed pace. He was a few feet from Kevin before he looked up and realized the boy had followed his progress every bouncing step of the way. Kevin was laughing quietly and Mike's gaze was riveted to a pair of sparkling brown eyes and a row of even, white teeth.

"You do that very well, Mr. Manning."

"It was the easiest way to get across the floor."

Mike turned to his dancing partners and bowed. "Thank you kindly." He patted the girl's hip, reached for the boy but thought better of it and withdrew his hand.

"Go right ahead," Kevin grinned, "he would love it."

"I think I've made enough of a fool of myself for one night," Mike all but yelled to be heard over the stereo and the din in the room.

"If Vicky knew Mike Manning was going to attend her party she would have cleaned up her act." Kevin waved his champagne glass over the crowd as he spoke.

"Not to mention the air."

"You remember me. It's been a long time, Kevin."

"Some place between prep school and college, I think. And how could I forget my mother's most celebrated friend?"

Mike nodded his thank you. "You haven't changed much."

Kevin shrugged. "The braces and pimples are gone."

"You never had either."

"Oh, then you did notice me." The boy was smiling broadly and Mike pretended not to hear the comment which was not hard to do as Vicky's guests began clapping to the disco beat coming from no less than eight speakers.

"Why aren't you at Trish Naughton's?" Kevin shouted.

"I came here to get you," Mike shouted back.

"What?" Mike took hold of the boy's elbow and began pushing him gently toward the hall. It wasn't much quieter there but at least the walls weren't vibrating around them.

"I said I came here to get you."

Kevin looked puzzled. "Why?"

"I want you to leave with me and not ask any questions until we get out of here." Mike's hand was still on the boy's arm. Kevin began to look uneasy but managed a smile.

"Are you making me an indecent proposal?"

"Hardly...I'm here at your mother's request." With the mention of his mother the boy became deadly serious and dropped his flippant air.

"You're not kidding, are you?"

"No, Kevin, I'm not kidding Where's your coat?"

A young man staggered into the hall, saw Kevin Lakewood and reeled toward him.

"Kev, baby, I've got two horny ladies waitin'..."

Without taking his eyes from Mike's face Kevin gripped the newcomer's arm and said, "Brad, this is Mike Manning. Mike... Brad Turner."

"Hello, Brad."

"Mike Manning...no shit." He stuck out his hand and Mike shook it. Brad Turner was shorter than Kevin but with a firm, muscular body that brought to mind the word Jock. His straight, dark hair fell in short bangs across his forehead and his vivid blue eyes appraised Mike Manning as their hands clasped. Brad would have to shave twice a day if he wanted to appear clean-shaven at the dinner table.

"I read your column every day...well, every other day. Between times I read Penthouse and jack-off."

"Brad's a class act with a one-track mind," Kevin explained.

"And right now the track is headed in that direction," Brad jerked a thumb over his shoulder.

"Nice meeting you, Brad...we were just leaving," Mike said.

"We?" He looked at Kevin.

"What about the girls? What about me? We came in your car and I was supposed to sleep at your place if all else failed... remember?"

"Something's come up, Brad, I'm sorry." Brad looked from Kevin to Mike Manning and the silly grin on his face went slack as he caught their somber mood.

"Say, what is this, New Year's Eve or a funeral?" The word

caused Mike to once again prod Kevin into action.

"Come on, kid, let's go."

"What about me?" Brad pleaded.

"One of those ladies is sure to have her own apartment," Kevin answered.

"They both do...they're roommates." Kevin patted his friend's cheek as he handed him his empty champagne glass. "You're going to be one busy little stud, Bradley. Happy New Year." Kevin began to mount the stairs with Mike right behind him.

Brad was speaking but what he said was lost to the perpetual roar of Vicky's party. Mike looked down and waved, silently wishing he could take Bradley Turner with them.

"My coat's in the back bedroom along with a hundred others...this might take a few minutes." The room was in partial darkness, lighted only by the ceiling light coming through the door from the third floor hall. Twin beds were both piled high with heavy winter coats. Kevin began to rummage through the assortment on the near bed when a sound, something between a gasp and a sigh, floated over the music coming from downstairs.

He paused in his search, turned his head and focused his eyes on a shadowed corner of the room. A young man, his eyes closed and the tip of his tongue visible between his teeth, was leaning against the opposite wall. His knees were slightly buckled and a girl's blond head, moving rapidly, covered the open fly of his tux pants. The rest of her was hidden by the mountain of coats covering the other bed.

Kevin looked over his shoulder to see Mike standing in the doorway. He also had his eyes fixed on the erotic tableau. Kevin located his coat and tiptoed to Mike.

"Do you want to leave," he whispered, "or stick around for the climax?"

"Move out," Mike ordered, and guided the young man into the hall and down the stairs. "And put that coat on...there's a blizzard raging out there."

"I think you're shocked," Kevin laughed.

"Nothing shocks me…except indiscretion."

"But we intruded on them."

"Keep moving," Mike sighed. Their exit from the townhouse was as inauspicious as Mike's arrival. He wondered if the very young ever communicated on a personal level and then recalled the scene in the bedroom on the third floor.

"Indeed they do," he thought, "but they seem to avoid the sublime and go straight for the ridiculous. Well…why the hell not?"

The snow was ankle deep and where the wind had piled it against buildings and parked cars it was a foot high. They climbed into the back seat of the Chevy and the driver turned on the ignition. It sounded like a death rattle and Mike held his breath. Then, as if by accident, the engine turned over and the car jerked forward.

"Can you get us back?" Mike asked.

"I'm gonna try," was all the driver would commit himself to.

"Now can you tell me what this is all about, Mr. Manning?" Kevin was nestled in a corner of the back seat, his hair wet and glistening.

"Don't call me Mr. Manning, it makes me feel as if I'm old enough to be your father."

"How old are you?"

"Thirty-five."

"I'm twenty-two. If you were a promiscuous thirteen-year-old you could be my father."

"If I were your father you wouldn't be at that party."

"You were shocked," Kevin laughed, "or embarrassed…or jealous."

The car made it to Park Avenue and was now heading south.

"Where are we going?" Kevin asked, sitting straight up.

"My place."

"I thought you said my mother wanted me."

"Kevin…Stephen Burke is dead." It was too dark in the back of the car to read the expression on the boy's face, but Mike did catch a sharp intake of breath. He waited, but nothing was forthcoming.

"Did you hear me, Kevin?"

"I heard you." If he was upset by this bit of news he was certainly doing a masterful job of concealing the fact. "How?… When?"

"About six this evening. Your mother shot him." How crude, Mike thought, but then how do you politely tell a young man that his mother has just murdered his stepfather?

"Jesus…"

Mike put his hand on the boy's knee and squeezed hard.

"What are you saying? You're crazy." He jerked his knee from Mike's hand. Mike thought of all the comforting clichés one is supposed to offer the bereaved but somehow none of them seemed to fit the occasion.

"I'm saying Milly shot Stephen Burke at six this evening and I'm sorry to be the bearer of the news. Look, kid…"

Kevin reached for the door. "Let me out of here."

Mike took hold of the boy's arm and pushed him back into the car seat. "Don't be a fool and where the hell do you think you can go, and why?"

"I want to see my mother." Mike could feel Kevin's body trembling under his grip. The arm he held jerked spasmodically.

"I want to be with my mother," he repeated.

"You can't…not now. She's with the police and Sam Saxman is with her. There's nothing either of us can do now except sit tight."

"You are so damn smug," Kevin shouted as he again withdrew from Mike's touch. "Sit tight? What the hell is that supposed to mean? If I can't be with her I want to go home. I'm not coming to your apartment." The sophisticated young man in black tie, leaning against a marble fireplace and holding a champagne tumbler, was fast giving way to a very frightened five-year-old.

"Listen to me and try to understand what I'm doing. As soon as the...the accident was reported to the precinct every newspaper, magazine, television and radio network sent a man to cover the story. Right now the old 19th must look like a cross between Times Square and a movie studio. The second stringers, freelancers and morbidly curious are digging in to spend the night across the street from your apartment building. And don't think anything as mundane as a blizzard is going to cut down on their number. They're all pros and they know they can't get near your mother. It's you they want. They want your picture...they want your statement...they want to see you crying or laughing or, hopefully, drunk and tossing snowballs at the press. You're young and pretty and rich and your mother has just confessed to murder one. They're going to make it a circus and a circus isn't worth a damn without a clown."

"Shut up," Kevin cried, "I've got the picture."

The car moved through the storm at a snail's pace and the two men in the back seat sat in silence, avoiding each other's eyes and touch. Kevin had once again pressed himself into a corner with his head turned toward the snow-streaked window.

Mike stared straight ahead, shivering in his wet shoes. He had handled it all wrong, was his only thought. But how else to handle it? Had he been as crude and insensitive as he sounded in retrospect? And why didn't the boy cry? If he cried Mike could take him in his arms and comfort him. Did either of them feel anything or had the human race lost its ability to respond to that sense?

A finger touched Mike's hand.

"I'm sorry, Mike." It was just a whisper. "You're trying to help and I'm acting like an idiot."

Mike took the boy's hand and held it gently. "Funny, I was just thinking it was me who had played that role."

"No...you did what you had to do. My mother sent you to get me, didn't she?"

Mike nodded. "Yes. She wants you to stay with me till we know what's going to happen next."

"You've seen her?"

"She called me right after...as soon as it happened."

"Tell me about it."

"There's not much to tell, Kevin."

"I'm glad he's dead, Mike. Does that shock you?"

"No, it just puts you at the end of a long line."

"Tell me about it," Kevin said again.

"Do you know a girl named Susan Kennedy?" Mike asked.

"I've seen her around."

"You mean she's not a friend? A good friend?"

"No...what's she got to do with this?"

"She was at your apartment earlier this evening. She was with Burke." He felt the boy's hand tighten over his.

"She's dead, too, Kevin." The boy let out a groan and doubled over, his head touching Mike's knee. Mike put his hand on the bent head, the hair under his fingers was as soft as a baby's.

"I'm sorry, kid. Christ, I'm sorry."

"Why?...why?" Kevin sobbed. Why? It was the right question but Mike didn't have the right answer. Who did? He was sure no one did, including Milly.

The old Chevy came to an abrupt halt. "We made it, Mr. Manning."

"What's your name?" The driver turned around just as Kevin raised his head.

"Frank Evans." He was a mature black man.

Mike fished into his wallet and pulled out two fifty-dollar bills. He handed them to Frank Evans. "You know how to keep your mouth shut, Frank?"

"Where I come from you don't live as long as I have by opening it."

Mike laughed and said, "When I call the service I want you as my driver...no one else."

"Thank you, Mr. Manning." Give and take...right now Frank Evans was ahead of the game but by next week...who could tell?

Inside Mike's apartment the first thing they did was take off their wet shoes and socks. Mike pointed, "The bedroom is that way and the bath is off it. We might as well make ourselves comfortable. There are a couple of robes in the closet; one of them should fit you."

"I'm two sizes smaller than you, so who usually wears that one?"

"I could kick you out in the snow, sonny."

"You could, but you won't. By the way, how long before your colleagues figure out where I am?"

"It depends," Mike shrugged, "on how far off the scent Saxman's put them. The smart ones won't believe a word he says and probably know right now. The others will get the message as soon as the first edition of the *Ledger* hits the stands."

"You phoned in the story?" Kevin made it sound like a criminal offense.

"It's my job, Kevin, and it'll be the only coverage that delivers a straight story. The rest will be soap-opera, bullshit and bank balances."

"I like a modest man."

"So do I." Mike started for the kitchen. "What are you drinking?"

"Whatever you are," Kevin answered, and Mike liked the way

that sounded. Mike poured two drinks over ice and then went into the bedroom to change. He heard the sound of running water coming from the bathroom and noticed Kevin's tux and shirt folded over the back of a chair. The boy's t-shirt and jockey shorts lay on the bed.

"Well…I did tell him to make himself comfortable." He marched back to the living room barefoot, stopping to pick up the drinks on the way, wearing jeans and a flannel shirt. A few minutes later Kevin joined him.

"It does fit," he announced, opening his arms to model the blue robe for Mike. "Your…er…lady friend is just my height. Tall for a girl or is that how you like them?"

"I can still toss you out in the snow. Sit down and drink this… you need it." Kevin sat on the couch next to Mike and sipped the offered drink.

"What is this?"

"Bourbon. Do you like it?"

"They all taste the same to me." He looked around as if seeing the room for the first time. "This is very comfortable. I'm thinking about getting my own place…"

The unfinished sentence shouted the uncertainty of Kevin Lakewood's future. He looked at Mike. "Tell me about it… please…everything."

"Okay," Mike nodded. "You have a right to know and by this time tomorrow you'll have read and heard a dozen different versions." He told the boy what he knew in a straightforward manner, dulling the rougher edges without altering the facts. Kevin listened impassively staring into his glass when he wasn't drinking from it.

"Jesus…the bastard," was Kevin's first comment when Mike had finished.

"He wasn't satisfied with screwing in every bedroom he could get a foot into, so he had to start doing it in our home. You're familiar with my stepfather's reputation?"

"I've heard stories," Mike responded.

Kevin held up his hands, palms facing, about a foot apart. "It was that big and who the fuck ever said size doesn't matter." Mike suppressed a smile at the somewhat exaggerated dimensions of Stephen Burke's prowess.

"Tell me about the girl, Kevin."

"What can I tell you? Susan Kennedy...I met her about a year ago at a party in the city or maybe out on the Island. I really don't remember. She was part of the crowd, whatever that is, and I saw her fairly often this past fall. That's all I know."

"Do you know anything about her family?" Kevin shook his head, which meant Susan was a hanger-on in Kevin Lakewood's crowd. The boy was being kind and Mike liked that.

"Did you ever date her?"

"Shit, no. I might have danced with her a few times but aside from that I don't think I was ever alone with her."

"Did your stepfather know her?" Kevin closed his eyes and rubbed his forehead with two fingers.

"I think so. But Christ, Mike, I'm not sure. I think she was at a party I had at the beach house. Yes ... she was, and Stephen and my mother were there so he must have met her."

"But what was she doing at your apartment?"

"I think that's obvious."

"Christ, you sound just like your mother," Mike shouted. "No, Kevin, it's not obvious. A man doesn't invite a girl into his home for a quick fuck with his wife present. And suppose he didn't invite her. Say she came on her own and he happened to be alone in the apartment at that moment. Does he take her into the bedroom when he knows his wife could return at any minute? Sure, everything is obvious, but the obvious doesn't make sense. Just wait till Saxman hears this story...Christ!" Kevin looked meekly at the man sitting next to him

"I'm sorry, Mike, but I don't know the answer."

Mike tousled Kevin's hair and sighed. "Sorry, kid, I wasn't cross-examining you. But what Susan Kennedy was doing in your apartment could mean the difference between premeditated murder and a crime of passion. Do you know what that means?"

"My mother could go free, get a slap on the wrist…"

"Or spend the rest of her life in jail," Mike concluded.

"Do you think my mother knew the Kennedy girl was coming?" Now it was Kevin's turn to shout.

"I don't know…do you?"

"But that's impossible."

"Prove it, sonny, prove it…that's what the prosecution is going to toss at Sam Saxman." They sat in silence for a few minutes before Kevin mumbled,

"Jesus…do you mind if I have another?" He stood up, showing Mike his empty glass.

"Help yourself, the bottle's on the counter." Mike watched a pair of straight, muscular legs walk toward the kitchen. He wondered where the boy's undershorts were at this minute.

"Shit…I've got the morals of a jack rabbit." Once again he used bourbon to diffuse guilt.

Kevin returned with a fresh drink and the bottle. He poured out a generous shot for Mike before resuming his place on the couch. Seated, he leaned back and put his bare feet on the coffee table which held their drinks and the bottle of bourbon. The front of his robe parted and the boy quickly pulled the divided flaps over his legs…but not quickly enough to leave Mike's speculation unanswered. The jockey shorts were still in the bedroom. Mike forced himself to think of something else and, under the circumstances, all he could come up with were Stephen Burke's clothes. Avoiding Kevin's eyes he asked,

"Was Burke exceptionally neat?"

The boy looked puzzled. "He was fairly neat, as far as I know, but not a fanatic about it. Why?"

"His clothes," Mike answered, "I mentioned that to you. There wasn't a trace of them in the bedroom, or the apartment for that matter."

"Well if he were…" Kevin began but Mike stopped him with an annoyed wave of his hand.

"That won't gel, so forget it. If he were getting ready for a love match that's all the more reason to believe he would undress and let his clothes fall where they may. If he were getting ready to go to sleep, which he wasn't, and hung everything up, there would still be something…socks, pajamas, a robe…lying about. Burke's clothes disappearing is as big a problem as Susan Kennedy's appearing."

There was another long silence until Kevin picked up his glass and raised it toward Mike. "Happy New Year, Mike."

"God…I forgot all about it. Happy New Year, kid. Did we miss the magic hour?"

"Slightly…the new year is almost two hours old." Kevin suddenly covered his face with one hand and his shoulders began to heave. Mike looked embarrassed.

"What a way to start a new year. I'm sorry, Kevin, I really am."

"Don't mind me. I always cry at weddings, funerals and the first day of the year."

"Come on, it's going to be all right." Mike put his arm around the boy and drew him close. Kevin buried his face against Mike's chest and sobbed openly.

"Go on, cry…let it all out. It's about time you did." He put down his glass and cradled the boy like a baby.

"Next year at this time we'll all be a little older, a little wiser and, I hope, a hell of a lot happier." Kevin raised his head.

"Thanks, Mike." As he moved, the front of his robe parted again. Mike reached to close it and his hand lingered on the spot a fraction of a second too long, feeling like a piece of lead as he raised it to once again embrace Kevin. The storm continued to rage outside as the man and boy sat in eerie silence, each comforted by the warmth of the other's body and reassured by the steady, even sound of their own breathing. One year ago to the very minute Mike had sat in this exact spot, holding a warm body encased in the robe which now covered Kevin Lakewood. He closed his eyes and for a moment pretended...

"Are you asleep?" Mike whispered. The head nestled against his shoulder stirred.

"Almost."

Mike gently freed himself and stood up. "Come on, it's been a long day." He led the way and Kevin followed. In the bedroom the boy took off his robe and Mike averted his eyes as he slipped out of his shirt and jeans. Kevin got into the bed as Mike turned off the bedside lamp and then cautiously slipped under the covers. Kevin rolled toward him and once again (so naturally, Mike thought) their bodies entwined.

"I feel safe with you," Kevin mumbled.

"I wish I could say the same," Mike answered, grinning into the darkness. Kevin Lakewood did not hear him. He was already sound asleep.

The persistent ring of the telephone roused Mike a few hours before dawn. He looked at the boy sleeping peacefully next to him as he got out of bed to pick up the phone on the nightstand.

"Saxman," the tense voice said without prelude. "I just left her. They booked her on murder one and there's no chance of getting to a judge before tomorrow. Today's a legal holiday. How's the boy?"

Mike felt a sharp pain in his chest which he immediately diagnosed as guilt. "He's asleep," he answered, and quickly diverted the lawyer's concern for the boy to that of his client. "How's Milly?"

"Not bad. She's a tough lady, Mike."

"Can you arrange bail?" Mike felt a hand touch his naked knee. He jerked his leg backward and looked down. Kevin was looking up at him, smiling.

"I think so, for about a million bucks." The hand moved up Mike's thigh.

"She's got it," Mike answered, hoping Saxman didn't notice the tremor in his voice.

"I know that." Saxman yawned audibly.

"I'm tired, Mike. I'll talk to you tonight. Take care of the kid."

The pain in Mike's chest sharpened. "Thanks, Sam."

"By the way, that was a damn good piece in the early edition."

One finger touched the masculine sack.

"It's my job, Sam, that's all." Mike hung up and looked down at Kevin. "Saxman...he thinks he can get Milly out on bail tomorrow."

"I heard...come back to bed." The hand continued to probe.

"Look, Kevin, maybe I offered too much comfort last night... murder makes me very protective...but one mistake a year is all I'm allowed so I've had it till next New Year's Eve." But Mike didn't move an inch from where he stood, shivering from more than just the cold of the pre-dawn winter day.

"You want to as much as I do."

"Christ, Kevin, don't do this to me."

"Then walk away. That's all you have to do, Mike, just walk away. I won't bother you anymore." He eased his tall frame back under the warm bed covers. His hand touched Kevin's shoulder.

"Kev?"

"Yeah?"

"I want you to bother me." Kevin laughed.

4

The city was covered under a half a foot of snow and overhead a wintry gray sky promised to deliver another six inches before the new year was two days old. The tranquil scene in the dimly lit bedroom was once again shattered by the piercing ring of the telephone. The sleeping bodies nestled under warm blankets stirred on the second ring; on the third the taller of the two kicked the bed covers off himself, rolled out of bed and disconnected the intruder by pulling the cord from the wall socket. But the damage had already been done and by the time Mike returned to the bed Kevin was sitting up, wide awake.

"Do you always do that when you don't want to answer it?" he asked, looking up at his host through eyes still swollen from sleep.

"No ... I usually pull it out of the wall before I go to bed. Why don't you go back to sleep."

"I can't...and I feel rotten, Mike." He ran a hand through his hair.

"Like a hangover without the benefit of having been drunk." Mike sat down next to the boy.

"The shock has worn off and reality is setting in." He patted a bare back. "And I suspect it's going to get worse before it gets better."

"Thanks for the lift."

Mike shrugged his shoulders. "If you want sympathetic bullshit, you've come to the wrong place."

"You sound like one of your columns."

"I am my columns. Why don't you hit the shower while I make the coffee. You hungry?"

"God, no. Just juice and coffee." Kevin got out of bed, stood up and stretched. His body was slim, finely muscled and tanned above and below the perfect outline of an invisible bikini swim suit. Mike wondered how such a garment could contain Kevin Lakewood. He tried not to stare as Kevin walked around the bed.

"About last night," Mike began…

"It was good…for me, anyway. Let's not analyze it." With that he picked up his robe and marched into the bathroom. Mike watched the door close and looked at it until the sound of the shower jolted him into motion. He put on his robe and went to brew a pot of strong coffee. When it was ready and he had poured himself a cup, Kevin entered the kitchen looking fresh and clean.

"I used your shampoo and razor but drew the line on your toothbrush."

"I appreciate the restraint but there's a new one in the cabinet under the sink." Mike poured coffee into a mug and pushed it toward Kevin. "You feeling better?"

"Not much…what's going to happen, Mike? I feel so helpless. I want to see my mother and I want to go home. I can't sit in this robe all day like an invalid…I'll go out of my mind."

"Let me shower and shave and then we'll talk. I don't want to do anything until we've had a chance to sit down with Saxman, but I think the police are going to catch up with us before we do that." And right on cue the telephone rang. Kevin turned with a start.

"Did you reconnect it?"

"If I had you would have known about it long before now." Taking his coffee cup with him Mike went into the living room. "This is a different line. A very private number."

"Your newspaper?" More fear than hope was conveyed by the emotion the simple question evoked and Mike began to wonder if the boy was going to need professional attention. Kevin's initial reaction, or lack of it, to his mother's predicament had been strictly veneer and now that the facts had time to sink in he was showing signs of running scared. And what was last night all about? An irrational attempt to thwart reality at any cost?

As he picked up the phone Mike began to feel as sick as Kevin Lakewood looked and the sound which greeted his polite hello did little to help.

"Is the boy with you?"

"And a happy New Year to you, too, Inspector Brandt."

"This isn't a social call, Manning."

"Obviously not. Yes, he's here."

"I want to see him."

"Officially?" Mike asked.

"I just told you, this isn't a social call."

"I'm told it's a legal holiday."

"I know that, Manning, and so does the rest of the world. It's very quiet here and most of the press is observing their day of rest." Mike hated himself for not having thought of that, almost as much as he hated Brandt for pointing it out to him.

"I'll bring him in. Give us an hour."

"Thanks. And happy New Year, Manning."

Mike put down the phone and with his mind still on Andrew Brandt he turned to face Kevin. The boy was a deathly white and looked slightly unsteady on his feet. Mike gripped him by the arm.

"Come on, Kevin, try to snap out of it. The call was strictly routine."

"What does he want with me?"

"He wants to question you, naturally. That's all. Just answer every question honestly and it'll be over and done with in less than an hour."

"What kind of questions?" Kevin moved away from Mike and began to walk aimlessly across the room. "Do you have a cigarette?"

"When did you start smoking?"

"When did you become a preacher?"

"One minute, young man." Mike raised his voice. "Stand still for one minute and look at me." He began to advance toward Kevin.

"I appreciate what you're going through but I'm not one of your mother's servants or a fraternity brother you're pissed off at. If you can't be civil, then keep your mouth shut. You're here because your mother's a very dear friend of mine and she gave more thought to your welfare than to her own when she asked for my help. Try to appreciate the fact even if you can't respect it."

Mike took a deep breath, "And…if you think what happened last night gives you the right to…"

"Forget what happened last night," Kevin shouted.

"I don't want to forget it," Mike shouted back, and was immediately sorry. They stared at each other for a brief moment and then Kevin sank to the couch.

"I'm sorry," he whispered. When Mike didn't answer he added,

"This is getting to be a habit. The explosion followed by the apology."

"If we're going to be roommates for another twenty-four hours, minimum, I think we should declare a truce." Kevin held out his hand toward Mike.

"Truce." Mike took the offered hand in his and shook it. An audible silence followed.

"Can I have that cigarette now?" Kevin asked, the slightest hint of a grin beginning to appear on his face.

"Scene two, take two…when did you start smoking?"

"I do on occasion," Kevin answered.

"Most occasional smokers do so when they have a drink or…" Mike tossed a pack of cigarettes to Kevin. The boy extracted a cigarette, lit it and exhaled a cloud of smoke without inhaling it.

"Or after sex…is that what you were going to say?"

"As a matter of fact…no."

"Come on, Mike," Kevin patted the cushion next to him as he spoke, "sit down and let's talk about it. That's what you want, isn't it?"

"I don't appreciate the condescending attitude." But Mike took the seat indicated. Kevin held up his forefinger like a teacher admonishing a student.

"Truce…remember?"

"Did it ever occur to you that what happened between us last night might be slightly traumatic to me? That it might have been more than a pleasant alternative to jacking off?"

Kevin put his hand over his heart. "Is this a proposal, Mr. Manning?"

"You're a baby," Mike replied as if making a remarkable discovery, but it did little to conceal the disappointment he felt.

"No, I'm not a baby, Mike, but you're acting like one." The look those brown eyes gave him told Mike something was about to explode, and then…"Did it ever occur to you that I would like to savor what happened between us last night before the inevitable vivisection hits the fan? To enjoy it in my own special, private way? Did it ever occur to you that I risked rejection and won but don't want to risk it again for fear of losing? I've had a crush on you since the day you took me to the zoo when I was twelve years old, but did it ever occur to you to drop me a note all those years I was away at school or make an effort to see me when I came home on holiday? I didn't expect anything big you understand, just 'Hello, Kevin, glad to see you're still alive' would have been fine. Did it ever occur to you that last night my moment came, finally, and I grabbed at it under the most hideous of circumstances because I didn't know if the moment would ever be right again? Do you think it was easy with my mother…"

Mike, bewildered, stopped listening when Kevin's words evoked the image of escorting a young boy around the Central Park zoo. A boy who had recently lost his father and who held Mike's hand in a tight grip as if fearing he might lose him, too, and be left alone with the caged animals in the strange oasis surrounded by brick and glass towers. The boy hadn't laughed or tried to break away from his chaperone as did the other children. Rather, he looked constantly up at Mike with sad, brown eyes that wanted only to please…and be loved.

"Kevin…" Mike, still slightly disoriented, tried to stop the embarrassing outpouring.

"If I wanted to jack off, Mr. Manning, I would have done just that. You're not an alternative…you're an obsession." And the moment ended as abruptly as it had begun.

When Mike finally answered he spoke more to himself than to the boy sitting next to him. "I feel like a wet towel being squeezed through a wringer. Not to mention being the perfect horse's ass."

"I feel the same way, so that makes everything even. Just the right climate for a truce." Kevin stood up and untied the sash of the blue robe. He took it off and stood before Mike stark naked as he handed him the garment. Mike looked up at an image that was at once obscene and saintly — an etching from a glossy pornographic magazine or the Archangel defending the gate of heaven. Suddenly Kevin became Eve, the robe a shining red apple and Mike heard the words, "Then just walk away."

"Have it laundered," Kevin was saying, "and give it back to its rightful owner. I know how to keep a secret and the robe can't talk."

"Neither can its rightful owner. He's dead."

Frank Evans was waiting for them in the same beat-up Chevy Impala. "Don't you ever get a day off?" Mike asked as he followed Kevin Lakewood into the back seat.

"Don't you?" Evans answered, without turning to look at his passengers.

Mike tried again. "Is this heap the only car available? Christ, it was getting ready to die last night." Now Evans turned to look at Mike as he answered. His wiry gray hair was cut close to his scalp and beneath the wrinkled black forehead his broad grin was ablaze with a row of sparkling white teeth.

"No, Mr. Manning, this heap ain't the only car available because the fact is there ain't no car available. This heap is mine and it's been getting set to die since the day I bought it, slightly used and a lot abused."

"Strike two," Kevin mumbled. "One more and you're out."

"Shut up," Mike answered as he settled back and began giving Evans directions. He was feeling slightly euphoric and knew the reason why.

Evans once again drove up First Avenue, overshooting their destination, and came down on Fifth. As they passed the Burke's apartment building Mike pointed to a dozen men grouped in a cluster directly across the street from the canopy upon which *Eight Thirty* was inscribed in white script lettering. They made an incongruous sight in the foot-deep snow and numbing cold.

Bundled in heavy top coats, mufflers, fur hats and rubber overshoes, a few brave ones sat on the icy park bench as others leaned against the stone wall which separated the Avenue from Central Park. Some drank from thermoses and others held cardboard cups of steaming coffee in their gloved hands. The cameras dangling from their necks announced their common bond.

"Have they been there since yesterday?" Kevin asked, his head turning as their car drove past the photographers.

"Some have, I'm sure," Mike answered. Again he got the feeling that Kevin Lakewood was running scared. Milly was a smart lady; the boy would have put on one hell of a show had he been allowed to face that group last night. Mike shivered inwardly at the thought.

"They're crazy."

"No," Mike replied. "Just trying to make a living."

"Did you ever do that?"

"On occasion…yes."

Kevin turned his head from the rapidly retreating scene and looked at Mike. "It's insane."

"Not really. It's the American way." He looked out the rear window and pointed. "Those news-hounds are the only thing standing between us and everyone who's out to pull a fast one on an always unsuspecting public."

"This is a private matter and none of the public's business," Kevin protested.

Mike shrugged. "That's a matter of opinion. Besides, you have to take the bad with the good. Selection is a form of censorship."

Kevin's jaw relaxed as he glanced at Mike sheepishly, a flicker of amusement lighting up his brown eyes. "Thanks for the lecture. Do you tutor political science on the side?"

"My hobbies are more…esoteric?"

"Are you asking me or telling me?"

Mike laughed. "I'm informing you. Make of it what you will." The car moved slowly down a strangely deserted Fifth Avenue. The city was either abed, nursing a monumental hangover, or else had burrowed in for the winter solstice. The freshly fallen snow, contrasted against a gray, still threatening sky, sparkled like a blanket of white diamonds. Its newness and brilliance relegated the weeks-old Christmas decorations of the famous thoroughfare to a drab and shop-worn oblivion. Mike, for reasons known only to his subconscious, thought of a bride walking down the white, satin-carpeted aisle of a grand cathedral.

Kevin, lost in his own thoughts, suddenly mused, "You're right, you know, we do have to accept the bad for the ultimate good."

Mike moved uneasily in his seat and looked at the boy. "I don't think we're talking about an informed public anymore." When Kevin didn't respond he continued. "Murder, for any reason, is never acceptable."

"The sacrifice of one to save the many?" Kevin tried to stare Mike down but failed.

"If you're talking about Burke, and I'm sure you are, who's the many his death saved?"

"My mother, for one."

"And the only one. I'm sure the rest of the female population wanted Stephen Burke alive and kicking. Sorry, but your rule doesn't apply. If it did, half the world's population could be legally liquidated. An eye for an eye...or a corpse for every bruised heart." Mike shook his head. "You're on the wrong track, kid. There are more conventional ways of dissolving a marriage."

"You don't understand," Kevin pouted, turning his head away from Mike and looking out the window. This was an irritating habit of the boy's Mike had noticed before. Whenever Kevin Lakewood didn't like what was happening in front of him he simply turned his head as if commanding the unpleasantness to disappear before he decided to once again grace the scene.

"A rich brat," Mike thought, but without malice. He wondered what it would be like to turn the rich brat into an interesting man. Without giving the speculation a moment's thought he decided to apply for the job and figured there was no time like the present to start.

"No, I don't understand," Mike began, "but even if I did I still couldn't condone the cold-blooded murder of two people. Forgive...maybe, but not condone."

"Very generous," Kevin said to the dirty pane of glass.

Ignoring the retort, Mike continued to lecture. "But it's not me who has to understand. It's a jury that has to be convinced and even Saxman is going to have to dip deeply into his bag of tricks to garner sympathy for a lady who was born and raised in the lap of luxury and has nothing more to occupy her time than deciding how to spend the interest on fifty million bucks."

"We don't have fifty million bucks," Kevin answered.

"Excuse me," Mike grinned, "twenty-five million. Do you think that will make the jury more sympathetic?"

"If they think like you do, no."

"But I'm not in command of the facts and presumably they will be."

Kevin opened his mouth to speak but changed his mind. Instead he tossed back his head and looked at the car's dilapidated ceiling.

"They *will* know all the facts?" Mike probed.

"They still wouldn't understand," the boy answered, as if bored with the conversation.

"Better let Saxman be the judge of that."

"Saxman isn't God." Kevin continued to talk to the ceiling.

"No, he's a trial lawyer, and aren't you lucky. If memory serves, Christ wasn't very successful with his jury." With that Kevin's sullenness disappeared and was replaced with an outburst of laughter.

"I like that one, Mr. Manning. I really like that one."

"You have a weird sense of humor, kid."

"And you know just how to tickle it." It was now Mike's turn to stare out the window.

The building which housed the 19th precinct in New York City was an anachronism. Built about the turn of the century, it stood in the heart of the city's plush, silk-stocking district looking like a Victorian workhouse squatting amid modern, high-rise apartment dwellings and stoically facing the elegant white brick edifice which houses the Russian embassy. Its facade could be used by an industrious filmmaker for a shot of Holmes and Watson entering Scotland Yard.

An enterprising photographer was rewarded for his persistent vigil by being able to snap no less than three photographs of Kevin Lakewood as he walked from the car to the door of the police station.

"Your pretty face is going to be on page one of the *Daily News*," Mike quipped as he all but ran to keep pace with the boy.

It was obvious that the remark did not tickle Kevin's sense of humor.

The interior of the old 19th proved to be in perfect harmony with its exterior. The entrance hall was huge, two stories high and designed to remind all who entered of their insignificance. The place was miraculously overheated by ancient, hissing iron radiators which appeared to be desperately trying to ward off renovation by proving their efficiency. Kevin stood in the center of this vast place as Mike walked directly to the desk sergeant. The boy wore his own black cashmere top coat with a blue and white Cambridge scarf he had found tucked away in one of Mike's dresser drawers. Below the elegant coat he sported a pair of Mike's jeans, the bottoms rolled up several times to display white athletic socks fitted snugly into his own black formal pumps. Given his surroundings Kevin Lakewood looked like a man caught in the act of shoplifting in a Madison Avenue men's boutique.

Mike beckoned and the boy followed him up a flight of ancient wooden steps. "You wait here," Mike said, indicating a bench in the upstairs hall.

"I want to talk to Brandt." Kevin sat, burying his chin under the scarf around his neck and sticking his hands inside the pockets of his coat. Mike felt like Mr. Bumble delivering Oliver Twist to a prospective buyer. Brandt's door was slightly ajar. Mike was about to knock when he heard Brandt call, "Who's out there?"

Mike pushed the door open with one finger and looked into the office.

"Where's the boy?"

"He's here. Can we talk first?"

"Be my guest." Brandt shuffled the papers on his desk as Mike sank into a chair. "What's on your mind, Manning?"

"A hundred questions concerning the murders of Stephen Burke and Susan Kennedy."

"And you think I have the answers."

"No, but I thought if we compared notes we might come up with a few."

Brandt stopped manipulating his reading material and looked directly at Mike. "You're a reporter, not a colleague, and you don't carry any weight around here. Bring in the kid."

"You're a damn good policeman, Inspector Brandt, and you know as well as I do that the scene we walked in on last night was only lacking a director and a cameraman. Something stinks and you want to know what it is. I know these people and their friends, intimately. It's my job. You need help and I can help you, so let's forget the fucking vendetta and get on with what we're paid to do...serve the public."

Brandt looked astonished for one second and then banged his fist on his desk. "Christ! All that's missing is a brass band and a shot of the marines hoisting up the flag on Iwo Jima."

Mike suppressed a grin. "You got the picture."

"I sure do. You are some piece of work, Michael Manning. Pure bullshit. You come walking in here like the answer to my prayers and think you can jerk me around with some half-assed patriotic speech all because you know a few pansies who live on Park Avenue."

Mike waved his hand at the Inspector in disgust. "Let's leave sexual orientation out of this."

"I'd love to, but when you're around it seems to creep into every conversation."

"You elicit it, Brandt — in fact, you seem to be obsessed by it."

"Get the fuck out of here."

"Did you find one article of Burke's clothing in that bedroom?" Mike sprang the question at Brandt like a cat pouncing on an unsuspecting mouse and the ploy worked. As Mike had stated, Brandt was a good policeman and couldn't resist the possibility of learning something about a case that was presently a complete mystery.

"You noticed that too, eh?" Brandt responded, albeit reluctantly, but he was hooked and Mike Manning knew it. Mike nodded.

"And without my magnifying glass."

"How do you figure it?"

"Right now I don't. Too much smoke screen, but the air will clear. It usually does." The mouse began to squirm but before it could get away Mike asked, "What did Milly tell you?"

"Same thing she told you." Brandt once again began fishing through the papers on his desk. "Here...I just finished reading the statement you gave Cookie."

"What about the timing? A lot of people left and came into that apartment in very short order."

Brandt picked up yet another sheet of typescript. "Mr. and Mrs. Burke and the boy." He began to scan the page.

"Kevin," Mike prompted.

"Yeah, Kevin." Brandt looked up. "He staying with you?"

Mike smiled and Brandt grinned maliciously. "Is he pretty, Manning?"

"Like a fucking jack-off dream, Inspector."

"You're a cocky bastard."

"You sniff a lot, Brandt, and then get upset when you pick up the scent you're after."

Brandt's fair complexion turned scarlet and his eyes threatened to burn holes into Mike's forehead. Mike pointed to the paper in Brandt's hand. "The time schedule...?"

Flustered, the policeman picked up where he left off. "Mr. and Mrs. Burke and the boy were at home all day. Mildred Burke left the apartment about four to do some shopping."

"Confirmation?" Mike cut in.

"The doorman...here...Joseph Stern...comes on duty at four and he remembers Mrs. Burke going out a few minutes after he relieved the guy who does the early shift. You can't get it any closer than that." Mike nodded his agreement.

"A short time later, maybe a half hour, the boy left all dressed up in a fancy tux."

"Joe wasn't any more specific about the time?"

"Joe? That's right, I forgot, you're an intimate. No, Joe wasn't any more specific. He's a doorman, Manning, not a timekeeper."

"And the girl?"

"She enters some time after the boy leaves. Let's say five o'clock. Stern announces her on the house phone and Mr. Burke says 'send her up.'"

"Then Milly gets back about six…"

"Catches lover boy with his wee-wee hanging out and bang, bang…we all do overtime on New Year's Eve."

"Time of death?" Mike asked.

"Unconfirmed as yet, but the doc says two hours before he viewed the remains sounds just about right which makes it six. Mrs. Burke didn't waste much time. I'm surprised she didn't blow his pecker off."

"You make me nostalgic for my crime reporting days, Brandt. It's the drawing room repartee I miss."

"If you want polite chit-chat from cops, watch television."

"What about the girl?" Mike asked.

"Not much. She shared an apartment in the Village with a roommate, Terry Allen. We checked with a neighbor this morning and Terry is visiting her parents for the holiday. The neighbor had no idea where her parents live so we'll have to wait on that one."

"Do you have that address in the Village?"

"No, Manning, we went around knocking on doors till we hit the jackpot. What you mean is, will I give you the address."

"Will you *please* give me the address?" Mike asked hopefully.

"It'll be in the official fact sheet we hand out to the press tomorrow morning."

"Susan was running around with Kevin Lakewood's crowd and I know most of them. I can ask some questions and learn more in an hour than your men can in a week." Mike dangled this new piece of bait cautiously.

Andrew Brandt was no fool. "And then I can read all about it in MIKE MANNING'S NEW YORK. You insult my intelligence, mister society editor. Now get the boy."

Mike raised his right hand. "Anything I get I give directly to you. I print only what you clear." It was a tempting offer.

Brandt knew Mike could deliver but he didn't know if he could trust him. "Put your hand down. You look like a boy scout."

"The address?"

"You fuck me, Manning, and I'll put your balls in a vise."

Mike was about to respond in kind but checked himself by taking a deep breath. At the moment Milly's welfare, and Kevin's, was more important than going round for round with Andrew Brandt. "You have my word on it, Inspector."

Brandt scribbled on a pad of paper and handed the sheet to Mike across the cluttered desk. Mike breathed a sigh of relief without flexing a muscle. He pocketed Susan Kennedy's address and headed for the door.

"And go easy on the kid. He's frightened and confused."

"So was Kenneth Farley," Brandt whispered loud enough for Mike to hear.

Manning swung around as if he had been knifed in the back. "You've had my balls in a vice since Kenny died and every day you turn the screw a little tighter." Two short steps and he was standing in front of Brandt's desk. He leaned across it, his face a foot from Brandt's staring eyes. "I loved him and I did what I thought was right. I didn't kill Kenny. You and your fucked-up police department killed him. Now get off my back, Brandt, and stay the hell off it."

"Think twice the next time you tell me what I'm sniffing

after," Brandt whispered with a vehemence Mike had never heard before. So that was it. The dig…the slight innuendo…the wound to his masculine pride which some inane sense of honor forced him to vindicate even if it meant defiling the dead. Mike shook his head to clear it and straightened his back.

"Go easy on the kid. He doesn't know anything."

5

After his interrogation Kevin seemed relieved when Mike announced he was going to abandon him and stick to his normal work schedule. "It's called making a living," he told Kevin in an attempt to harass the boy out of his apparent depression.

"What am I supposed to do, vacuum and put up a pot roast?"

"Come to think of it I haven't had a home-cooked meal in years."

"Well if you wait on me it's going to be a lot more years before you do."

"Out," Mike ordered as the car pulled up in front of his apartment building. "Unless you hear from me I'll be back around five."

"Thanks, Dad."

"Out," Mike said again and when Kevin obeyed he immediately directed Evans to the address Brandt had given him. If Terry Allen had gone home for the holiday and tomorrow was a work day there was one chance in a hundred she would be back in her apartment this afternoon. It was a long shot, but right now it was the only odds being offered. Mike settled back, lit a cigarette and asked Frank Evans how long he had been a driver.

"If you count last night, two days," came the reply.

"What?" Mike sat up in his seat.

"You are connected, in some way, with the driving service…I hope."

"Mechanic. Been with them twenty years."

"So last night…"

"When you called all that was left in the garage was the dispatcher, my car and me. You're lucky you didn't get the dispatcher."

"How do you like being a driver?"

"Seem to do more waiting than driving."

"That's the way it goes. Do you think we could up-grade our wheels the next time around?"

"Hush up. She's a temperamental lady and doesn't take kindly to insults. Hate to see you pushing us down Second Avenue in this weather."

Mike groaned. "Maybe we should reconsider this alliance, Frank."

"If you're worried about my lack of experience you can consider today my second year on the job."

"Did you ever think of being a writer?"

"No. What did you have in mind?"

"A politician's press agent, what else?"

When they reached their destination Mike got his first lucky break in the case. Terry Allen was home. The address on Charles Street was a brownstone and Terry's apartment was, naturally, on the top floor, rear.

"Mike Manning, I can't believe it," the young lady exclaimed for the third time. Mike had been trying for years to come up with a suitable response to this one-liner but to date his only reply was a dazzling smile.

"I hope I'm not intruding," he began, "but…"

"No, no, not at all," she said a little breathlessly. "Please sit down, Mr. Manning."

Terry Allen was a petite girl with brown hair, a sincere smile and as similar to the stereotypical secretary as the copies which roll endlessly out of their Xerox machines. As she spoke her eyes darted nervously around the small living room and her face expressed the unspoken lament, "Why didn't I clean this place last Saturday." The Christmas tree, dry, drooping and lackluster, seemed to be the focal point of her misery.

"You're here about Sue," she continued. "I couldn't believe it.

I mean I just couldn't believe it. I heard it on the television last night. We were waiting for the ball to drop...you know, Times Square...and they had this news brief thing they do now and there it was...Susan Kennedy murdered. I couldn't believe it. I mean I still can't believe it. Daddy said there were probably a lot of Susan Kennedys in New York but I knew it was my Susan, Mr. Manning, I just knew it." She spoke rapidly, her face rotating between Mike and the sad Christmas tree.

Terry Allen was very upset and, Mike thought, had every right to be. "What made you so sure, Ms. Allen?" he asked.

"Terry, please. Or Theresa. But you couldn't call Susan, Suzie. God, she hated that. How was I sure? Because of him, how else?"

"You mean Stephen Burke?"

"I used to read about him...in your column. Mike Manning, I can't believe it. And remember the elopement? God, was that romantic. But look how it ended..." The girl shivered for emphasis.

"Did you know Stephen Burke, Terry?"

"Me? Did I know Stephen Burke? What a question. What would Stephen Burke want to know me for? Now Sue was different. I mean she had class and style and clothes...God did she have clothes." Mike's sympathy for Terry Allen was fast giving way to exasperation. He wanted to take hold of her by the shoulders and shake her till she made sense. In lieu of that he decided to take charge of the situation and once again turned on his dazzling smile.

Before she could say, "Mike Manning, I can't believe it," he plunged right in.

"Terry, I'm here as a working reporter and you don't have to answer any of my questions."

The girl started to protest, but he cut her off with a wave of his hand.

"I'm here as a working reporter trying to put a story together. But the police are going to question you and demand straightforward, honest answers." Terry's eyes widened.

"They were here this morning. Margie told me. She's got the front apartment. When she moves I'm next in line for it. Do you know some guy tried to marry her for that apartment."

Mike began to believe there was, after all, such a thing as justifiable homicide. "I'm going to ask the questions and you're going to answer them calmly and to the best of your ability. I'm even going to give what you tell me to the police which should make it a lot easier for you when they come for your statement."

"Thanks, Mr. Manning."

"First…do you know how to brew a pot of coffee?" Terry was so startled by the question she actually jumped out of her seat.

"Sure I do and I should have thought of it. I'm not usually like this, Mr. Manning, but it's been a very strange day and every time I see that ball drop…you know, on Times Square…I'm gonna think…" Her voice faded but was never completely silenced as she went to the kitchen. Mike hoped that performing a normal task would put the girl in a more receptive state of mind.

There is nothing like a domestic chore to bring us back to reality…like making a pot roast. He thought of Kevin and wondered what the boy was doing right now. Sleeping, probably; God knows he didn't get much rest last night. Mike grinned at this last thought and felt a delightful tingle about the base of his spine. Mike Manning liked a good pot roast.

"Would you believe they want eight hundred a month for this place?" The exclamation filled the room before the speaker appeared. She entered a few moments later carrying a tray which held two steaming mugs of coffee.

"I don't know how I'm going to swing that kind of rent alone."

Mike winced inwardly. Was this the ultimate concern of all New York apartment dwellers who lost a roommate to marriage, mayhem or murder? He was sure Theresa Allen didn't think she was being gross. After refusing cream and sugar Mike began trying, with more hope than expectation, to find out what Susan Kennedy was all about.

"How did you meet Susan?" Mike asked

"Would you believe through a roommate service?"

"How long ago was that?" Mike asked, hiding his disappointment. A roommate referral service was as reliable as a con man's testimonial.

"Almost two years ago. She moved here from some place on Long Island."

"Do you know anything about her family?"

"Her mother died just before I met her. She sold the house they lived in and moved to the city. She never mentioned her father and I never asked. These days, who knows? You know what I mean?"

"Did she have any other family?"

"If she did she never mentioned them to me," Terry answered.

"Where did she work?"

Terry named a prominent Madison Avenue advertising agency which Mike knew very well. He extracted a small pad and pencil from his jacket and began to take notes. "Do you mind?" he asked.

"Not at all. I feel like a movie star and you're Rex Reed."

Mike winced again but this time for an entirely different reason. "What about boyfriends?"

"At first, none at all. Sue was a real classy gal. No one was good enough for her. I told her, you gotta bend a little. Like Prince Andrew isn't gonna walk up four flights...you know what I mean?"

"And then?"

"And then a year ago she meets this guy...gentleman she called him...and her whole life changed."

Terry shook her head. "Did it ever change. Clothes...I never saw anything like it. Bergdorf Goodman, Henri Bendel, Bonwit Teller and those east side boutiques where they charge you just to touch. You know what I mean?"

She seemed completely relaxed now as she expounded on what was obviously her favorite topic. "And parties...she was going to those parties you write about and was running around with a crowd that was strictly top drawer, Mr. Manning."

Terry finally paused to breathe. "But I never dreamed the guy was Stephen..."

"You never knew who the man was, did you, Terry?"

"No, but..."

He stopped her again. "We're putting together the facts, not speculating. You never knew who the man was," he stated again.

"No," she answered, sounding a little miffed.

"Did Susan ever go away with this man? Weekends, vacations, anything like that?"

"No, that was the funny part of it. And she slept right here every night." Terry pointed toward the wall which meant the adjacent room was their bedroom.

"What people do is none of my business, Mr. Manning, don't get me wrong, but if they were balling it was strictly matinee time. But now that we know he was married..."

"You're doing it again, Terry. We don't know anything of the sort. Susan told you that she met a man she liked. He gave her some very expensive gifts — or a lot of very expensive gifts — and introduced her to a smart crowd. But he never went away with her or spent the night with her...are those the facts?"

Terry nodded her disappointment. What good was gossip when all you did was stick to the facts?

"Did you like Susan?" Mike asked.

"Yeah," she said, a little sadly. "She was a real classy gal. Not that any of it rubbed off...you know what I mean? But she taught me a lot and I'm a quick learner. Yeah, I'm gonna miss her.

I told her how much I was gonna miss her and not only because of the rent, either."

Mike, who was mentally composing his parting remarks, thought he had misunderstood Terry's eulogy. "You told her... you knew she would never come back to this apartment again?"

"Sure I knew."

"How?" Mike almost shouted. He wanted to strangle Theresa Allen with his bare hands.

"How did you know?"

"Because she paid her half of the rent for December and told me she was leaving. She was going away with her gentleman friend."

"Holy shit."

And then a bomb exploded in Mike's head. "Are Susan Kennedy's clothes here?"

"Of course not." The girl looked at Mike as if he were demented. "She was packing when I left yesterday."

"Where were they going? Did she tell you?"

Terry waved her hands in the air. "Who knows? London, Paris, Rome, Hollywood. Stephen Burke has all the money in the world."

"Stephen Burke didn't have the price of a subway token."

"What about those clothes and some nice pieces of jewelry I forgot to mention. That's a lot of subway tokens, Mr. Manning."

"We still don't know who gave them to her," Mike insisted.

"I think that's obvious."

"What's obvious?" Mike asked with a sigh.

"That she was running away with Stephen Burke and his wife caught them in the act...that's what's obvious, Mr. Manning."

Mike looked at the girl with a mixture of sympathy and envy. To people like her everything was black or white and always crystal clear. It wasn't a case of being unable to see the trees for the forest, but rather believing a forest existed because someone had erected a row of trees on the horizon. And there was one born every minute.

"About as obvious, young lady, as the sun revolving around the earth."

Before he had descended one flight he heard Theresa Allen scurry across the hall and knock on her neighbor's door. The obvious was about to be annotated.

Outside, the air was cold and damp. The day-old snow had been shoveled, swept and trampled into a sculptured landscape of frigid mountains and valleys. It was just four in the afternoon but dusk was already beginning to engulf the city. He signaled Frank Evans to stay put and hurried toward a phone booth he spotted on the corner. Without bothering to search his pockets for the proper coin, Mike punched out the emergency number and asked the operator to connect him with the 19th precinct. He was mildly surprised when she did. By the time the call went through to Inspector Brandt his fingers and toes were numb.

"Manning. I just spoke to the roommate."

"She's back?" Brandt was either uninterested or else distracted by a more immediate problem. "I'll send a couple of men down. What did she tell you?"

"You'll have it all as soon as I get it down on paper."

"I'd better."

Ignoring the comment, Mike asked, "Did you search Burke's bedroom?"

"You've got to be kidding. What do you think the police do, Manning, write gossip columns?"

"Were his clothes where they belong?" Mike shifted his weight from one foot to the other, then back again, in an effort to keep his blood from solidifying.

"Two big closets full and more drawers than I care to recall. The problem is nothing was out of place, remember?"

"The problem is, Inspector, we don't know what the problem

is."

The threatening clouds kept their promise and snow once again cascaded from sky to earth. Mike and his newfound roommate lay stretched out in front of a fire that whispered and hissed more than it roared. In the darkened room the flames rose and fell, highlighting and shadowing their naked bodies like a passionate but bashful lover.

"I haven't lit a fire in...I don't remember how long."

"Can we safely say it wasn't last July?"

"I should have tossed you out last night."

"And I should have burned you a pot roast."

Kevin's reference was to their dinner. When Mike returned to the apartment, cold and weary, he thought he had walked into a French restaurant by mistake. The aroma coming from his kitchen warmed his heart and reminded him that he had skipped lunch in favor of an interview that had raised more questions than it answered.

"If that tastes as good as it smells, I'll marry the cook."

Kevin beamed. "I left the pot roast recipe in my other apron and substituted this from memory." The substitution was beef bourguignon, swimming in a delectable gravy which did indeed taste better than it smelled. The salad was made of ingredients unobtainable at any green grocer in New York in January and wine was served in flute glasses Mike Manning never dreamed of owning. Kevin had not only managed to get the best caterer in town to deliver on short notice, but also got them to bring a load of firewood along with the gourmet meal.

"You have one great dialing finger, kid."

"You said something about marrying the creator."

"The cook, Kevin. I said the cook." Later — content, warm and all appetites sated — Mike's hand traced an invisible line from Kevin's neck, down his spine and over his buttocks.

"The fire's warmed you like a piece of toast."

"If you touched me like that in an igloo I'd feel warm."

"Good line. Have you used it before?"

Kevin sighed and rolled over on his back. "I feel a major question coming on."

Mike's hand once again tested for skin temperature, moving from smooth chest to flat belly to an exhausted but still valiant masculinity. "You and Brad Turner?"

"Oh…you were impressed."

"Just curious."

"Mike Manning is only curious about what interests him."

"You sound like an agent," Mike said, laughing.

"You sound like a dirty old man." Mike squeezed and Kevin pulled his knees upward.

"Okay…okay…Brad is a jock, a womanizer and takes his pleasure where he finds it."

"What's that supposed to mean?"

"Make of it what you will." Then Kevin withdrew, but not in typical fashion. He didn't change his position or turn his head. He simply tuned Mike out so that the rapport which existed between them a moment before was replaced by a mental barrier more physical than a stone wall. The fire, more glow than flame now, haloed the boy's head, turning his hair a reddish-brown. His face, flushed and brooding, resembled a painting some old Italian master might have done of his assistant or stable boy. His aloofness made him as desirable as an unobtainable Renaissance model. Mike drew the boy to him, pressing the full length of his body against a vision that was fast becoming his nemesis.

"Where are you?" he whispered.

"Staying out of your way…and your fantasies of Bradley Turner."

"You're acting like a baby again."

"Because you treat me like one."

"Kevin, in the past twenty-four hours I've treated you in many ways, but like a baby wasn't one of them."

"Would a one-night-stand be more accurate?"

"Christ…all because I happened to mention Brad Turner."

"Mentioned? I was contemplating our future and you practically asked for his phone number."

I already have his phone number, was the first thought to pop up in Mike's mind and he hated himself for thinking it. The morals of a jack rabbit? An instant later he honed in on the word future.

"You're a very handsome young man, Kev, and sexier than any I've had the good fortune to meet. But I told you I allow myself one mistake a year and I think I'm working on number three…and it's still January 1st."

"What does that mean?…and don't tell me…"

"It means," Mike cut in, "that if I had been a promiscuous thirteen-year-old I could be your father, remember?" And, he wanted to add, if I had accepted your mother's offer I would now be your stepfather…or a corpse and not because of Susan Kennedy. This last thought made Mike want to sit up and shout, "Why assume Burke was killed because of the girl?"

Was she one of those trees on the horizon behind which stood absolutely nothing?

"I've been had," he heard Kevin saying.

"But in the nicest possible sense. Come on, Kev, smile."

"Sure, why not. And let's do it again. That should just about pay for my room and board."

"If anyone else said that to me I'd punch them right in the gut."

"I feel as if you already have."

Mike reached for his cigarettes, lit one and handed it to Kevin. "You're very young," he told the boy, "and I'm fast approaching what is euphemistically called middle age."

"You look twenty-five." Kevin passed the cigarette back to Mike.

"Thanks, but looking and being are two very different things. It's how we think that makes the difference." Mike touched his forehead. "Right now I'm thinking about Milly and the trial and all the shit that's going to go down the tube between now and then."

"Do you think I've forgotten about it? Christ, I'm not an idiot."

"I know you didn't forget it," Mike said gently.

"But a cozy fire and a few glasses of good wine put it in second place to a rose-covered cottage in the not too distant future."

Before Kevin could protest Mike stopped him again. "I'm also thinking that your mother is one of my oldest and dearest friends. Did you know that when you were a teenager, just after your father died, your mother and I were what the gossip columns call an item?"

"She told me."

"Did she also tell you she wanted to marry me?"

"Yes," Kevin answered with a note of triumph in his voice.

Mike was surprised but tried not to show it. "So now I take her son as my lover? Come on, Kevin, it's grotesque at the very least."

"You can't take me as your lover but you can make love to me? That, Mr. Manning, is fucking grotesque." Kevin's accusation was followed by a silence as still as death. The fire, now reduced to a steady glow, had ceased to hiss. Even the constant hum of traffic from the street below was muted and hushed by the snow. Mike tossed his cigarette into the hearth and a tiny flame erupted where it struck the smoldering log.

"There's a difference," he finally answered. "And I'm not talking about right and wrong. You think like a brash young man and I, hopefully, think like a mature one. Both are valid but the two seldom mesh. I wanted you five minutes after I spoke to you last night but I would never have made the first move."

Now it was Kevin who looked embarrassed.

"I want you now and I'll want you tomorrow and probably next New Year's Eve, too. But there's more to a relationship than making love. One has to fill in the between times on some common ground and we can't count on a murder trial a year to keep us otherwise occupied. And, dammit, you're still Milly's son. Jesus, Kev, she would murder me." The words were out of his mouth before he realized their horrendous implication.

"You have just heard a mature man put his foot in his mouth," he offered in a vain effort to salvage all that had gone before the unintentional blunder.

Kevin chose to ignore the faux pas and answered simply, "My mother knows I'm gay." Some intimate conversations have passed between Milly and her son, Mike thought.

"When you're married to a man like Burke," Kevin continued, as if reading Mike's mind, "you turn to the next of kin for comfort. My mother and I have no secrets from each other."

And she knows my story, Mike continued to speculate, yet she asked me to look after the boy whose desirability wouldn't go unnoticed by a Trappist monk. Curious? Does the plot thicken or is it another tree on the horizon? If this continues we'll have enough trees to make a real forest. To hide what?

Then Kevin asked a question which brought Mike back to the present with a resounding thud. "Does that blue robe have anything to do with all of this?"

"It has to do with none of this," he answered impatiently, his tone gruffer than intended.

"Then we seem to have run out of common ground."

Kevin began to rise. "I think I'll turn in."

Mike's hand gripped the boy's wrist. "Wait...wait...I'll tell you. I owe you that much."

"You owe me nothing, Mike."

"Then I'll tell you because you asked. Is there more wine in that bottle?"

"A little, but it's warm." Mike held out his glass.

"No matter. They say wine loosens the tongue." Kevin poured the remains of the bottle into Mike's glass. He sipped and then spoke to the fire which was now a pile of white ash surrounding one glowing ember.

The story Mike told contained all the prerequisites of a Hollywood script, circa 1950. It was happy, sad, romantic, tragic and unique only because it was a page out of the life of the narrator. However, this particular scenario would never reach the screen unless major alterations, namely as to gender of one of the leading characters, were made between the writing and the filming.

Mike Manning was a cub reporter for the *Ledger*, covering the crime beat. Kenneth Farley was a rookie policeman. Both were young, handsome and ambitious. A journalist and a cop whose paths crossed because they were both involved, albeit from different aspects, in the pursuit of justice. An ideal in which they both believed but which was, in the end, to repay their obeisance with malice.

Mike was brash and as sure of himself as the young men in the glossy ads he still occasionally posed for to the tune of a hundred bucks an hour. Ken, a product of the American Midwest, had never outgrown the teenage awkward stage of existence. He seemed to be more legs than body, more arms than torso, and both appendages very often refused to obey the commands of his very intelligent mind. His blue eyes looked upon New York as if seeing was not necessarily followed by believing. His dark blond hair, cut and styled in a tonsorial establishment he could not afford, reverted to its own natural state of relaxed ambivalence ten minutes after the blow drier had thought it won.

They met in court rooms (Ken tripped while walking to the witness box), in morgues (Ken turned a sickly green and had to be physically removed from the scene) and in detention halls where Ken was reprimanded for being too polite to the inmates. Ken Farley wanted to be everything Mike Manning was and showed it by being as rude to the reporter as he was kind to his prisoners. Mike was dismayed by his attraction to Ken and thought the infatuation would disappear if he constantly reminded himself and the policeman of the latter's shortcomings.

Mike: "We meet in the nicest places."

Ken: "It's my job. You could be showing your capped teeth to a camera and picking up a week's salary in an hour."

Mike: "Don't trip over any clues, Farley."

Ken: "The only clue I'm looking for is how they let you in here. This is police business, Manning."

Mike was working night court when Ken and a dozen colleagues arrived with a paddy wagon full of prostitutes.

Mike: "You have some taste in women, Farley."

Ken: "And they all have your name in their little black books. Whoever would have thought pretty-boy had to pay for it."

Mike: "If my name is in their books it's as a consultant, not a customer."

The fisherman had baited the hook and the fish, while not taking a nibble, didn't swim away from it either. That night, for the first time, they had a drink together and communicated socially outside the line of duty. Neither could ever attest as to how this came about. One or the other could have made the offer or they could have found themselves walking in the same direction and drifted into the deserted bar off Foley Square as naturally as two commuters who routinely stopped for a beer before boarding the five-fifteen to Scarsdale. They were both struck, separately and privately, by the ease with which they went from working acquaintances to friends without any shifting of gears.

Mike: "What are you doing in that uniform? You should be teaching English in a fancy New England prep school."

Ken: "You should be on your way to Hollywood, where you

could dazzle the world in your jockey briefs."

Mike: "Which tells me you read the Sunday *Times* magazine section...including the ads."

Ken: "Actually, only the ads. Tell me something, Mike, do they air brush the crotch or are you really that flat down there?"

Mike: "Cute, Farley, real cute."

As naturally as they had had their first beer together they began to have dinner together a couple of times a week. To Ken, dining out was eating a Salisbury steak seated at a table as opposed to eating a hamburger at a counter. When Mike treated him to his first meal in one of the better restaurants in town Ken was awed by the bill but secretly thrilled at being in a bistro frequented by celebrities and with a companion the waiters knew by name.

Then they started to go to the films together. Because they usually worked nights this was an afternoon outing. They discovered they both liked old musicals and second-rate mysteries. Mike introduced Ken to a movie house which featured nothing but this type of vintage fare. They spoke of their work, of school, of growing up and of life in the city...by what seemed to be an unspoken agreement, they never discussed what they did when they were not with each other. Mike thought his lifestyle would appear frivolous to Ken Farley and Ken feared his mundane existence would bore the sophisticated Mike Manning. Mike bought theater tickets and refused Ken's offer to pay his share. Mike did it again and Ken refused to go.

Mike: "Death Trap...a real good mystery."

Ken: "Okay...but dinner is my treat."

Mike suffered, happily, through a Salisbury steak and fries. It went on this way for almost a year. Mike Manning, whose sex life was never wanting and whose track record included a movie star, a popular rock singer and a Washington gentleman whose name often turned up on page one of the *New York Times,* was actually courting and living the life of a celibate while in the process.

Then one afternoon, seated side by side in an almost empty

movie house, their hands touched, hesitated and finally clasped one into the other. Both breathed an inaudible sigh of relief.

Mike: "My place or yours?"

Ken: "Yours…it has an elevator."

This new intimacy enhanced their old friendship. Having nothing in common lent a note of mystery, interest and the joy of discovery to a relationship they drifted into as easily as they had drifted into each other's lives. They didn't exchange vows of eternal love or map out a future of perpetual togetherness. The fact that they continued to seek each other's company was the only proof needed of their commitment; the present too satisfying to warrant contemplating the future.

Mike, the more worldly of the two, waited for the ennui to set in. Eight years later he was still waiting. Ken Farley rose to the rank of sergeant. Mike Manning became society editor of the *Ledger* with his own by-lined column. Both were in the public eye and therefore in sensitive positions. They continued to maintain separate apartments and to move in different milieus. When their work brought them face to face in public they played the roles of friendly adversaries.

Mike: "Don't trip over any clues, Farley."

Ken: "I get all my clues from your column, Manning."

When they weren't working, they were together. Each considered the other's apartment home. There were beach weekends and ski weekends. Vacations in Europe and the Caribbean. Apart, their lives were full and productive; together, they were reflective and at peace. All in all it worked. Only a few intimate friends knew of their relationship. Milly Burke was one of them.

Oddly enough Ken's boss, Inspector Andrew Brandt, was another. How this came about proved to be the beginning of the end of their ideal. A policeman in a small southern town was fired after ten years of exemplary service with all accrued benefits forfeited. His crime was marching in a gay day parade in the community he had sworn to defend against such usurpers of the common good.

"The only crime I committed," he was quoted as saying, "was living a lie all these years. I lost my job and gained my self-respect. I have a hunch I won."

The incident and the quote drew national attention. Mike Manning went to bat for the underdog. His point of view was neither emotional nor prejudicial. He used his mighty typewriter to strike a blow against injustice in all its forms, shapes and guises. He printed responses, pro and con. He flew to that bastion of the common good where he was applauded and spattered with dung. The policeman was not reinstated. Injustice survived the onslaught. But if he had made one reader in a million more aware and more tolerant then Mike Manning had a hunch he too had won.

Ken encouraged the crusade and patted Mike's back after each stinging column saw the light of day. Mike accepted the compliments with more unease than grace. Both of them knew that their war on social injustice had landed a salvo in their own back yard. He was writing about a cop from the Bible Belt but thinking about a cop in New York. He was addressing the masses and found himself in the crowd. Mike Manning thought a man should practice what he preached.

Mike: "I'm starting to look for a bigger apartment. Two bedrooms should be just about right."

Ken: "No way."

It wasn't so much a fight as a series of philosophical arguments. More pros and cons, not from faceless readers but from the hearts and souls of two sophisticated and frightened men.

They talked of leaving their jobs and the city, but that would be quitting before the race had even begun and neither of them were quitters in any sense of the word. They composed the most convoluted of stories to announce their proposed living arrangements, but that would only compound the original lie. Finally Mike offered a compromise he knew they could both live with.

Mike: "We share a place and continue living just as we have been. No announcements, no waving of flags, no carrying of signs. Not lying doesn't mean shouting the truth from the top of the Empire State Building. We'll live the way we want to live and fuck anyone who doesn't like it."

Ken: "I have a feeling they'll fuck us...figuratively, not literally."

Ken, now a detective, said he would discuss it with his boss, Inspector Brandt. Mike encouraged this. Being upfront in that area was the best possible start.

Brandt: "You're a cop and a damn good one. What you do on your own time is your own fucking business. But flaunt it...even one fucking inch...and you're out."

Ken said he needed time to think. Mike said he could have all the time he needed, but continued to push, gently. He understood his friend's position. All the reporter had to lose was his column. The cop was betting all he loved and all he had worked so hard to achieve and the going odds were a million to one against him. Mike watched Ken go from fighting form to dull and at times even listless. Was it his imagination or was Ken actually losing weight?

Mike: "Is Brandt giving you a hard time?"

Ken: "No. It's something I've got to work out."

Mike: "Something we've got to work out. Now snap out of it and let's let it ride for a while. I want my old Kenny back with or without his own apartment. Christ, we'll rent two apartments apiece if that'll make you happy."

"...And then, just about a year ago, we talked on the phone as we usually did when we didn't see each other. He sounded fine. He said he wanted me to know that he thought I was right and that no matter what happened I should stick by what I believed. He said he would even pitch a tent in Central Park and share it with me. I told him he was overreacting but that I liked the idea. I had my old Kenny back. When he hung up I went to bed and he took out his service revolver, loaded it and blew his brains out."

"My God!" Kevin gasped.

Mike stared into what was left of their fire, his face a rigid mask.

"But why?" Kevin was saying. "Why? Nothing was decided. You told him you would go along with anything he wanted. Then why?"

"Because I was forcing his hand...because Brandt was harassing him because he was afraid to live in the sun and thought it cowardly...take your pick. There are a million reasons. I choose a new one every day but always come back to the one with my name on it."

"But you told him he could have it his way," Kevin protested. "It doesn't make sense."

"A lot of things don't make sense, young man, but we encounter them every day, big as life and certain as death."

Kevin touched Mike's arm. "I'm sorry." His tone reflected the inadequacy of the words. Mike shook his head. The gesture could have been in response to Kevin's sympathy but was more likely a reaction to his own silent thoughts.

Suddenly Kevin felt like an unwanted mourner at a stranger's funeral. He got slowly to his feet. "I'm going to bed...unless you want me..."

"I'd like to be alone."

"Good night, Mike."

"Good night, kid." The fire was now all ash, its heat only a memory. Mike reached for a cigarette and when it was lit derived no pleasure from the habit he had been trying to rid himself of for years. "Why?" he whispered. Would the story always end with a question mark?

"I would pitch a tent in Central Park and share it with you."

Mike heard the words and thought, "Please, God, not because of me." Had Brandt taunted Ken and was he now hounding

Mike to assuage his own guilt? Had Brandt been jealous? A psychopathic closet case who would see the object of his desire dead before allowing himself to face his true feelings? So many answers...but was he asking the right questions?

"Mike." He awoke from his reverie and looked up to see Kevin standing in the doorway. The boy was wearing a white robe.

"I bought it today," Kevin said. "You see, I don't want to fill anyone's robe. I want you to like Kevin Lakewood."

Mike smiled. "You don't give up, do you?"

"You would hate me if I did."

"I don't think I could ever hate you."

"Good night, Mike." Kevin retreated as silently as he had approached. Mike tossed his cigarette into the cold ashes. Milly would be coming home tomorrow and then what?

"Why the girl, Milly?" Mike whispered.

"Temporary insanity, isn't that what it's called?"

"He wasn't satisfied with screwing in every bedroom he could get a foot into, so he had to start doing it in our home."

"...Catches lover boy with his wee-wee hanging out and bang, bang..."

"She was running away with Stephen Burke and his wife caught them in the act...that's what's obvious, Mr. Manning."

It was the right question, but all the answers were wrong. Mike was sure of that. And now there was something else bothering him. A persistent gnawing deep inside his brain told him that he had missed something he should have seen, or ignored something he should have paid attention to. A link...that was it. There was actually a common denominator to all this madness, but what the hell was it? A link...a common denominator...funny, all he could come up with was New Year's Eve. Well why not, the new year was only one day and one hour old.

6

The ancient Impala proved its usefulness the next day. It was the type of vehicle one expected to see pull up at the service entrance of 830 Fifth Avenue.

"Tell Milly I'll be in touch," Mike said as Kevin opened the door.

"Thanks, Mike."

"What for?"

"Everything...especially..."

"Move out before those bloodhounds around the corner smell a rat." The young man who emerged from the car, wearing rolled up jeans and muffled to the nose, didn't warrant a second glance as he hurried from the curb and down the alley which led to the rear of the building. Crouched low in the back seat Mike noted, as the car turned south on Fifth, that Milly Burke's entrance was going to be as sensational as her son's was mundane The crowd surrounding the blue canopy was legion. He had expected nothing less.

"They should bring her home by helicopter," Frank Evans mumbled. "Roof's plenty big."

"And disappoint the press and sightseers? They would crucify her in print and Saxman knows it. What the lady needs is sympathy, not a reminder of her privileged status."

"What the lady needs is a one-way ticket to Brazil."

Mike laughed. "Can I quote you?"

"How much do you pay for a quote?"

"Nothing. People usually bribe me to get a mention."

"You just met the exception to the rule, Mr. Manning ."

Andrew Brandt was in his office when Mike arrived. When he finished reading the report on Theresa Allen he tossed it on his cluttered desk and leaned back in his chair.

"Just about what she gave us, which makes it all as clear as mud. Where are Susan Kennedy's clothes?"

"A locker in Grand Central or the bus terminal?" Mike ventured. Brandt shook his head.

"We're way ahead of you, Manning. Those things are good for twenty-four hours. If she deposited her luggage before she went to see Burke the lock would have been forced and the contents confiscated sometime yesterday afternoon. We checked them all, Grand Central, Penn, Port Authority, and the only suspicious thing we uncovered was two pounds of pot. Good stuff, too."

"It's going for a hundred bucks an ounce on the street. Nice New Year bonus for your crew."

Brandt didn't rise to the occasion. "Do you really believe the police do things like that?" he asked with more pity than indignation.

"Some do, I'm sure…and you know it."

"And I suppose you believe that Stuart Symington uses the police department like it was his own private stud service."

"In some cases, yes…and you know that, too."

"The only thing I know is that I have been trying to nail that bastard for a year and I'm gonna do it, Manning, you just watch me."

"The Florida business? I thought that was a dead issue."

"The kid Symington was playing house with is dead, not the case." Brandt leaned forward as if about to confide in his listener. "What do you know about it, Mike?…as an intimate, so to speak."

Mike? It was the first time Brandt had ever used his Christian name and it didn't go unnoticed. When Andrew Brandt wanted to butter up someone he certainly knew how to do it. Mike wondered how far the policeman would go to learn what he wanted to know. Interesting bit of speculation, if nothing else.

"I know as much or as little as you do," Mike answered.

"When the police didn't prosecute I dropped it. I'm not out to nail anybody ... Andy."

"You think I'm after his blood because of his...what's the word this week? Orientation?"

"I think if you had anything on him a year ago he would be behind bars now and if you had anything on him now you wouldn't be talking to me about it."

Brandt shrugged. "So where does that leave Ms. Kennedy's clothes?"

"Are we sure she didn't have her bags with her when she went to see Burke?" Mike asked.

"According to Joseph Stern she carried nothing with her but her purse. By the way, the guy sounds like he's at death's door."

"Lung condition. He's had it for as long as I've known him. Look, she packed everything she owned when she left the Village apartment and she arrived at upper Fifth Avenue with only her purse. Her luggage has got to be somewhere between those two points."

"Between those two points is half the island of Manhattan and more floor space than you can find in the entire state of Kansas. We have to work with what we know and what we know is that she was having an affair with Burke and they were about to blow town together."

With a gesture of impatience Mike stood up and answered, "If that's the theory you're working on, you know less than I do."

"What do you know?"

"I know Stephen Burke. If there was one thing he loved more than himself and sex it was money. Christ, he had his pick of the women in this town, some of them prettier than Susan Kennedy and all of them a lot richer. So much for sex. He was married to a millionairess. He had everything he wanted and you're trying to tell me he was going to give it all up for a penniless secretary and live happily ever after on her two hundred and fifty bucks a week? I hope you're kidding, Inspector."

"What about the clothes and jewelry he was buying her?"

"Now you sound like the roommate. We don't know who Susan's sugar daddy was or if she had one. All we know is that she turned up in the wrong place at the wrong time and got in the way of a bullet. The rest is pure speculation."

"Sit down, Manning, you make me nervous."

Mike sat. "I told you I know these people. Stephen Burke didn't have a dime of his own. He depended on his wife for everything. Her accountants doled him out a small allowance for pin money and not a cent more. Everything else was charged on Milly's account and if clothing other than male or jewelry turned up, the bill would be rejected first and questioned second. His wife put up with a lot of shit from that guy but drew a very firm line when it came to her money. The ladies he courted were the kind who could pick up the tab because it was a cinch he couldn't."

"Someone was buying her clothes and someone introduced her to Burke's crowd. If it wasn't Burke then who was it? And if it wasn't Burke what was she doing in his bedroom, both of them in their birthday suits, when his wife caught them?" Brandt was just as adamant as Mike had been.

Mike raised one finger in the air. "Error number one. Introduced her to Kevin Lakewood's crowd, not Burke's. She was half Burke's age at the very least. If she knew Burke, she met him through Kevin, didn't the boy tell you that?"

Brandt nodded. "He did. He also told me he hardly knew the girl and can't remember who introduced them or when. But the fact remains she was intimate with Stephen Burke, or do those people you write about usually entertain casual visitors in the nude?"

Mike began to rise, thought better of it and settled back in his chair. "Error number two. Assuming that Burke and the girl were getting ready for a party when Milly walked in on them. Think about it for a minute and you'll realize how foolish the idea is. The man's wife went out shopping and could walk in at any moment. Stephen Burke wasn't a teenager in heat. He was a mature, experienced man."

"Then what the hell were they doing?" Brandt shouted.

"I don't know," Mike answered.

"I just don't know. But I do know it wasn't the obvious."

"Do you think Milly Burke did it?" Brandt asked.

"Who else?"

"Kennedy's mysterious benefactor?"

"How did he get past the doorman?"

"I forgot about that. This case is beginning to get to me. None of it makes sense. But why does it have to?" Brandt added. "Milly Burke confessed to the crime, she was alone in the apartment, except for the two corpses, and her prints are on the gun. Why don't we forget it and let the D.A. do battle with Sam Saxman?"

"You won't forget it because you think something stinks to high heaven and you want to know what it is. Well, I think the same thing and I'm ready to find out what it is."

The words triggered a reminder of Ken Fancy's suicide and Mike wondered if Brandt was thinking the same thing. "Milly is a good friend and I owe her."

"A good friend, but she won't level with you," Brandt said.

"Maybe there's more at stake here than we know."

"More than her life? Those are some stakes, Manning."

"We've got to find out more about Susan Kennedy."

"Why? I thought she didn't matter."

Brandt sounded as if he were having fun at Mike's expense.

"What she was doing in Milly's apartment is all that matters. I know you put a trace on the girl…how far did you get?"

"About from here to that door. I think she was born the day she moved in with the Allen girl."

"What about that roommate service. They make out applications, don't they?"

"The place is out of business," Brandt sighed. "They come and go like gypsies. The tenement it was housed in is now a forty-story condominium. Two years in this town is like a lifetime anyplace else."

"Her job at the ad agency," Mike continued. "I know some people there if you need any help."

"Conners and Walsh," Brandt answered. "We got a line on that this morning. She gave the Charles Street address as her current and a previous address on the Upper East Side that doesn't exist and told them her previous job was as a freelancer...whatever that means."

"Christ, didn't they check anything?" Mike asked.

"Why should they? She made a good appearance, she could read, write and speak English and knew how to type. In today's market she's called a blessing. You don't ask too many questions for fear you might find out something you don't want to know."

Mike was about to speak but Brandt stopped him. "She applied for her social security number a week before she got the job. She could have come from Mars for all we know."

"A complete change of identity," Mike said.

"You've seen it before."

"Sure. But who was she before she was Susan Kennedy?" The two men stared at each other, each waiting for the other to answer the unanswerable. The only sound in the small office came from the radiator which hissed, rattled and clanked as it over-performed.

"I've been reading your columns," Brandt said thoughtfully, breaking the spell. "For background on the Burke shooting. Six months of Mike Manning's New York. Jesus, you've got a lot to say."

"More fun than the comic books. What did you find out?"

Brandt shrugged. "Not much...except that Burke and Symington were pretty friendly."

That again, Mike thought. "What gave you that idea?"

"You did. They seem to have turned up at quite a few parties together."

"Not together, Brandt, just part of the same crowd. The rich are incestuous, they band together to compare bank balances. Besides, who else have they got to invite to their parties?"

"But they did know each other," Brandt insisted.

"Sure they did and if you're going to implicate everyone Stephen Burke knew you'd better start giving out numbers."

Mike's face lit up with a wide grin. "You don't think old Stu Symington was the sugar daddy? Oh, how he would love you for that, Inspector. Stu Symington, stud…I think I'll hint at it in tomorrow's column. A good laugh is what this case needs."

"You're not funny, Manning."

"No, but you are. Tell me something, what makes you so sure Stu did in the boy?"

"What do you remember about it?" Brandt asked.

"All I got was the official statement your people put out which wasn't much and rumors. But I could fill two columns a day with rumors about Stuart Symington. Do you know a story once made the rounds that had it Stu would only bed one of your finest if the guy was uncut?"

Did Brandt blush or had the radiator finally gotten to him? Now Mike was having fun.

"Why didn't you ever follow up on it?" Brandt asked a little too quickly. "He's a natural for an exposé piece."

"Follow up on it? What did you want me to do, a short-arm inspection of all Stu's partners?"

"I was talking about Florida."

"Okay…okay…just a little joke. I didn't follow it because I thought it was just another Symington rumor. When the police dropped it I was convinced there was nothing to it." Mike looked at his shoes. "And a few weeks later something happened in my life that made everything else insignificant."

Would he ever have a conversation with Andrew Brandt without being reminded of Ken's death? Maybe it was Ken, exercising some mysterious power of the dead, who insisted on coming between the two people he most loved and respected. Mike felt cold in the overheated office. The murders of Stephen Burke and Susan Kennedy were beginning to have a weird effect on him, too.

"Who knows what happened to the kid," Brandt said after a slight pause.

"Drugs, wasn't it?"

"Was it? A twenty-year-old boy from the Bronx. Italian descent. Ever see a photo?"

Mike shook his head.

"Looked like a Botticelli angel. No record, no history of drugs and his friends told us he didn't even drink. If Robert Cimino was a hop head I'll turn in my badge."

"How did he meet Stu?" Mike asked.

"A party…one of the bars," Brandt made a gesture of despair. "Symington doesn't remember. Remarkable what people forget, isn't it?"

"What's Stu's version of the weekend?"

"He invited Cimino to Palm Beach the weekend after Christmas. The boy accepted and they flew down by commercial carrier on Friday."

"A party of two?" Mike interrupted. "That doesn't sound like Stuart. He liked a crowd, especially when he was flaunting a new conquest."

"So I've heard. But he insists it was just the two of them…for a relaxing weekend on the beach. Symington says the kid wanted to stay so he gave Cimino his return ticket and Symington flew back to New York on Monday morning."

"Why did he want to stay?"

"You ask the right questions," Brandt said with as much

respect as he had ever accorded Mike Manning. "According to Symington the boy said he had friends in the area. The Florida police combed Palm Beach and points north and south…"

"And didn't come up with a soul who knew Robert Cimino," Mike finished.

"You got it."

Mike's interest was aroused and habit forced him to reach for a cigarette. "You mind?"

"Yes, but don't let that stop you." Andrew Brandt was being very polite. Too damn polite, in fact. He wanted information and he thought Mike could supply it. As for Mike, if he did tell Brandt what little he knew, would he be helping a homophobe entrap an innocent man or avenging the death of an innocent youngster?

"Where did he leave Cimino?" Mike asked, deciding that he knew too little to help Brandt and it was much too late to help Robert Cimino.

"Not at Symington's house, if that's what you're getting at. Cimino left the Palm Beach house before Symington…according to Symington. There are no witnesses, or none we know of."

"Don't the Symingtons keep a staff down there?"

"They do," Brandt nodded, "when mama is there, but when her favorite son goes down for party time the staff goes on holiday."

"Where did the police find the body?"

"On the beach, about ten miles from the Symington mansion. This was the following Tuesday morning."

"Official cause of death?" Mike asked.

"Drug OD."

"Had he been sexually assaulted?"

"Not that we know of," Brandt answered.

Mike digested what Brandt had told him and concluded, "Outside of your own suspicions you haven't got one piece of concrete evidence against Stuart Symington."

"Thanks for the reminder."

"Then why don't you let go? It's not because the police couldn't find anyone down there who knew Robert Cimino. So the kid lied to Symington. Young men are known to do that... and he had a free round-trip ride so why not stick around and check out the action without Stu breathing down his neck? If he had gone down with Stu he wasn't opposed to being well tipped for services rendered and Palm Beach is prime territory for that game. Or his supposed friends were dealing or taking drugs and turned scared shitless when Cimino was found dead and clammed up. But you realize all this, so why not call in the bloodhounds? The scent is not only cold; it was never there in the first place."

"First of all, the boy was not a known drug user. We've established that fact to our satisfaction." Brandt held up his hand. "I know...there's always a first time and the kid could have gotten his on his maiden voyage. Possible, but I doubt it. Now I'll answer the question you didn't ask. How did Stuart Symington get back to New York?"

"I know he didn't swim, but what's that got to do with anything?"

"It's got to do with everything." Brandt said. "Now listen carefully. Symington had a reservation on a noon flight to New York. That was on the Monday. We know Robert Cimino didn't make that flight, but neither did Stuart Symington because when that plane left Palm Beach Symington was lunching with mama in their Park Avenue apartment."

Mike raised his eyebrows. "He took an earlier flight?"

"Indeed he did," Brandt answered.

"A much earlier and nonscheduled flight. The Symington Company jet was at Newark airport, all fueled up and ready to take the company's board of directors on a junket to Mexico City. Departure time was set for ten a.m. that Monday. The pilot was called at five that morning – you hear me, Manning, five a.m. — and told to change his flight plans and leave for Palm Beach as soon as he could arrange it with the airport, pick up the prodigal and get him back to New York as soon as possible."

Brandt paused for effect. "Stuart Symington was very anxious to end his relaxing weekend on the beach...like hysterical to put as much distance between his ass and Florida as quickly as possible."

Mike was impressed. "I didn't know any of this. Why did you keep it quiet?"

"Because it was all we had to connect Symington with the boy's death and we were afraid a leak would blow it. Symington said he suddenly remembered promising his mother he would attend her lunch party. At five in the morning he remembers, then bumps some very important people off the company plane — they didn't leave for Mexico till five that evening which means they waited at Newark for seven hours — so he could share a sandwich with mama. Bullshit, Manning, pure bullshit."

"I agree," Mike offered. "And the only thing Stu ever promised his mother was to get the boys out of his bed before the upstairs maid went in to make it up."

"The famous lunch party," Brandt continued, "was for a charity committee Mrs. Symington sponsors. We questioned the people present. Stu was there all right but the committee never remembered him attending one of their meetings or even taking an interest in their work. So much for Stuart Symington's dedication."

"Do you know when the boy died?"

"The medical people are pretty sure he had been exposed on the beach for about twenty-four hours. That means he went there, or was put there, early on Monday. Actual time of death has more than a twelve hour margin, either way, because of the time lapse."

"So the boy could have died long before Stu left Florida or long after," Mike concluded. "In either case he never got very far from the Symington house."

"I don't think he left the Symington house alive," Brandt

added.

"What you have is not even circumstantial," Mike said, shaking his head at Brandt. "And what Stu says is plausible, but certainly not probable. Does all this remind you of something?"

Brandt nodded. "The Burke case. All the figures are correct, but they don't add up."

"Sorry, but I can't help you with this one and you seem to know more about it than I do." Mike stood up and began to put on his top coat. "But if I hear anything, pro or con, I'll pass it on."

"I'll hold you to that. What are you going to do about Burke?"

"Stick with it...for a while anyway. Nosy around, see what I can pick up. Reporter business, I won't step on any toes."

"Keep me posted," Brandt said.

"I will if you help when I holler."

Brandt grinned. "Depends on what you're hollering about. How's the kid? Kevin, isn't it?"

"Kevin it is. And he's bearing up, as the expression goes." Mike put his hand on the door knob and waited for Brandt's dart to hit its mark.

"Did you take him home?"

Mike nodded without turning his head.

"And is he still a virgin?"

Now Mike turned to face the policeman.

"Let's say I delivered him in the same condition I got him."

"You got balls, Manning...you really got 'em."

7

Who was she before she was Susan Kennedy? It was Mike's lead for tomorrow's column. True, he had borrowed it from Andrew Brandt, but why let that stand in the way of a solid opening which so accurately described his theme? He had decided to devote a week of space to the Burke- Kennedy murders, giving his readers a serialized account of the life and times of Stephen Burke, complete with the colorful people and places which comprised the rags to riches to violent death mosaic. This, in addition to the hard facts he was feeding the news editor, put the *Ledger* in the enviable position of being first, with the most extensive coverage, as the sensational story unfolded.

Besides being the type of thing Mike did well (his delineation of Theresa Allen brought the reader into the living room on Charles Street) the ploy left him the free time he needed for his sleuthing. Right now, however, the only sleuthing going on was inside his own head. It had happened again. That gnawing sensation in the back of his mind which told him he had seen or heard something significant and had ignored it while trying to debunk what everyone was calling the obvious. It had started when he left

Brandt and it had stayed with him as he worked at his typewriter. A link…a common denominator…but what was it? The gnawing persisted but the breakthrough never came. New Year's Eve was still all he could come up with and that was as stale as yesterday's headlines. The first thing Mike noticed when he arrived at 830 Fifth Avenue was that Joe Stern was not on duty.

"Sick," Joe's replacement informed Mike, "Real sick," he repeated, thumbing his own chest repeatedly.

Mike didn't know if Joe's lungs had finally given up the ghost or if the old man's heart had been unable to keep pace with the love life of his seventeenth floor tenants. As Mike walked to the elevator he recalled the man's pleading voice on that fateful night and wondered if he should have listened to Joe. Was this the link that kept evading him?

He was surprised to see an elevator operator in attendance. The cooperative must have decided it needed more protection from those within than without the plush digs. Relieved of the necessity of having to press a button Mike again thought of Joe Stern and concluded that anything the man had to say he had said to the police. His incoherency that night was understandable. So much for Mike's missing link, but he made a mental note to get Joe Stern's phone number and give him a goodwill call by way of an apology for his abruptness.

The widow Burke looked spectacular. Mr. Kenneth, or Mr. Mark, or whatever Mister was currently in vogue, had obviously been sent for and had arrived with scissors, comb and make-up kit to erase all traces of prison life and restore Milly to a countenance in keeping with her surroundings. And, Mike noticed, the lady's spirits were in keeping with her appearance.

"I can't thank you enough," she said, kissing Mike as he entered. The maid, Betty, who had shown Mike in, retreated discreetly and for a moment Mike wondered if Stephen Burke would suddenly pop into the room and say "What's new, Michael," as had been his habit.

"You look great," Mike greeted her. "Crimes of passion must agree with you." He was a little sore at Milly and didn't try to conceal his feelings. Burke had been a bastard, but some respect for the dead, especially those whose exit you helped, was little more than civilized.

Milly looked as if she were about to celebrate New Year's Eve after the fact. The lady smiled as she moved to the liquor cabinet. "Martini?"

"Why not straight whiskey and make it a real Irish wake?"

Milly began mixing their drinks, her serenity unbroken by Mike's barbs. "Did you expect to find me in widow's weeds with dark circles under my eyes?"

"No, but I didn't expect to find you combed, curled and primed for a party either. Can I assume the unpleasantness in your bedroom has been removed?" Mike accepted the glass Milly handed him and saluted her with a silent nod.

"All but the decor," she answered. "I'm redoing it in green to match your eyes."

"I get the feeling we played this scene before...after the demise of husband number one to be exact. Better cool it, Milly, before people start talking trash." She sat and motioned toward a comfortable chair for Mike.

"After the last few days there won't be anything left to say. Mildred Hamilton Lakewood Burke has been talked about ad nauseum, or don't you read what you write?"

"What I don't want to write is your obit, but if you start appearing in public like this that's just what I'll be doing. Didn't Saxman caution you?"

Milly gestured toward herself. "This is just for tonight and you. Yes, Sam warned me, but I have no intention of appearing in public for a long, long time. When I do I'll look properly contrite and widowish."

She sipped from her glass. "Do you know Sam told me to let my hair go grey, for effect I guess, and when I told him I didn't have a grey hair on my head he seemed disappointed."

"Sam tends toward the dramatic, but he's the very best, Milly. Listen to him. What's his prognosis at this point?"

"Not now, Mike, we're celebrating my freedom."

Had Milly's hairdresser curled her brains along with her hair or had a Dr. Feelgood administered to the lady, too? Mike could tolerate the cheerful appearance and demeanor but drew the line when she started to talk like a damn fool. "Your freedom is temporary and the worst is before us. Come on, Milly, let's start talking sense. The trial is going to be a circus and Sam is going to have to come up with some solid facts to get you acquitted. I'm here to help."

"My father once told me the three greatest lies I would ever encounter are, one, I'll respect you in the morning ; two, the check is in the mail ; and three, I'm from the government and I'm here to help."

Mike laughed. "I would have liked your father, but I'm not from the government."

"No," she said, "but I was hoping you were here to see me." Mike moved from his chair to the couch and settling next to Milly he took her hand in his.

"I said I'm here to help which means I care very much. Granted, I'm getting a lot of mileage out of this as a reporter but I swear, Milly, if there wasn't one line of news in this I would still be here wanting to help."

She leaned toward him and kissed his cheek. "I know you would," she answered. They looked at each other for a long moment and then she whispered, "You are so handsome, Mike," in a tone that bespoke a long-repressed passion.

"Compliments will get you every place," he answered, trying to make light of this sudden intimacy.

"But you don't want to go every place," she told him.

"There are times when I think I've been every place and back again." He started toward the liquor supply. "And I'm having another; how about you?"

"Not right now. I've been nursing a hangover since the incident."

"The incident!" Mike struck his forehead with the heel of his hand

"A double murder, headlines all over the country…all over the world, for all I know…and you call it an incident. As my friend Andy Brandt would say, you got balls, Milly, you really got 'em."

"What do you want me to call it, my murders of passion? No, thank you, I'll stick to incident. Anything else would glorify it and don't start preaching to me. Kevin told me you were a born

Sunday school teacher."

Mike didn't suffer a twinge of guilt or even a slight pang of remorse at the mention of Kevin Lakewood. He had decided sometime during his busy day that Kevin was a man, not a boy, and the man had made all the right moves and gotten exactly what he wanted. The only problem now was that Kevin wanted more than Mike was ready to give.

When he had finished mixing his drink he turned to face Milly, thought of her as Kevin's mother and headed for his original seat as he asked, "Where is he?"

"In his room. I told him I wanted a few minutes alone with you."

"Good," Mike said as he sat, "I think we have some talking to do."

"Before we do I want to thank you for taking care of Kevin."

"A minute ago I was Elmer Gantry. I take it Kevin has mixed feelings about his rescuer."

Milly smiled. "I think he enjoyed the preaching. He likes you a lot, Mike."

Milly knows her son is gay, Mike thought, and the two, according to Kevin, have no secrets from each other. He began to get the uneasy feeling that he was being manipulated with a mink-lined velvet glove and wanted to know if it was covering a wad of coarse sandpaper.

"Why didn't you tell me he was gay?" Mike, as usual, entered the water without testing the temperature.

"You never asked," she said, avoiding his gaze.

"Did you…discuss it with him?"

"We talked about a lot of things and that might have been on the agenda."

If she wanted to play games he was ready to give her a run for her money.

She reached for a cigarette. "It doesn't really matter, I think it's just a phase of growing up." Mike picked up the lighter before Milly reached for it and leaned forward as he ignited the wick. He watched her closely as she lit the tip of the cigarette and marveled at the steadiness of her hand and the calm composure of her jaw as she performed the ritual.

Milly was acting like a soldier about to enter his first battle and determined, for the sake of honor, not to let a soul know he was petrified. Was there something more at stake here then Milly Burke's life? Honor? But whose...Milly's, Stephen Burke's or Susan Kennedy's? He had a triangle with one viable angle and suddenly Kevin's sex life, not the relationship of the dead members of the trio, was about to be hung on the clothesline.

Mike thought he could feel the sandpaper beneath the velvet. Two days ago Mike's only concern with the double murder had been for Milly. Since then, like it or not, Kevin had been added to the list. Now, more than ever, he had to find out why Milly had killed her husband and a strange girl. If he was going to establish a relationship with Kevin Lakewood, on any level, there were a lot of hurdles to get over and a thirteen-year age span was the least of them.

"He's twenty-two, Milly, not twelve," Mike said, more in response to his own thought than to Milly's statement. She looked directly into Mike's eyes as she answered.

"In some ways he's still very much a twelve-year-old."

Mike felt the guilt and remorse he thought he had rationalized to oblivion.

"Kevin has always been somewhat of a loner," Milly continued. "He was devoted to his father and when he died the boy was inconsolable. I thought..." She paused and moved her hands in a gesture which indicated that the truth could no longer harm her son. "I thought I would have to get help...medical help...for him. Then he went away to school and the problem took care of itself."

She smiled at Mike. "Kevin is just fine now."

"If you think his father's death made him a homosexual,

you're wrong. Dead wrong." Mike lectured. "If every boy who lost his father…"

"I think he's looking for the father he lost," Milly countered.

Is that why you sent him to me, Mike wondered. Strange choice, unless she wanted to divert Mike's attention from more serious matters. Could Milly be capable of such a diabolical scheme involving her son? Forty-eight hours ago he didn't think she was capable of murder and yesterday she confessed to two, which proved that anything was possible. Of one thing he was certain. Milly was erecting a smoke screen and he didn't like it one iota.

"Let's drop it, Milly, and move on to something more pressing, like your chances of staying out of jail for the rest of your life. Does that interest you at all?"

She handed him her glass. "I'm ready for another now."

He took the glass from her, none too gently, and went to the makeshift bar again. "You can procrastinate from now till Kevin is fifty, mentally and chronologically, but I'm not leaving until I get the truth out of you," he announced, waving a vodka bottle in her direction.

"What truth are you talking about, Mike?"

"Why you killed Steve. I think the girl just happened to be in the way, but we'll get to that later. Why did you do it, Milly?"

"I told you why and I told the police why. How many times do I have to repeat the shabby story?"

"Until the pieces fit," he answered, placing her glass in front of her. "I'm not buying the story you told, nor is the good Inspector Brandt and, I'm sure, neither is Sam Saxman."

"Suppose I told you I don't give a tinker's damn what you, the police or Sam think. What happened, happened to me and not any of you. Just because it doesn't happen to fit some pattern or mold doesn't make it a lie." The lady was mad and she let Mike know it.

"Christ, no one is trying to fit it into a mold. We're just trying to make some sense out of it. Do you really want to tell a jury that while you were out shopping a young lady came to call, unexpectedly, and your husband entertained her by undressing and neatly stowing away every article of clothing he was wearing and when he was finished you entered and shot them both.? Do you really want to stick with that, Milly?"

"I have no choice. It's the truth." Milly pounded her cigarette to death in an ashtray and immediately reached for another. "And why is everyone so concerned with Steve's clothes? You're making a major case out of a man hanging up his pants and jacket."

Steve's clothes had struck a sensitive cord and Mike was sure it wasn't the first time. Hadn't Milly reacted, or over-reacted, in the same way when Mike brought up her husband's missing clothes on the night of the murder?

"What about his underpants and socks and shoes and shirt... and tie, if he was wearing one? I can make a major case out of that."

"All I can tell you is what I know and I've done that." He looked at her long and hard and knew he wasn't going to get anything more out of her.

"I talked to Susan Kennedy's roommate," he said, trying a different approach. "She said Susan gave her notice that she was leaving the apartment for good, packed her bags and went off to elope with her lover."

"Steve?" Milly exclaimed.

"Your guess is as good as mine. But a funny thing happened on her way uptown. She lost all her luggage."

Milly gave this a moment's thought and then answered, "She stopped some place before coming here. Her boyfriend's apartment probably."

Mike nodded. "I thought of that. Now level with me, Milly, how well did you and Steve know Susan Kennedy?"

"I've given that a lot of thought," she said, then quickly added, "you see, I'm not completely indifferent to the situation. I'm now positive I met her for the first time last summer. It was at our beach house and she was part of a crowd of young people Kevin had invited to a party Steve and I were giving. I talked to Kevin about it and all he can remember was that he met her through friends sometime last year and saw her a half dozen times since then at social gatherings. At the beach you invite two people to a party and ten show up. You know how the young are."

Mike wondered if she kept repeating the word young on purpose. Just what he didn't need now was a case of paranoia. How young was young and how old was thirty-five?

"What about Steve?"

"As far as I know he knew her about as well as I did. She wasn't Steve's type, Mike, unless she had a couple of million bucks hidden away that only he knew about."

"I'll go along with that," Mike said.

"About her clothes..." Milly raised her arms in a gesture of disgust. "I don't want to hear about anyone's clothes, Mike, especially hers."

"I'm afraid you're going to have to whether you like it or not. You see she didn't have a couple of million bucks or anything beyond her weekly salary...but her wardrobe was strictly first class. Someone was dressing the lady in a style to which she was not accustomed."

"Not Steve," Milly all but shouted, "and I can prove it." She seemed overjoyed at being able to prove something concerning the case. "My accountant pays all the bills and keeps all the receipts. If there's even one with Steve's signature on it and it isn't legitimate I'll eat it. Steve got an allowance of a hundred dollars a week pocket money and everything else was charged. He couldn't buy Susan Kennedy a fancy wardrobe if he saved for a year, which he most certainly didn't do."

"I know." Mike nodded his agreement.

"And I told the police as much, but I did want you to confirm it. The trouble is, Milly, the one thing we seem to know for sure will be the most damaging to Sam's case."

When she gave him a questioning look he continued, "Don't you see? The fact that Steve wasn't her lover and that he knew her only casually turns your so-called crime of passion into cold-blooded murder. And if the D.A. can prove that you wanted Burke out of your life…well, do I have to go on?"

"Whether they were lovers or not isn't the point," Milly protested. "I caught them in the act and lost my head. That's the truth, Mike."

"Caught them in the act of doing what?" Mike asked. "Exactly what were they doing when you walked in the bedroom?"

"Steve was showing her his magic wand." Both Milly and Mike were slightly startled and turned abruptly at the sound of Kevin's voice. The young man sauntered leisurely into the room, his arms gesticulating as if he were leading a symphony orchestra.

"He was showing her his magic wand," Kevin repeated.

"Now you see it…abracadabra…now you see more of it."

"Kevin, you're not being amusing," Milly snapped at her son.

"I'm not trying to be amusing. I honestly think that's what Steve was doing. God knows it was the biggest tourist attraction in this town."

Mike struggled to keep from smiling. It wouldn't do to encourage that kind of talk in front of Milly. He made an instant, and firm, decision never to act as referee between mother and son. Instead, he looked at Kevin Lakewood and tried, without success, to remain aloof. Kevin was wearing his own jeans which fit as if they had been tailor made for him — and probably were. The denim was properly faded and hugged his slim form in all the right places. Atop, he sported a t-shirt upon which was printed in black, bold lettering, READY, WILLING AND ABLE (Mike could attest to the validity of all three pronouncements) ; below, a pair of beat- up sneakers. He didn't look twelve years old but he didn't look twenty-two either. Mike opted for sixteen trying to pass for eighteen and prayed he could keep Kevin Lakewood at arm's length, knowing God would turn a deaf ear on his less than fervent plea.

"What do you think they were doing, Mike?" Kevin asked as he sat next to his mother.

"Not what everyone thinks they were doing," Mike answered. "But I've said that before and I'm sticking with it."

"I take it you don't like my magic wand theory."

"If there was one thing your stepfather didn't do, it was give free shows," Mike said. "He was strictly a cash and carry guy. But what they were doing doesn't interest me. Why she came here on New Year's Eve does."

There it was again. Mike was engulfed with the eerie feeling that the answers to all the questions boiled down to a single point...but what was it? There was now no doubt that New Year's Eve was the link but he had no idea where or how to connect it.

"Were you and Steve planning on going to Trish Naughton's for the new year or did Steve have other plans?"

"We were going," Milly answered, "but not for dinner. I told Trish we would stop by later. It's always such a long night and I didn't see any sense in starting out any earlier than we had to. Steve agreed."

"What were you going to do about dinner?" Mike asked.

"We weren't going out. In fact, with Betty away for the holiday, Steve had threatened to whip up his famous cheese omelets for the both of us." It all sounded very homey and normal. Perhaps a bit too homey for Stephen Burke, Mike thought. He shrugged his shoulders hopelessly.

"The more we probe the more meaningless Susan Kennedy's presence becomes."

"Why don't we just play it as it lays," Kevin offered.

Now that's a novel idea, Mike thought cynically and wondered what other sage advice Kevin had been feeding his mother.

"Because it won't play as it lays," Mike answered, "and it never will until we know what the girl was doing here and who she really was."

"You mean she's not Susan Kennedy?" Kevin looked mildly surprised.

"If she was, she was born last year," Mike told him.

Milly, who had been following the exchange between Mike and her son, suddenly cut in. "I've had enough of this. I've been questioned to death by the police, incarcerated, and just when I thought I was going to get a blessed night of peace it starts all over again. I know you're trying to help, Mike, but I just can't take any more of it. I really can't."

She looked on the verge of tears and Mike immediately acquiesced to the lady. "You're right," he sighed, "and I apologize. I guess I got carried away." It was an awkward moment as mother and son looked at Mike as if expecting him to now amuse them in compensation for his harassment.

"Well," he said, "what's on the agenda for this evening?"

"Betty is fixing me a salad and then I'm going to bed," Milly replied. "Why don't you and Kevin go out for something."

"My treat," Kevin exclaimed with a smile that implied that more than food was going to be on the menu.

Mike answered without hesitation. "Get dressed and you've got a date."

"I am dressed." Kevin stood up. "All I need is a jacket. Is it still cold?"

"Freezing," Mike cautioned as he watched Kevin march out of the room.

"Do you like him, Mike?" he heard Milly ask.

"Very much," he answered honestly, turning toward her. "Reminds me of his old lady."

"Actually, he's very much like his father." She looked sad and forlorn in spite of her new coiffure and impeccable dress. "I want so much to protect him from all of this."

"He's a man, Milly, not a little boy."

"I feel responsible for all the problems in his young life,"

Milly said, disregarding or not hearing Mike's comment. Was she referring to Kevin being gay?

Mike checked his anger at the implication and answered with a mild, "I don't think Kevin has any problems and if he does I'm sure they're not much different than those of any young man his age."

Milly shook her head. "I replaced a father he loved with one he hated. Not every young man has grown up with Stephen Burke to contend with."

"As bad as all that?" Mike asked.

"From the moment they laid eyes on each other," Milly answered. "I think it had something to do with Kevin's allowance being bigger than Steve's."

She smiled at her feeble joke. "It's all my fault, Mike. First I brought Steve into his life at exactly the wrong moment and now this mess just when the boy is starting out on his own. It's not fair...it's just not fair."

He went to her and sat in the spot Kevin had just vacated. Putting his arm about her fragile shoulders he drew her to his chest and was shocked at the rigidity of her body.

"It's a bum rap, Milly, but you've got to face it. As for Kevin... well, he's very young and they have a remarkable capacity for recovery."

"I'm counting on you to see him through this, Mike." He felt the mink-lined glove stroke him ever so gently.

"I know he's not your responsibility but..."

"I've made him my responsibility," he cut in and the statement, perhaps spoken a bit too harshly, seemed to reverberate in the room. She gave no indication of understanding his meaning or chose to ignore it.

Her response was a whispered, "Thank you."

"It's you I'm worried about," he said gently. "Why are you turning from everyone who's trying to help you?"

"But I'm not," she pleaded. "I'm telling the truth and you and Sam and the police are turning from me because of it. What else can I do, Mike?"

"Is it the truth, Milly?"

"I swear to you it is."

"I believe you," he said and felt her body relax for the first time since taking her in his arms.

When he and Kevin got to the lobby Mike asked the man on duty for Joe Stern's telephone number. "What's that for?" Kevin asked.

"I'm told he's sick and I think a call might give him a lift," Mike answered, stuffing the scrap of paper handed him into his pocket.

"You're a soft touch," Kevin said.

"And who should know that better than you?"

When they arrived at Mike's apartment Kevin lit a fire with the one log remaining from their previous evening. Mike watched the boy as he knelt, struggling with sheets of newspaper and matches, and felt a contentment he had not known in a long time. He had been alone and chaste since Ken Farley died. He now realized he was never meant to be either. It was time for letting go and Kevin Lakewood had been handed to him just when he needed someone to pin his hopes on.

Handed to him? What a strange way to phrase it. The piece of wood hissed and spat black puffs of smoke at its executioner. Mike saw only Kevin's face, intense with determination, the clear complexion slightly flushed, the brown curls rolling down the furrowed forehead only to be pushed back abruptly by a hand that had more important business to attend. Mike's eyes moved over the bent back and to the exposed flesh where the t-shirt had pulled away from its confinement and finally to the denim-encased behind which wiggled, tensed, relaxed, then tensed again as the log finally surrendered to the inevitable.

"I did it," he cried, leaning back so that the raised heels of his sneakers dug into the flesh which had captivated Mike's attention. Mike felt a longing he thought had died from the fatal wound of a service revolver. The hardness between his legs was a tantalizing ache and his entire being, his only reason for existing at this moment, in this time and place, was centered on that ache.

"Stand up," he whispered. Kevin obeyed. As he rose the fire suddenly engulfed the entire log and a solid flame of yellow heat ascended with him. The boy faced Mike as he dug his fists deep into the back pockets of his jeans, his belly thrust forward, the tight mound under his crotch accentuated.

"Do you think I could model?" he asked as if completely unaware of Mike's gaze. Mike shook his head slowly, his eyes never leaving the vision before the fire.

"You're too perfect," he finally answered. "A model can't distract from what the advertiser is trying to sell. They want the reader to buy, not jack off."

Kevin grinned.

"You're better looking than I am and you modeled for years."

The 'for years' hurt. The 'for years' also brought back the gnawing sensation which Mike was beginning to hate. Years… New Year's Eve…for years…what the hell did it mean? Mike didn't want to think about that now and he shoved it aside like a glutton who had just spotted the dessert tray. This mixture of emotions threw him off balance, made him incapable of logical thought. All he could feel was the throbbing ache which demanded satisfaction before it would release him from its grip.

"It's very warm in here," Kevin said.

"You know what you can do about it," Mike answered, surprised at the almost cruel intensity of his tone. Kevin pulled the t-shirt over his head. The brown curls once again danced across his forehead as the flickering shadows of firelight licked his torso. He opened his belt ; the zipper rode over the arc; the jeans were pushed downward. He bent to free them from his legs.

"Can't do that," he announced. "Gotta take the sneakers off

first." He sat on the floor, the pants below his knees, the gleaming white briefs straining to contain him, fingers tugging at laces and sneakers. He looked up at Mike.

"Are you enjoying this?" The question intended to elicit an emotion, not an answer. It succeeded admirably He removed the jeans then raised his behind and the shorts followed the pile of denim. He leaned back on his elbows and looked down at himself.

"I feel a little foolish with you fully dressed."

Mike stood up. "You won't feel that way very long."

8

It would be months before Milly's trial convened. During that time both factions would work feverishly to build their case. Sam Saxman had entered a plea of 'guilty by virtue of temporary insanity.' The District Attorney's job was to refute that. It was going to be an important trial, one that would garner media coverage on a daily basis. The people involved were pretty, rich and famous. Their tale was pure soap opera with just enough of the macabre to whet the appetite of a public bored with fictional facsimiles. The D.A. was counting on a conviction to boost him up the political ladder. Saxman needed a win to re-establish himself as the best trial lawyer in America, a position he had recently relinquished to one Melvin Belli.

"When I'm finished with my character portrait of Stephen Burke," the lawyer told Mike, "he's going to make the devil look like Little Mary Sunshine. You're going to see a picture of a six-foot penis masquerading as a man." Oddly enough, the D.A. was going to embellish Saxman's painting of Stephen Burke as the classical satyr: Saxman sought to depict a wife sinned against to the point of total despair, the D.A. to portray the same woman seeking revenge. The singer, not the song, would ultimately sway the jury.

Everyone knew that witnesses to Burke's escapades would be called upon to testify and suddenly New York society was on the move. Trish Naughton announced her intention of making an extended tour of the Far East.

"The further the better," some quipped. One matron, long married to a maestro who took a special interest in pubescent male prodigies, established residence in Brazil, where she would devote her time and considerable fortune to the problems of third world nations.

"On the Copacabana?" friends tittered over their breakfast trays.

The men who were close to Stephen Burke sought legal advice, consulted public relations firms and doubled their charitable contributions. Except for Stuart Symington. "I can't wait for my subpoena," he stated loudly whenever in earshot of several ladies who had been unkind to him in the past.

Those who knew Burke only casually stayed put, fearing any sudden move would make them appear part of the stampede. Everyone was speculating, pointing or packing. The undercurrent at social affairs bespoke the calm before the storm. In the eye of the impending hurricane sat Mildred Hamilton Lakewood Burke: calm, cool, collected and unreachable. True to her word Milly did not appear in public and only ventured forth with Mike Manning and her son for an occasional dinner out at restaurants her friends didn't know existed on the island of Manhattan.

"My two favorite men," the lady remarked on one of these outings.

"We're like a family." Mike lost his appetite. The handsome, sophisticated reporter-at-large was also losing his cool, the reason being a 22-year-old 'brat' whom Mike could not decide if he disliked intensely or loved with the same fervor. Did Milly know of the affair? If she did, she gave no indication of condoning or condemning the relationship. What she did do, in Mike's presence, was encourage her son to look upon Mike as teacher, advisor and father figure. Mike felt he was being coerced, especially when Kevin took to whispering, "Hi, Dad," behind Milly's back. It was not only disconcerting, it was also strangely erotic.

However, if there was one thing Kevin Lakewood didn't need any advice about it was the erotic — strange or otherwise. The boy would avoid Mike for days and just when Mike thought he was free of his addiction Kevin would appear, as charming as ever, and give himself to Mike with the trusting innocence of a child and a masculine passion that never failed to astonish. The 'shot' was administered at just the right intervals to keep the addict hooked. Kevin continued to keep up with his crowd and when running into Mike the boy always made a point of proudly exhibiting the pretty girl on his arm or, if his companion were male, introducing the young man to Mike.

"What did you think of him?" Kevin would ask later.

"Brad Turner he ain't," Mike always answered. If Kevin knew how to tease, Mike knew how to inflict a stinging wound. But when Kevin returned to the fold the petty childishness was forgotten and Mike again became captivated by the intelligent, witty and always sexy young man.

Sexy was the pivotal word. Could one base a relationship on sex? The answer was probably no, but what man wouldn't want to spend a life time testing the axiom? Now, more than ever before, Mike longed for Ken Farley and the union they shared. A union that was never defined, therefore knew no bounds. A passion that contained no highs and lows, but burned with a steady glow of fulfillment and contentment. A relationship that was taken for granted because it would be unthinkable to exist without it. To have experienced this once in a lifetime was as much as one could hope for ; to expect it to happen again was courting disappointment.

Mike never knew what the next day would bring: a dizzying joy or a relentless sense of despair; a giddy abandon or a sobering reality. Was he in love with a memory...a new passion...or was he allowing a rich brat to tease him like some two-bit hustler? As this bitter cold January drew to a close neither Mike, Sam Saxman, or the police could shake Milly Burke's story. Nor could any of them come up with a shred of evidence to prove her story true or false. The police turned up empty-handed in their search into Susan Kennedy's past. Mike questioned everyone who had, or might have, come in contact with the girl. The answers he got were inevitably the same.

"I met her at a party...she was introduced to me by...I thought she was a friend of...she sort of turned up one day..."

Andrew Brandt kept up with Mike via Mike's daily column and a twice-weekly phone call.

"Anything?" Brandt always began. Mike had nothing to offer and neither did the policeman.

"How's Symington?" was another question Brandt never failed to ask.

"He can't wait to appear as a witness," Mike commented.

"On whose side?"

"He couldn't care less. All he wants to do is trash every lady in this town who ever called him a fag."

"That's a lot of ladies," Brandt chuckled.

"Stu's got a big mouth," Mike answered. Both men knew their new found camaraderie was based on a common need and neither was ready to turn the truce into permanent peace. But Mike enjoyed these talks and, he suspected, so did Andrew Brandt. They had a great deal of respect for each other and had suffered a common loss, two attributes which go a long way in soldering a common bond. More out of a need to act than with any hope of accomplishment, Mike called Theresa Allen.

"I framed the column, Mr. Manning. You know, the one where you talk about me." Mike smiled broadly, thankful that he wasn't face to face with the girl. When Theresa Allen didn't annoy she could, unwittingly to be sure, amuse.

"Do you know why I'm calling?" he asked.

"You want to know where Susan lived before she moved in here. The police want to know the same thing, Mr. Manning. They've been hounding me to death. My father thinks it's extreme mental cruelty and wants me to get a lawyer."

"It's their job, Terry, and knowing more about Susan Kennedy is terribly important."

"But I told them all I know," she cried. "She came from Long Island, that I remember. If she ever mentioned the town, which I'm sure she didn't, I forgot it."

"When the roommate service sent her to see you, she didn't just move right in," Mike said. "Didn't she have to inspect the place and didn't you have to decide if you wanted her as a roommate?"

"Well, sure. She came over that first time and we talked for about an hour. I liked her right off and she liked the place but I didn't want to appear too anxious. You know what I mean? It's like with guys. If you're too anxious they expect too much too soon but if you're not anxious enough you never see them again." It was very easy for Theresa Allen to couple any subject with the care and feeding of men.

"Then did you call the service or call Susan directly when you decided you wanted her to share with you?" There was a long silence during which Mike held his breath and vowed to give up smoking if the girl came back with the answer he wanted to hear.

"You know something, Mr. Manning, I think I called her," came the slow, methodical reply. Mike wanted to shout for joy but didn't dare in fear of upsetting that delicate balance which was Theresa Allen's brain. Instead he reached for a cigarette.

"So she must have given you her phone number," Mike said as gently as his pounding heart would allow.

"What did you do with it? Think, Terry…please think."

"That was two years ago," she squealed, "and in spite of what you might think, I do clean this place regularly."

So the Christmas tree is gone, Mike thought. "Don't you keep a book or a listing of personal phone numbers? Most people do."

"Sure, but I update it every year. You know, when I send out my Christmas cards. I add some and toss some…like most people do."

"But her phone number might still be someplace in the apartment. Please look for it, Terry. Just gave it a try. Maybe inside an old purse or between the covers of a book you were reading at the time. Look, Terry, for me…please." Again silence and then,

"For you, Mr. Manning, I'll look." Mike hung up, stared at the cigarette dangling between his fingers and decided he got exactly what he deserved. Then something happened that completely obliterated the search for Susan Kennedy's origins.

"Joe Stern is gone." Brandt's voice came over the wire as cold and crisp as the winter air outside Mike's windows.

"So it finally happened," Mike answered, suddenly remembering that he had been carrying the doorman's phone number around for weeks but had never called.

"What do you mean?" Brandt sounded confused.

"He had a lung disease. I'm surprised he lasted as long as he did. I take it you have his signed statement."

"I didn't say he was dead, Manning. I said he was gone… disappeared, bag and baggage. All he left behind was what he couldn't carry."

Now Mike was certain he should have listened to what Joe Stern wanted to tell him the night of the murders. That pleading voice took on a new meaning. It wasn't the ranting of a bemused old man but a cry for help. What did the doorman know? What had he seen? And why hadn't he told the police?

Mike was furious with himself and twice as determined to find out exactly why these two senseless murders had taken place. The stupor he had fallen into over the past weeks gave way to a new vigor. He finally had a clue that told him what he had long suspected. Something occurred at 830 Fifth Avenue the last night of the year that, if presented at the trial, could win the case for Sam Saxman…or the District Attorney.

"I have no idea," Milly said when Mike presented her with the fact of Joe Stern's disappearance. "Why, I hardly knew the man. I mean I've known him for years but don't think more than a civil good evening and thank you ever passed between us. Is this a bad omen for us, Mike?"

"It could be," Mike told her. "He was the only witness who could substantiate your time table."

"But he gave that information to the police. Surely they'll attest to that."

"There's nothing like a witness who can give a first-hand account and, more important, the jury is going to want to know why the old man fled if he was telling the truth and had nothing to hide. The D.A. can build his whole case on that, Milly, and a damn good one."

Kevin was no more helpful than his mother. "Christ, how would I know? What did he say to you when you called him?"

"I never called," Mike answered.

He even put the question to Frank Evans. Mike had taken to sitting in the front seat, beside his sometimes driver, and the two would hash out the problems of the world while trapped in the perpetual snarl of mid-town traffic. "A man runs for one reason," Frank said after a moment's deep thought. "'Cause he's scared."

"I had that figured out for myself," Mike replied, not too kindly.

"But you didn't follow through."

"Follow through? With what?"

"A lot of scared guys want to run but they can't because they lack the means."

Frank took one hand off the steering wheel long enough to rub his thumb and forefinger at Mike. "Money...loot...cash to get you where you want to be and comfort you once you're there."

He was right. Someone had given Joe Stern the means to escape. And not just carfare money. Joe was a sick man and jobs for old, sick men are not easy to come by. According to Brandt, Joe was a childless widower who maintained a shabby apartment in the Bronx. His bank balance wouldn't carry him through two consecutive weeks without a regular pay check.

Who wanted the former doorman out of the way and who had the means to achieve that? Milly Burke had the means but certainly not the desire. Joe was to be Saxman's star witness. It was in Milly's best interest for him to be present at her trial.

That left someone who was rich and wanted to harm Milly. Susan Kennedy's benefactor was rich. Did he send the girl to the Burke's apartment on New Year's Eve especially to cause trouble for Milly and then get more than he bargained for? Now that Milly had a fifty-fifty chance of getting away with it, was he trying to cut those odds by getting rid of Joe Stern? It made sense. Susan's lover wanted to hurt Milly but he didn't want to see his girlfriend dead. But she was dead and Milly was the murderer. He would see to it that Milly paid. But who was he?

"You should be a detective," Mike complimented Frank.

"I thought you said I should be a writer."

"Then you should write detective novels," Mike compromised.

"How's the lady's kid?" Frank asked.

"Kevin? He isn't a kid. He's twenty-two years old." Mike was getting tired of telling people how old Kevin Lakewood was.

"My, my, ain't we touchy about age," the black man grinned.

"The light's green, Frank, let's move it."

"He's pretty for a white boy, too," Frank continued.

"He would be pretty if he were green," Mike huffed.

"But he ain't green, Mr. Manning, he's twenty-two and you're..."

"Not old enough to be his father." Mike moved uneasily in his seat. "Maybe this driving business isn't such a good idea, Frank. Maybe you should go back to repairs and lube jobs."

"Let's not talk about lube jobs, Mr. Manning," came the retort along with a flash of startlingly white teeth.

Mike presented his new theory to Andrew Brandt.

"Sounds logical," the policeman said, "but who's out to get Milly Burke? Any ideas?"

"Not even one," Mike replied. "She doesn't have an enemy in the world."

"We all have enemies," Brandt told him. "Some we know about but most we don't."

"This kind of enemy you would know about, Inspector,

unless you were deaf, dumb and blind."

"So ask the lady."

Mike did and got the same bewildered look Milly had given him when he questioned her about Joe Stern.

"Mike, you've known me for years ... and all my friends. Is there anyone you would even suspect of wanting to hurt me like this?"

"No," he confessed.

"Well neither do I." All the roads led to Susan Kennedy. A girl Mike had thought an innocent victim was shaping up to be the star of the show. If Susan Kennedy wasn't the culprit, she was certainly his tool. Who was she and who had honed her to taunt Milly Burke? The only thing Mike was sure of was that the mysterious someone was one methodical and diabolical bastard.

"A madman," Mike concluded. "One fucking madman."

He was tired of thinking, tired of speculating and tired of waiting for Kevin whom he had not seen in almost a week. He considered calling a pro tennis player he had long admired and had met over the holidays.

On parting, Mike had said something like, "I look forward to seeing you again," and received, "On or off the court?" for a reply. This tantalizing response had left Mike with happy expectations but Milly's 'incident' had delayed the fulfillment... or disappointment. But when the phone rang he hoped, in spite of his daydreaming, to hear Kevin's voice answer his brisk hello.

"I found it, Mr. Manning," Theresa Allen shouted breathlessly. "I found Susan's old phone number."

9

Mike was so startled by this unexpected bit of good fortune that he only half listened as the girl babbled on about the remarkable find.

"The Christmas tree ornaments…I was decorating the tree that day she came to look at the apartment. I remembered as I was taking down the tree…dropped in one of the ornament boxes…and there it was…in that box for almost two years…"

Mike blessed Theresa Allen's inept domesticity. "I'm going to wine and dine you," he cut into the testimonial, "in the best style this town has to offer."

"Do you mean it, Mr. Manning?"

"Of course I mean it. The best, Terry, nothing but the best for you. If you were here now I would kiss you." The silence this evoked on the other end of the line made Mike wonder if the girl were trying to decide what degree of anxiousness to ascribe to the offer. He thought, as a special reward, he might even introduce her to Kevin Lakewood but instantly changed his mind. He liked Theresa Allen and didn't want to witness her premature demise from frustration.

"I think you're great, Mr. Manning," came her somewhat docile response.

"I'll call you and let you know how I make out with the number."

"What about our dinner date?"

"I'll call you about that, too." He stared at the number he had scribbled on his desk pad and tried to keep his hopes from soaring. It could connect to a motel or another roommate who knew as much about Susan Kennedy as the persevering Theresa Allen. This logical assumption did little to quell his apprehension as he began to dial. It rang twice before a recorded voice came on the line and told him the number was no longer in service. So

it could have belonged to the home Susan Kennedy had sold…
or a defunct motel.

The *Ledger* had a formidable research department. The police,
he knew, had an even better one but he wanted to track this down
as far as he could before turning it over to Brandt. Because of Joe
Stern he was beginning to feel a personal involvement in Milly's
case. If the old man had fled in fear it was because Mike had not
listened to him. Right now he could do more for Joe and Milly
by finding out who Susan Kennedy was than where Joe Stern
was…and he was sure the police had already put a tracer on the
doorman.

The research people at the newspaper had some pull with
the phone company and in twenty-four hours Mike had a
name, Pasternak, and an address on Judy Terrace in a town
called Massapequa on Long Island's south shore. Now came
the legwork and some fast talking, but he couldn't do it himself.
If he were recognized and blew his cover Andrew Brandt, as
promised, would have his balls in a vise.

Mike had never allowed the *Ledger* to run his photograph
in conjunction with his daily column. He wisely believed that
a reporter should be as inconspicuous as possible. But the
endorsement ads and numerous television talk show appearances
which came with success had made his face as well-known as
his name. What he needed was someone Susan Kennedy's age,
preferably male, who could ask questions without raising any
dust.

A cub reporter on the paper's staff might do, but they tended
to congregate in pubs with other cub reporters where they drank
too much and talked too much. Kevin Lakewood was out of the
question, but his name immediately led to someone who would
fit the bill to perfection. Mike wondered how far Sands Point was
from Massapequa as he reached for the phone.

He drove himself, feeling that one pretty white boy at a time
was more than enough for Frank Evans to cope with. As he
crossed the mid-town bridge and headed east he was surprised
to see piles of snow still lining the curbs and driveways. In

Manhattan it disappeared two days after it stopped falling. The expressway was mercifully uncongested and he moved along at a fast pace, the air cool and clear and a warm glow of anticipation egging his foot onto the accelerator. He hadn't felt this good in weeks.

Brad Turner had answered the phone himself and seemed delighted to hear from Mike.

"I was hoping you would call," the boy had blurted and Mike wondered what Brad Turner had meant by that. Probably nothing more than polite youthful enthusiasm, Mike told himself, but he didn't allow that to dampen his expectations when he recalled how excited Brad had become when learning the reason for Mike's call.

Had Mike been a bit too dramatic in describing his simple request? Had he made it sound too cloak and daggerish? Well, when one was recruiting one had to make the offer as attractive as possible, Mike lied to himself.

He turned off the expressway and drove north, marveling at the scenery which surrounded him. Acres of gleaming white fields sprouted giant oak trees now morosely dark and barren except where patches of snow cleaved to their barks and limbs. A schoolhouse, long, sleek and modern, stood on a lawn as big as a football field. Clusters of neat houses with meticulously shoveled driveways were speckled with groups of hooded and muffled children building empires with the raw material of nature.

He was in the shadow of the Empire State Building but could have been on another planet. He continued to follow Brad's directions and the clusters of houses began to dissolve into spacious homes which in turn gave way to gracious mansions he could now and then glimpse from the road because winter had disrobed their mighty sentinels.

He turned into the Turner's driveway and before he could see the house he spied a familiar figure jogging a few yards in front of his car. He rolled down his window as he cruised smoothly beside Bradley Turner.

"It's too damn cold for that," Mike greeted his host. Brad was wearing a gray, baggy, sweat suit which did nothing to conceal his trim, compact physique.

He grinned down at Mike, his eyes a startling blue in the stark winter light. "How fast are you going?"

"About ten."

"Move it up to fifteen." Mike obeyed and the runner kept pace. He was so engrossed as to be taken completely by surprise when the house suddenly loomed in front of him. It wasn't ostentatious, just big and rambling and very inviting.

Before Mike was out of the car Brad had the front door open. "Wipe your feet," he shouted. "I have to clean it up. Everyone's gone south."

The house was just as inviting inside as it had looked from the outside. A lot of space, a lot of light and a riot of good furniture that was obviously for use and not for show.

"Why are you still here?" Mike asked as he followed the gray sweat suit up a broad flight of stairs.

"Waiting to hear about a job." That was refreshing

"Doing what?" They crossed the second floor landing and began to mount another flight of steps.

"You won't laugh?" Brad asked.

"Cross my heart," Mike answered.

"Assistant to a Broadway producer. I want to be a director. Theater, films…" His voice trailed off.

"Why would I laugh at that?"

"I don't know. People usually do." He stood aside and allowed Mike to enter before him. "I hang out up here."

It was a huge room with windows facing north and south. Without having to look Mike knew the northern exposure commanded an imposing view of Long Island Sound. It was a man's room but all about were traces of the boy who had grown up in it. A model sailboat, athletic trophies, framed photos of little baseball players, little campers and scrubbed and polished prep school graduates. It was the kind of room Mike had expected Brad Turner to hang out in.

"I admire your ambition," Mike said. "And it's an admirable profession. Stick with it. If you have talent you'll make it."

"And if I don't have talent?"

"You'll suffer in opulent splendor," Mike sighed, waving his arm about the room.

Brad looked a little embarrassed. "Would you like something? I have a little kitchen up here, believe it or not."

"I believe it. Would a beer be possible?"

"You got it." Brad moved through a narrow doorway and came back with two cans of beer.

"Don't drink that on my account," Mike said, indicating the beer. "Stick to your tiger's milk."

"You putting me down, Mr. Manning?"

"The name's Mike and I'm not putting you down. It's just a little unnerving to catch you running the mile while waiting for me. You're a cool man, Bradley Turner."

"Not really. I was wearing out the carpet up here and decided to put the tension to use. It's not every day I get asked to help Mike Manning solve a crime." It was an honest statement, spoken without a hint of self-consciousness. Now Mike felt he had been put down, but with a great deal of care and pampering.

"Thank you," Mike said as he raised his beer can toward Brad before taking his first swallow. They drank in silence, Mike looking at Brad and Brad looking at his feet, the ceiling and finally, like a reluctant magnet, his eyes met Mike's. Suddenly, the boy burst into action.

"Have a seat. I'm going to shower and change...don't worry, I'm fast...and you can tell me what I have to do. I don't own a gun, but I guess I can borrow yours."

"I never touch the things. They have a nasty habit of hurting the wrong people."

Mike sat and watched Brad remove his sneakers. "I take it you know all about Kevin Lakewood's mother?"

Brad nodded. "I talked to him a few days after Vicky's party. Remember? Christ, I couldn't believe it. Tried to get him the next day, when I read about it, but couldn't. He told me he had been staying with you."

Brad stood up and pulled the sweat shirt off his body. Mike filled the boy in with as much information as he needed to reveal. "By the way, did you ever meet Susan Kennedy?"

"Kev told me I had, but I don't remember. Guess I was completely underwhelmed." He took off his pants and stood facing Mike in a pair of one-piece long johns.

"How do you like 'em?" he grinned at Mike.

"Not very sexy, but practical." Mike laughed and couldn't help compare Bradley Turner with Kevin Lakewood. The two young men were as different as night and day. Everything Kevin did, the way he walked, talked and undressed, seemed calculated to entice. Everything Brad did was practical ... but just as enticing. Perhaps even more so.

He wondered aloud, "How did you and Kevin ever become such good friends?"

"Kev? We've known each other for ages. Shared a room at Ryder Prep, hated each other and continued sharing and fighting right through college. Why do you ask?" Brad began to unbutton the long johns

"You're exact opposites, that's why."

"They say opposites attract." The underwear came off and he stood in his jock strap, his body as relaxed as if he were fully clothed. His torso was well defined, muscular without being overbearing; the stomach hard and flat ; the legs at once graceful and athletic. The dark hair on his chest narrowed down to a tantalizing line which disappeared under the taut elastic band.

"I never believed that for a minute," Mike answered. "Mind

if I smoke?"

"Not if you don't mind a little pot. I'll need it for courage."
Brad took the paraphernalia from a night table drawer and began
rolling his joint. He moved about with the grace of a dancer and
the masculine assurance of one long accustomed to the ambience
of the locker room. He inhaled deeply, kept the smoke in his
lungs for the required length of time and exhaled with a sigh.

"That's good," he announced. He pushed the jock strap down
his legs, allowed it to fall to his ankles and then stepped out of
it. With a flourish of his right hand he juggled his testicles and
the appendage they supported like one petting a dog too long
confined to a cage. Then he sat facing Mike, took another toke
and asked,

"Well, what do you want me to do?" This, Mike thought, is
too damn much.

"Why don't you shower and dress and I'll tell you on the way
to Massapequa. But first get me another beer." Mike sat back and
watched the naked youth parade across the room and then back
again. The view, from both directions, was fascinating.

Brad, a road map spread across his lap, gave directions and
Mike drove. The plan he proposed to the boy was quite simple.
Brad was to pretend to be a friend of Susan Kennedy.

"Say you knew her at college and lost touch. You tried calling
her number, learned the phone had been disconnected and came
to her house hoping to find out where you could contact her. But
find out as much as you can," Mike pleaded. "Try to keep them
talking. Most of it will be meaningless but something significant
might pop up."

"Who are them? I mean who lives there now?"

"I have no idea. You're the director ; see what turns up and
improvise."

"But suppose the house was resold since Susan Kennedy
left?" Brad asked.

"Then we're back to square one," Mike answered truthfully.

Massapequa was a typical suburban town and Judy Terrace a winding street dotted with small, ranch-style houses. As Mike pulled up in front of the house a pretty girl, obviously pregnant, emerged, followed by a toddler. The boy began kicking snow in the air with his tiny rubber-booted foot.

"Danny, stop that," his mother reprimanded but Danny had a mind of his own and took another whack at the snow, taking a good bit of lawn with it.

"You're on," Mike said as he gently shoved Brad toward the door. Mike waited in the car and watched. The young mother seemed pleasant and animated as she spoke to Brad. Judy Terrace, on the other hand, was about as animated as a graveyard. The girl was probably happy for Brad's company, however brief it might be, to break the monotony of her day. Danny gave up kicking the snow in favor of kicking Brad in the shins. Five minutes later mother and son got into their car and Brad returned to Mike's.

"The kid kicked me."

"I saw. What did you find out?"

"She's nice," Brad said. "Her husband's a fireman."

"Is that what you found out? Holy shit…"

"They bought the house two years ago," Brad teased, "from a man named Pasternak."

"Home run," Mike shouted.

"Not exactly…but I think I made it to first base." The young couple had bought the house two years ago from one Vladimir Pasternak, an old man who was the original owner. He had occupied it with his sister and niece.

"Susan Kennedy," Mike exclaimed. Brad shook his head.

"She didn't know anyone named Susan Kennedy. She and her husband only dealt with Pasternak. They met him once when they viewed the house for the first time and after that their only one-on-one was with a real estate agent who carried the listing and finally put through the deal. The agent told them that

Pasternak was retiring to Fort Lauderdale, and that his sister had recently died."

"The sister has got to be Susan Kennedy's mother. It figures. She told Theresa Allen her mother had just died but made up a little story about it being her house that was sold. It was actually her uncle's. So Susan's mother's maiden name was Pasternak but what was her married name? Kennedy is probably as phony as the girl herself."

"Sorry Mike, but Danny's mother didn't know that."

Mike drove in silence, looking as depressed as he felt.

"Not even first base, eh," Brad offered, looking as sad as Mike.

"You were great," Mike said, snapping out of his pensive state. "We have Vladimir Pasternak in Fort Lauderdale and that was more than we had an hour ago."

When they got back to Brad's place the boy asked, "You want to come in for another beer?"

"I'll take a rain check," Mike told him. "I want to get back to town before the five o'clock traffic hits the fan."

"I had fun today, Mike."

"So did I," Mike answered.

"But all you did was watch."

Mike grinned. "I repeat...so did I." Did Mike see a glimmer of a smile on Brad Turner's face?

"Will I see you again?" the boy asked.

"I certainly hope so. How about the theater some night?"

"Now you're talking my language." Brad looked as pleased as he sounded.

"I don't mean a dingy loft in Soho where they mumble. I mean the theater."

"A compromise?"

When Mike nodded Brad continued. "Off-Broadway in the

Village. I'll arrange the tickets."

Mike stuck out his hand. "You've got a date."

He drove back to Manhattan wishing, once again, that he could take Bradley Turner with him. The first thing Mike did was call a stringer in Palm Beach. Mike asked the man to try to locate Vladimir Pasternak in Fort Lauderdale and when he did to ask him one question: What was his niece's name? Then he called Andrew Brandt and told him what he had been up to. Brandt was furious.

"We had a deal, Manning," Brandt shouted. "You clear with me before you act, remember?"

"The deal was I write nothing until I clear it with you," Mike corrected him. "All I did was lay the groundwork."

Brandt ignored this. "Are you telling me everything?"

"As much as there is to tell."

"What's that address in Massapequa?" Mike gave it to him again and then asked if they had turned up anything regarding Joe Stern.

"We're still laying the groundwork," Brandt snapped and the phone went dead. Mike hoped little Danny would kick the shit out of Brandt's men. He spent the evening making the rounds of clubs and parties, gathering fodder for his column. Milly Burke was still topic number one, with all focus now on the missing doorman.

"I don't know if I want him found," Sam Saxman confided to Mike. "I'm afraid of what he's hiding."

"Don't you want to know the truth?" Mike asked.

The lawyer shrugged dramatically. "I don't know. Do you?"

The call from Palm Beach came through the following afternoon. Vladimir Pasternak had died one year ago. Susan's phone number, the house in Massapequa and now Pasternak — three strikes and Mike Manning was out.

Then it began again. The gnawing, the restlessness, the mental itch that Mike couldn't shake once it took hold of him. But what it was trying to tell him was no clearer now than it had been weeks before. All roads led to Susan Kennedy and all of them were cul-de-sacs. He called Kevin and got Milly. Kevin was skiing in Vermont. He called Bradley Turner and got no one. He called the tennis pro and got himself a date.

10

The offices of Conner and Walsh were located in an old Madison Avenue building boasting high ceilings, huge elevators and a marble and gilt lobby. The space occupied by the advertising agency, however, exhibited none of this grandeur. Its partitions and dividers gave one the feeling of traversing a series of railroad cars when walking from the reception area to one's destination. But Conner and Walsh offered Mike Manning his last, meager hope of learning who Susan Kennedy was. So meager in fact that he would have skipped the visit had he not been putting off for weeks a meeting with the agency concerning an endorsement one of their clients had proposed for Mike.

"Finally," Jerry Hagen exclaimed as Mike walked into his office. "We're offering you a deal that can make you rich and you avoid us like we were your dentist."

"Good to see you, Jerry, and I haven't been avoiding you. Just otherwise engaged."

"Sit down," Hagen said. "Can I get you something? Coffee, a cold drink?"

Mike declined as Jerry Hagen looked at the former model he had used to enhance dozens of successful advertising campaigns. "You don't get older, Mike, just better. A cliché, I know, but it's true. If you were still working I'd put you in every Calvin Klein ad and make you a star."

Mike laughed in appreciation. "I am working, in case you don't read, and I am a star, in case you haven't heard."

"I read," Hagen said with a nod, "and these days mostly about Milly. Sorry about that, Mike. How's she doing?"

"Holding up," Mike answered. "Well…what do you have for me?" They talked business for the better part of an hour and when Jerry Hagen thought he had Mike sold and a solid piece of business for the agency, Mike brought up the subject of Susan

Kennedy.

"Can't tell you anything more than I told the police," Hagen said. "She did her job and got the usual number of complaints. Nothing exceptional, just the run of the mill."

"This business about her employment application never being verified," Mike stated, "is that the usual or an exception?"

"The exception, we told the police that."

"So what happened?"

"Mike, hundreds of people pass through our personnel department every year. Some get hired, some don't. The ones who do we check out but every once in a while we fuck up. She was that once in a while." Mike shook his head.

"It seems impossible that she should be the exception to the rule. Did you know her, Jerry?"

"Just in passing. She didn't work for me personally." Then he added reflectively, "Funny, she never struck me as Burke's type."

"She wasn't," Mike agreed.

"What do the girls in the office have to say about her?"

"Again, what they told the police. Susan was quiet, not very friendly and some thought a little haughty. She seemed to think she was a cut above the nine-to-five secretarial routine."

"Any comments about her clothes?"

"Plenty," Hagen waved his hand in the air, "especially around a place like this. Nothing goes unnoticed. Was Burke paying the bills?"

"That's what everyone thinks," Mike said.

"But you don't."

"No, Jerry, I don't." Hagen held out his arms in a gesture of despair.

"Sorry I can't be of more help."

"Not your fault." Mike stood up and prepared to leave. "You'll give them my terms?"

"That I will." Jerry also rose and extended his hand. Then a mischievous smile curled his lips. "Tell me something, Mike, strictly off the record. Did Stu Symington ever get his three hundred bucks worth?" The question, so out of context, took Mike by surprise. When he realized what Hagen was referring to he started to laugh but in the middle of the mirth he suddenly turned deadly serious.

"This is the Symington Company's agency," he muttered as if the fact were a revelation.

"We call it bread and butter," Hagen said. "I sent you on that job. Don't you remember?"

Mike walked toward Jerry Hagen's desk, pointing a finger at the man. "Tell me something, Jerry, and no bullshit. If Stu wanted to place a secretary in this agency, no questions asked, could he?"

"Are you kidding? Stu Symington could name a monkey Vice President of Conner and Walsh and we'd thank him. We're talking billings of twenty-five million a...Christ...Susan Kennedy?"

"Yeah, Susan Kennedy," Mike whispered in somewhat of a trance.

"Stu Symington and Susan Kennedy? You're losing it, Mike. The girl was a girl, not a pretty boy."

"But it has to be Stu," Mike insisted.

"Why?"

"Because it's all I have to go on." Mike was euphoric as he headed for the door. "I love you, Jerry, and screw my terms...tell your client I'll accept any offer they want to make."

"Are you serious?" Hagen would never know the answer because Mike was already racing for the elevator.

But it wasn't all Mike had to go on and he knew it. There was more...so much more that Mike was amazed he had only laughed when Andrew Brandt had suggested Stu as the girl's benefactor. Stu Symington had the money to keep the Kennedy girl in fancy clothes and anything else she might want. Stu Symington had the connections to introduce her to all the right people...like

Kevin Lakewood's crowd. And, most of all, Stu Symington had no inclination to detain the girl overnight.

"That was the funny part of it," Mike could almost hear Theresa Allen's voice..."she slept right here every night." But why...why...why? What was in it for Symington and how did it all connect with Stephen Burke? A nondescript girl from Massapequa being treated like royalty by Stuart Symington? The man was known to wine and dine and dress boys, one of whom even turned up dead like Susan Kennedy. The more Mike thought about it, the more excited he became. And the more excited he became the madder he got at Andrew Brandt. It was Brandt who had brought Symington into the picture and Brandt who had suggested a connection between Symington and Stephen Burke.

"They seem to have turned up at quite a few parties together." What game was Brandt playing and what did he know that he wasn't telling Mike? There's a bar on New York's east side, just a few blocks from Mike Manning's apartment, that deals in dreams — all the dreams money can buy. Its polished parquet floor is trod upon by dreamers, slightly past their prime ; its mirrored walls, on any given night, reflect an array of handsome, young dreams. The dreams parade before the dreamers to the tinkling airs of Cole Porter provided by a cocktail pianist.

It's all very civilized...and very expensive. The word hustler would be too crude to ascribe to the young men who work this beat. They are artists of the genre, selling not merely sex but fantasies come true. They know the essential tricks of their trade...it's all in the packaging. Their guises are perfect; their acting skills worthy of the stage.

A young executive, fresh out of college and on his way up. A teenage athlete, his shoulder bag bulging with the gear of his sport, his clothes slightly mussed after a quick change in the locker room. A boy with a shy smile and outdated crew cut you would swear had just gotten off the bus from Ohio and had wandered in here by mistake. And the tough looking lad in the far corner, so pensive, had to be a prince of the Mafia.

Some pity the dreamers. This is a gross error. They can make their dreams come true as long as their stamina and money hold out. Lament the dreams. They last but a single night and, should they recur, are labeled nightmares.

The first time Mike Manning had walked into the dream bar he had taken it all in and concluded what wise men have long known…"There's no such thing as a naked sailor…" and never went back again.

Returning now, he was recognized immediately and every eye in the place followed his progress down the length of the bar. He went directly to the rear, a dimly lit area furnished with plush chairs, glass cocktail tables…and Stuart Symington who watched Mike approach, raised his drink in the air and said, "Welcome… are you buying or selling?"

"Not your concern," Mike answered. "If I were buying you wouldn't interest me and if I were selling you couldn't afford me."

Stu clapped his hands without making a sound. "Very good, but it won't win you any friends around here. The approach is more subtle." Stuart Symington was thin, with dark hair brushed straight back, dark eyes and a nose tilted in such a manner as to give the impression he was forever sniffing some foul odor.

Mike sat, without being invited, at Symington's miniscule table. "I'm not here to make friends, Stu, just to chat with an old one."

"I'm flattered. And appreciative; everyone is staring at us. Thanks to you, we're the main attraction."

"Your money doesn't exactly repel."

A waiter, who looked like a movie star playing the part of a waiter, interrupted their banter. "Can I get you a drink, Mr. Manning?"

"Bourbon over ice."

As the boy retreated, but before he was out of earshot, Symington blurted, "I've had him. Seventy-five bucks. I'm so old I remember when a good piece of trade went for ten and was happy to get it."

At that moment Mike hated Stuart Symington more than he thought it possible to hate another human being.

"I'm forty, Mike, how old are you?"

"How old do you think I am?"

"If I didn't know any better I'd say twenty, but you've been around too long for that. Wasn't it ten years ago when we had our...er...little incident?"

"Fifteen years and I was twenty then."

"Have you come to repay the three hundred or to celebrate our fifteenth anniversary of boyhood innocence and fraternal devotion?"

The waiter placed Mike's drink on the glass table. "Put that on my tab," Symington told him.

"It's on the house, Mr. Manning," the waiter spoke to Mike without acknowledging Symington's existence. It was the boy's moment of triumph and he played it to the hilt. Mike silently applauded the performance as he nodded his thank you.

Symington mumbled something that sounded like *bitch* and then turned his attention back to Mike. "So, what are you doing here?"

"I told you. I came to talk to you."

Symington began to look a little uncomfortable. First he shifted his position, then he reached for a cigarette. As he lit it he looked across the room as if he were expecting company. "You know what I like about you, Mike? You know everything. You haven't been in this place for years, if ever, but you knew I'd be here as sure as you know the back of your hand. Tell me, do you really have spies in all the watering holes in this town?"

"You don't need spies to know what's happening," Mike told him. "You need big ears. Mine are gigantic."

"If you know so much, what do you want with me? I don't know anything."

He's anticipating, Mike thought, feeling like a hound who had finally picked up a viable scent. "Susan Kennedy," Mike said.

Symington managed a tight, false smile and shrugged. "Burke's girl? What about her?"

"She's dead," Mike answered.

"Aren't you a bag full of hot news." He leaned toward Mike. "Now stop the bullshit and tell me what this is all about."

The fox was going on the offensive. It was a valiant but pathetic try. Stuart Symington didn't have the heart for battle. He had, for too many years, hired mercenaries to fight them for him.

"I want to know who she was."

"She was Burke's girl and Burke's wife shot her. Is that all, Mr. Manning?"

"She was being kept by a rich man and Burke wasn't rich. The relationship was chaste and Burke wasn't the chaste type. She was a phantom hired by an advertising agency who couldn't pay the rent if they lost the Symington Company's account."

Symington was visibly shaken but he kept up a good front. "Who do you think you are, the police?"

"I'm an investigative reporter verifying his facts."

"You're a fucking menace and there are laws to protect us from people like you. You have any more questions for me, you submit them to my lawyer. Now get the fuck out of here, Manning."

Mike could taste Symington's fear and savored it like a starving gourmand. A long shot had finally paid off. If one stab in the dark had hit its mark, why not try another?

"The police are still working on the Cimino case, Stu."

Symington turned pale under the dim light, his face tense and ugly. "The *Ledger* is never going to see another Symington ad and if that doesn't get you where you live I'll sue you and that rag of yours from here to the gate of hell and back again."

Mike rose, towering over Symington. "Thanks for the

information, Stu."

"I didn't tell you a thing."

"An old reporter once told me a 'no comment' was the most blatant statement a person could make. Good night, Stu." On the way out Mike slipped a ten-dollar bill into the waiter's pocket.

"You don't have to do that, Mr. Manning."

"I know I don't, but I want to."

"I get off at four a.m."

"That's too late for me," Mike smiled, "or too early, depending on how you look at it."

"For you I'll walk off the job."

"Don't ever sell yourself short, kid."

"I don't sell myself, Mr. Manning. Symington is full of shit."

"I agree."

The night was cold and so clear the sky glittered with stars in spite of the perpetual glare of midtown Manhattan. Mike walked home feeling that for the first time since he had taken up Milly's cause he had made a slight dent into the mystery that surrounded Susan Kennedy.

Symington was scared out of his wits. The mere mention of Susan Kennedy had him calling his lawyers and the name Robert Cimino had turned him into a screaming hysteric. Mike wished he could have stayed longer to needle Symington until he got the truth out of him, but doing so might have tipped his hand. It wouldn't have taken long for Symington to realize Mike knew absolutely nothing about either victim. As it were he had left Symington with just the right dose of apprehension and enough innuendo to make him grossly paranoid. He would give a fortune to know what Symington was doing at this very minute. Choking on his martini, he hoped.

Kevin Lakewood was waiting for Mike in the lobby of his apartment building, a red, heart-shaped box of candy in one hand and a bottle of champagne in the other. He was wearing a fur-lined parka, a ski tow tag dangling from the zipper, and looking exceptionally young, healthy and handsome.

"Did Vermont run out of snow?"

When they got to Mike's apartment the boy handed over his offerings. "Happy Valentine's Day."

"Aren't you a little early?"

"A day or two, but I'm here to protect my turf and inform you that I play a mean game of tennis myself."

"Christ," Mike moaned, "is nothing sacred? Who's stringing for you, Kev, Roger Mudd?"

"As a matter of fact, you're your own enemy," Kevin answered. "I read all about it in Mike Manning's New York. You gave the pretty *enfant terrible* of the tennis world two mentions in two days but when you wrote 'Jack confided to me over dinner at Le Cirque' it got me right in the balls."

"Nasty, nasty," Mike wiggled a finger at Kevin and started to enjoy himself. "Here, have a bonbon, it'll sweeten your tongue."

Kevin pushed the red box back toward Mike. "Have you ever seen me in a pair of tennis shorts?"

Mike pretended to contemplate the question. "No...but I've seen Jack Montgomery in 'em and it's a sight one is apt to remember."

"Maybe I should leave."

"Come here," Mike beckoned.

"What for?"

"Shut up and come here." When Kevin was standing in front of him Mike unzipped the parka and put his arms around Kevin under the warm lining. "I missed you," he whispered. "More than I care to admit, I missed you."

"Maybe I'll stay a while," Kevin answered.

"You're a spoiled brat but in spite of all the complications I think I'm hooked," Mike said.

"The only complications are the ones you dream up." Mike's hand opened Kevin's belt and found the top button of the boy's jeans. Kevin stood perfectly still, his body relaxing to Mike's touch. Mike had the feeling he could do anything he wished at this moment, knowing Kevin would follow, without pause, wherever he was led. It was a tantalizing feeling, filled with visions which dwelt in the darkest recesses of the mind. Kevin Lakewood, saying nothing and doing nothing, dared Mike to bring them to fruition.

"No thermal underwear?" Mike teased. "It must get chilly on the slopes."

"It has other things to keep it warm."

"I wasn't referring to that it."

"No…but you were thinking about that it."

Later they sat sipping champagne, Mike smoking a cigarette and grinning contentedly as Kevin inspected a set of black and white glossies of Jack Montgomery.

"Did he give you these?" Kevin asked, none too kindly.

"I asked for them. He's going to win at Wimbledon this year and I'm going to run one of those on page one."

Kevin put down the photos. "All he does is ham it up for the television cameras."

"That's what television cameras are for, or haven't you heard?"

"I heard Jack Montgomery swings both ways," Kevin responded.

"What, his tennis racket?"

Kevin tossed a pillow at Mike. "My mother says she hasn't seen you in over a week."

"I haven't seen you in over two weeks." Mike tossed the pillow back.

"I went skiing What have you been up to?"

"Working, as a matter of fact. Which reminds me, do you know Stuart Symington?"

"Stu? I've seen him around," Kevin said. "Always reminds me of a Scott Fitzgerald character slightly out of context with the times."

"I think he knew Susan Kennedy."

Kevin appeared unimpressed. "So what? I knew her, too, and so did a lot of other people."

"I think Stu was the guy who was introducing her around town and paying her bills." Mike leaned forward and spoke in earnest. "Could Stu Symington be the one who introduced you to Susan Kennedy?"

The boy shook his head. "Stu Symington never introduced me to anyone and I think you're way off base. Stu Symington and a girl?"

"Everyone seems to think Symington was allergic to women," Mike answered, slightly annoyed. "Well, he wasn't. Quite a few ladies played up to him and he loved the attention. A lady of title once made a fool of herself over the man."

"If you're talking about the Duchess, forget it. The Duke was long on pedigree and short on cash. The lady would have courted a zebra if it were rich enough."

Mike laughed. "You must have been fourteen when all that was going on."

"I cut my teeth on your column. But why this sudden interest in Symington?"

Mike filled him in on what had transpired since Mike's visit to Conner and Walsh. "And I think I struck gold," he concluded.

Kevin remained unimpressed. "If the ad agency is your only tie-in between the girl and Stu Symington I think you're on pretty thin ice. The Symington Company isn't their only account and Susan could have gotten the job on her own. It happens every day. Your evidence is less than circumstantial."

"If the agency was the only connection, I would agree with

you," Mike nodded. "But I'm basing my case on Symington's reaction to my questions. He wasn't just disturbed, he was scared shitless. Why would an innocent man act like that?"

"Innocent of what or guilty of what?" Kevin exclaimed, losing patience. "We both know who committed the crime...and didn't Stu have a nasty brush with the law not too long ago over some hustler who doped himself to death at Stu's Palm Beach place?"

"The boy wasn't a hustler and Stu's part in it was more than circumstantial." Now Mike was angry. He had been ready to hang his hat on the Symington connection and now Kevin Lakewood was hacking away at the peg. Mike didn't like it.

"What the kid was doesn't make any difference. The point is Stu had a lousy experience with the police so why shouldn't he turn chicken when you come along and try to involve him in something he knows nothing about?"

"I think he knows more than he'll ever tell," Mike was almost shouting, "and whose side are you on, anyway?"

"My mother's," Kevin answered, "whose side are you on?"

This response, spoken with passion, was totally unexpected and silenced Mike for the moment. Kevin Lakewood never ceased to amaze. Every time Mike thought him as young, frivolous and self-serving, the boy said or did something that belied the impression. What Mike had been thinking this evening was how little concern Kevin exhibited for his mother. He seldom lamented her situation and almost never talked about her in connection with the case. But Kevin's involvement at the moment showed that he cared a great deal, although Mike failed to see the reason for the boy's obvious resentment toward implicating Stuart Symington. Rather than speculate he asked Kevin to explain.

"Saxman thinks my mother has a good chance of walking away from this," Kevin told him.

"My stepfather's reputation speaks for itself and catching him in the act in our home is all Saxman needs to mount his case."

Kevin, Mike thought, was beginning to sound like Sam Saxman.

"I know you want to help but if you start sticking your nose into every crack that looks suspicious all you'll accomplish is covering a lot of people with mud. I don't care about other people, but I do care about my mother. Half-truths and hints that there's more here than meets the eye can only help the D.A. It won't bring anyone back to life or change the fact that Mother did what she did."

Kevin looked pleadingly at Mike. "Now do you understand why I'm upset? Open a can of worms labeled Stuart Symington and God knows what you'll come up with...and when you do, what will it prove?"

Rather than admit that Kevin was a hundred percent correct, Mike asked, "What about the truth? Don't you want to know why your mother did what she did?"

"I want to see my mother go free. That would be justice. I don't give a fuck about the truth."

Now the boy sounded exactly like Sam Saxman. Funny how no one involved in Milly's crusade wanted to know the true story. Mike seemed to be the exception to the rule and he was going to stick with it regardless of Kevin's reservations.

"Just leave well enough alone," Kevin said with an air of bravado but a trace of fear plainly visible in his brown eyes. Ken Farley had made a similar request and suddenly Mike was afraid...afraid for himself and afraid for Kevin.

But those who allow fear to grind the mill of justice get only the injustice they deserve, Mike reflected. "Don't worry," he said gently, "I won't open any closet doors." Kevin came to him and nestled himself in Mike's arms. Mike stroked the soft, curly hair and thought how easy it was not to give a damn about anything but the here and now.

11

Andrew Brandt looked up from his duck a l'orange long enough to ask, "Do you always lunch like this?"

Mike shook his head as he cut into his steak. He glanced at the red meat under its black crust with a look of satisfaction and then answered, "No. It's usually a tuna sandwich on the run followed by indigestion. I thought we both needed a break."

"Which means you want something from me."

Mike looked hurt. "Bribe the police? Andy, what do you think I am?"

"A fast talker and a faster worker," Brandt answered.

"Is the duck good?"

"It's better than sex."

To each his own, Mike thought, knowing better than to voice the opinion. "What do you think of my conversation with Symington?" Mike finally asked, breaking with tradition and bringing up business before the coffee was served. He had given Brandt all the details of his talk with Stuart Symington via phone and Brandt's response had been a maddening silence. Mike then arranged a meeting in the fancy bistro to see what he could learn from the man after he had been wined and dined in regal splendor.

"I bet this lunch costs half my weekly pay check," the policeman now speculated.

"Hardly, and if it offends your sense of modesty don't blame me. You could have refused."

Brandt very discreetly waved his fork to the left and right of his plate. "And miss all this? I couldn't get in here unless someone was stabbed to death with their silver paring knife." He nodded toward an actress of legend sitting a few tables from them. "It's her in the flesh, isn't it? What a pair of knockers. Are they real?"

Mike leaned forward. "Real…and eager. The last time I was on the coast she tried to get me to screw her in her dressing room."

The duck a l'orange suddenly took second place. "You're kidding?"

"I am not. She kept grabbing for my pecker and I had to keep pushing her away. It's very distracting when you're trying to conduct a serious interview." Mike cut himself another piece of the perfectly broiled steak. "Close your mouth, Andy."

"Then what happened?"

"I told her I had a headache."

"Why do guys like you get all the offers like that?" Brandt asked.

"Guys like me? Do you mean me as in Mike Manning or fags collectively?"

A slight flush crept up Brandt's neck. "You know what I mean."

The actress and her companion rose to leave and passing behind Mike the lady bent, pressed her ample bosom into his shoulders and kissed him in a sisterly fashion. "I'm staying at the Plaza," she whispered before moving on. She left behind, besides the lingering odor of very expensive perfume, her red lip prints on Mike's clean-shaven jaw.

"I guess I'll have to fake another headache," Mike sighed.

Brandt attacked his wild rice with a vengeance and sublimated his frustration by enjoying a heartier appetite than was his want. "I think you scared the pants off Symington," he said, but not a minute before the steaming cup of coffee was placed before him.

"I know that," Mike said, "I was there. But why? That's what I want to know."

"And you think I can tell you?"

"I think you can tell me more than you already have," Mike said, relieved that they were finally getting around to the point of the meeting. His contentment was short-lived as yet another actress entered the room on the arm of a writer more celebrated for his foppish behavior than his prose. Brandt's eyes followed them from their conspicuous entrance until they were seated.

"It's not polite to stare," Mike reminded him.

"What's she doing with that bird-brain?" Brandt asked.

"He's sleeping with her husband," Mike answered.

"And she's having lunch with him?" Brandt was astonished.

"He's also writing the screen play for her next film. When she's sure he's given it his best shot she'll toss him and her husband out of her home and life."

Brandt shook his head. "Some people you know, Manning."

"Me? I don't know them. I just know about them, it's my job. Now can we get back to Symington? I'm not on the city's payroll and have to end our little tete-a-tete before the sun goes down."

"What do you want to know?"

"Why you thought to link Symington to the Kennedy girl and Stephen Burke. Either the police department has a crystal ball that works or you have a hard piece of evidence to substantiate the tie-in. And how does it connect to the shoddy business in Palm Beach?"

Brandt reached into his jacket pocket and brought out a piece of worn, folded newspaper. As he carefully opened it to its full size he said, "Not a hard piece of evidence...just this," and then he passed it over to Mike. "It was run in one of those small, local papers in Palm Beach that print nothing but social news."

Mike was looking at a photo of a senator and his wife smiling for the camera while reclining in deck chairs on the beach.

"Look in the background," Brandt prompted. When Mike did he let out a long, low whistle and shook his head in disbelief. The background depicted Stuart Symington, a young man and Stephen Burke, all of whom appeared to be walking toward the camera when the photo was snapped. A pair of masculine legs could be seen behind the trio but the man's torso was obliterated by Symington and Burke. Whether he was part of the group or just a straggler was impossible to determine.

"That," Brandt said, "was taken the weekend the boy died. Saturday, to be exact."

"I take it the kid is Cimino." When Brandt nodded, Mike continued, "Did you question Symington and Burke about this?"

Brandt nodded again. "Symington said he ran into a lot of people on the beach that weekend and Burke might have been one of them. I showed him the photo and he said he guessed Burke was one of them."

"And Burke said the same thing."

"Right. Symington and Burke together in Palm Beach and a boy from the Bronx, a nobody, turns up dead. Then Burke and a girl, another nobody from Massapequa, turn up dead. So I played a hunch."

"And I think it paid off," Mike said. "I don't know why Symington was playing with Susan Kennedy, but he was. The fear on his face was as plain as a written confession."

He looked at the news photo again. "But I think you're wrong connecting it to the Palm Beach incident. These people do run down to Florida for a weekend and they do run into each other on the beach or in a club. I've seen it countless of times. A nod, a hand shake and then they move on. The camera could have caught Symington and Burke during the few minutes they happened to be in the same place at the same time."

"So my hunch got us one out of two. Symington and the Kennedy girl." Brandt shrugged. "Not bad considering the fact it was nothing more than a guess to begin with."

"Not bad at all," Mike agreed. "Now what we have to do is keep on Symington till he breaks."

"We can't get too close," Brandt told him. "We have nothing to charge him with and his lawyers are very sharp. I've dealt with them before, remember?"

"But I'm not the police," Mike reminded the Inspector.

"Yeah," Brandt said slowly, as if mulling over that fact for the first time. "You could keep on Symington's tail with more impunity than the police."

"And if someone's head has to roll guess whose neck will be conveniently stretched out for the axe."

"You don't have to do it," Brandt answered, as if not caring one way or the other.

"But you know I will and I know this is what you've been angling for while running up my lunch tab. I thought I was going to get something out of you today but the canary seems to have swallowed the cat."

"Your first mistake was to think of me as a canary, and you did get something out of me," Brandt indicated the newspaper photo Mike was still holding.

"Can I keep this?" Mike asked

"Be my guest. I've got more of 'em."

Mike refolded the photo and slipped it into his pocket. "Anything new on Joe Stern?"

"Still missing but presumed alive. We talked to neighbors and think he's gone to Arizona."

"So do I. His lung problem. He was always talking about retiring to Arizona but never had the money to actually do it." The two men looked at each other knowingly.

"Stuart Symington," Brandt said.

"The train always stops at the same station."

"But why?" Mike said, exhibiting the frustration the question aroused.

"That's what I'm hoping you'll find out," Brandt said calmly.

"Did your men turn up anything in Massapequa?"

"Nothing more than you got and Uncle Vladimir, as you told us, is happily dead. We seem to be top heavy with dead people, Manning."

"How much digging did you do in Ft. Lauderdale?"

"Not much. Susan Kennedy was murdered and Milly Burke has confessed to the crime. Why waste a lot of time and money investigating a corpse?"

"Sounds like the D.A. read you the riot act," Mike said sympathetically.

Brandt dismissed the District Attorney with a wave of his hand. "Something like that and according to the policeman's bible he's right."

"I take it the D.A. is not interested in Symington," Mike reflected, knowing the answer.

"On the contrary," Brandt grinned. "The D.A. has his eye on the big office in Albany and Symington is known as a heavy hitter when it comes to political contributions...for politicos he likes, that is." The grin faded. "I never even mentioned Symington to him in connection with the Kennedy girl."

"Did you ever hear the story of Stu Symington and the last presidential campaign?" Mike asked.

"No, but I could use a good laugh."

"Stu backed the winner with big bucks," Mike began, immediately warming to the subject, "and received a framed, autographed picture of the man himself for services rendered. Stu mounted the picture in his room and one day his mother came wandering in, saw the photograph of the president of the United States and said, 'I knew you chased actors, Stuart, but I didn't know you liked them so old.'"

Brandt laughed.

"And," Mike added at the height of their new-found conviviality, "if I ever find out you're on Symington's case simply because he's gay I won't get off your case until you're back pounding a beat in Flatbush."

Lunch ended with the truce as tenuous as ever between the two adversaries. When Mike got back to his apartment the doorman handed him an envelope. Inside was a theater ticket for a play he had never heard of being presented in a theater of similar obscurity. His answering service had a dozen messages for him, including an invitation to the opening of a new Broadway musical which the press had ballyhooed into something tantamount to the second coming. It took less than one minute to decide which one he would attend.

He called his stringer in Palm Beach and asked him to see what he could learn from Pasternak's neighbors in Ft. Lauderdale. If Brandt could find out by questioning neighbors where Joe Stern went, there was no telling what Pasternak's neighbors might come up with. He grinded out his column, mentioning the two actresses and author he had seen at lunch and told his readers he had broken bread with Inspector Andrew Brandt, the man in charge of the Burke case. Brandt would verbally rebuke him for this and silently relish every line.

He showered, dressed casually and headed downtown. The theater was located in the east Village and wasn't the nightmare Mike had expected. Situated in what must have once been a fraternal meeting hall it exhibited some semblance to a theatrical setting. The fact that it wasn't in an unheated loft or an overheated basement made it the Shubert of the off-Broadway circuit. He presented his ticket at the make-shift box office and found Brad Turner waiting for him in the make-shift lobby.

"Thanks for the advance notice," Mike greeted the boy.

"Big opening uptown tonight. I thought you would go there." Brad's sweatshirt was a walking advertisement for the play Mike was about to see.

"Did you plan it this way to test my loyalty?"

"Maybe," was all Brad would commit himself to. "I got you the best seat in the house," he continued abruptly as if embarrassed by Mike's question. He pointed to a row of uncomfortable looking folding chairs fronting the make-shift stage. "I'll see you later."

Before Mike could protest, Brad walked briskly across the stage and disappeared into the wings of the theater. Mike found a cheaply printed program on his seat and perused it as soon as he made himself as comfortable as he was ever going to be in the hard, wooden chair. When he found what he was looking for he grinned happily.

"Bradley Turner...Assistant Stage Manager." The boy was as modest as he was charming.

The play was mildly entertaining and little else. The young man of ideas and ideals, misunderstood by his girlfriend, jeered at by his peers and encouraged by his father, an older man of ideas and ideals who long ago abandoned both for the easier path of conformity. Five minutes into the first act Mike realized the lead actor was completely wrong for the role of the suffering youth.

Brad reappeared at intermission. "What do you think?" he asked as soon as he had elbowed his way through the thin crowd and stood before Mike.

"I get the feeling I'm watching a revival," Mike answered truthfully. "It's not exactly fresh ground."

"I know it's a hack," Brad agreed, "but the writer does have talent."

Mike nodded. "He does, and it'll blossom if he stops licking his wounds and gets down to business. His story is not unique. And..."

"The lead is all wrong," Brad anticipated.

"So you noticed."

"I knew when he auditioned but I'm not the director. What the role needs is a Montgomery Clift or Jimmy Dean type. What they got is a blond Sly Stallone. How can you sympathize with a guy who looks like he could punch his way out of a steel cage?"

Mike laughed. "You've got a director's vision but not the job. Which reminds me...why didn't you tell me you were stage managing the show?" The second act curtain buzzer sounded.

"I've gotta go," Brad said and was gone before Mike could elicit an answer to his question. After the final curtain Mike waited a half hour in the freezing cold for Brad Turner. When the boy finally emerged, his shoulders hunched under the parka he wore over the lettered t-shirt, he walked shyly toward Mike.

"You waited."

"You invited me here with two hours' notice, placed me on a hard wooden chair and left me to suffer in silence and now you're surprised that I hung around hoping you would offer to buy me a drink. You're one hell of a date, Mr. Turner."

"I didn't know I was your date," Brad answered.

"You're not. I'm yours. Come on, walk, before I freeze my tail off. I'm not wearing long underwear."

"They all know you saw the performance," Brad said as the two began walking toward the West Village.

"Who are they?"

"The cast, the crew…the whole damn company. They think you're going to give the play a mention."

"Well I'm not," Mike answered emphatically. "Mostly because it's not worth mentioning Was that why you sent me the ticket?"

Brad stopped abruptly. "Fuck you, Mr. Manning."

"Grow up, Bradley…and keep walking."

Brad hesitated a moment and then hastened to keep pace with Mike.

"I asked an honest question and I expect an honest answer. Save the dramatics for your chosen profession."

"I didn't tell you I was stage manager," Brad shouted, "because I didn't want you to think I was looking for a hand-out and I sent you the ticket a few hours before the curtain because I didn't want you to nosey around and find out I was stage manager for the same goddamned reason."

"I know that," Mike replied calmly.

"Then why the hell did you ask why I invited you?"

"Because I want to know…and I still do."

Exasperated, Brad once again raised his voice. "I asked you because I wanted to see you again."

Now Mike stopped walking and faced his companion. "Thank you."

"You're a bastard, Mike."

"I call it honesty…but a rose by any other name and all that jazz…and now that that's behind us, where are you taking me for a drink?"

"Down here you have two choices. A gay bar or one of those places that smells of urine and disinfectant where aging hippies meet to talk about the good old days. Your move."

Mike thought it over and decided that he had already pushed Brad a step further than the boy was willing to go. On the other hand, the prospect of aging hippies, not to mention the promised aromas, turned him off completely.

"I know a place uptown you might like," he finally offered as he raised his hand to flag a passing cab.

When they got to Mike's apartment Brad commented, "Very nice and no cover charge. I think I like it." Mike mixed drinks, then he and his guest settled down to amiable conversation for the better part of an hour. They talked about the theater, Brad's ambitions and Mike's work. Mike, though he tried to avoid it, found himself once again comparing Bradley Turner to Kevin Lakewood. But it was an unfair comparison because both young men succeeded in their own particular fashion. Kevin evoked a sexuality that was pure lust; a viable asset he plied for all it was worth. Brad was a long fuse attached to either a firecracker or a box of TNT ; the temptation was to light a match and gladly suffer the pop or explosion.

"Anything come of our sleuthing in Massapequa?" Brad asked when Mike returned from refilling their empty glasses.

"Uncle Vladimir, if he was Susan Kennedy's uncle, is conveniently dead."

"Of what?"

"Not murder," Mike assured Brad. "My guess is he was done in by happy retirement. I understand it's usually fatal." He handed Brad his drink. "Here's to a long career and a pox on retirement villages."

"So that link to Susan is a complete wash-out." Brad sounded genuinely disappointed and Mike wondered if this was prompted by the fact that Brad's part in the drama was destined for oblivion.

"That link, my boy, was the only link I had...except for..."

Mike sipped from his glass and when he continued he spoke as if he were embarking on a completely different topic. "Do you know Stu Symington?"

Brad grinned. "The playboy of the western world? Our paths have crossed."

"Did he put the make on you?"

"Not as crudely as you make it sound. He asked me if I would audition for a Symington Company T.V. commercial."

"He put the make on you," Mike said with conviction. "I speak from experience."

"I didn't know you did T.V. commercials," Brad answered with a smile that was as mischievous as it was infectious. A stubble of beard now appeared on his smooth, clean-shaven face. The blue-black covering had the texture and consistency a man usually confronts the first thing in the morning and not eleven o'clock in the evening. For some strange reason this feature made Brad Turner look younger, not older than his twenty-two or so years. Beneath the sparkling blue eyes he reminded Mike of a boy masquerading as a man.

"I don't," Mike responded curtly.

"What did you say to Stu's offer?"

"I told him I didn't shop the Symington stores."

"Good for you," Mike laughed.

"I don't think Stu shops them..."

"You know, Mike," Brad interrupted, "I just thought of

something."

"What?"

"Susan Kennedy."

"What is it?" Mike leaned forward in his seat as if ready to physically draw anything concerning the Kennedy girl out of Brad's furrowed brow.

"The first time I met her," Brad began slowly, "was at one of those big charity balls. My mother bought the tickets from…"

"Mrs. Symington. Stu's mother. It was a benefit for the charity she sponsors."

Brad was impressed. "How did you know?"

"An educated guess, laddie, an educated guess." Mike was excited. Here was yet another tie-in between Susan Kennedy and Stuart Symington.

"The theme of the ball was hearts and flowers." Brad spoke rapidly as the incident emerged clearly from his subconscious. "So that would make it Valentine's day, about a year ago."

There it was again! The flash of insight that told Mike all the pieces of the puzzle lay under his nose and all he had to do was fuse one into the other to complete the picture which would tell him what actually occurred in Milly Burke's bedroom on New Year's Eve. There was now no question that New Year, or simply the word year, triggered the response. But why? The only pieces of the jig-saw which locked properly were the ones labeled Susan Kennedy and Stuart Symington. Where was the piece that would link them to Stephen Burke? If it was a piece tagged year… what year? New Year? last year?…its jagged edges melded with nothing on Mike's drawing board.

"…Kevin was there," Brad was still recalling his first meeting with Susan Kennedy. "And just about everyone else who was home from school for the weekend and forced to go. You know the routine. The tickets are a hundred bucks apiece…shouldn't go to waste…all your friends will be there." Brad was obviously quoting his mother.

"Do you think it was the first time Kevin met her, too?"

Brad shrugged. "Could be. How's Kev doing?"

"He'll live," Mike answered.

"The tragedy hasn't cut into his skiing or put a moratorium on his social life." The mischievous smile reappeared on Brad's face. "Kev's been giving you a hard time?"

"I wouldn't say that," Mike replied, angry at himself for being angry at the implication of Brad's question.

"Be careful, Mike, Kevin is addictive and lethal."

"Are you speaking from experience?"

"Now that would be telling, wouldn't it?" Brad's blue eyes seemed to bore right through Mike as he spoke.

"Honor among the fraternity and all that shit?"

Brad raised his eyebrows and pointed a finger at himself. "Oh, I'm not a member of the fraternity."

Mike was too wise to be put off by the pointed retort. He knew something was in the offering and after three strong bourbons he was ready to find out just what it was. Besides, he had spent two hours on a hard seat, watching a lousy show, and he fully expected something for his trouble. He had given and the time to take had arrived. Brad was holding out the pastry tray but Mike couldn't see what was on it. If the dessert proved too rich he could always say he was on a diet and call it a night. The time to ignite the long fuse that was Bradley Turner was at hand and Mike happily struck a match.

"You could have fooled me."

Brad looked at his feet. "Is my slip showing?"

"Come off it. If you had played your scene on the stage tonight you'd have had a winner."

"I never tried to fool you." Now the boy was all wide-eyed innocence.

"I refer to the strip tease at your home last week followed by the parade of the nude jock. I thought I was getting a preview of things to come."

"Shit, I was just getting dressed. What did you expect me to do, duck behind a screen like a prima donna?"

"I didn't expect you to do anything." Mike's amusement was beginning to give way to boredom.

"Besides," Brad continued with a shrug, "I sort of like it." He rose, walked aimlessly for a step or two and ran his hand under his t-shirt. "I mean if a guy wants to look at me, why the hell not. I'm not a prude. What's the harm in helping a buddy get off?"

The t-shirt was now up to his pecs and his hand ran a circle over his flat, tight belly as he talked. The pastry tray was being uncovered and Mike looked it over like an undecided window shopper. The t-shirt was suddenly gone and Mike stared once again at the broad shoulders and hairy chest.

"I think I liked it better unstaged," he said, but continued to look. Mike reasoned that he couldn't beg off via the diet route because what was being offered was definitely the lo-cal special. Brad stepped out of the loafers he wore and unzipped his jeans.

"Do you think we'll have more snow?"

The whole fantasy trip, Mike thought, as boredom reverted back to amusement. "Too cold to snow."

"Hot in here," Brad said as the jeans came off. He was wearing a jock strap and Mike wondered if the garment was Brad's usual under attire. The short, stocky athletic body posed itself languidly in front of the somewhat reluctant voyeur. It was everything Mike remembered and more...Brad was mildly aroused.

Mike contemplated the tableau. "The only thing missing," he mused, "is the towel draped casually around the neck." Brad turned and left the room. Mike watched his retreating legs and for amusement rated them against Kevin Lakewood's and Jack Montgomery's. He decided it was an even match and saluted his good fortune with a sip of bourbon. When Brad returned the towel was in place, the jock strap was gone and the mild arousal had grown to serious proportions.

"Better?" Brad clutched the loose ends of the towel with his fists as he once again struck a pose. "Do you think the Yankees will make it to the pennant this year?" Brad rubbed the towel across the back of his neck. "They have no hitting power and their pitching is for shit."

"Poor Yankees," Mike lamented.

"But Boston looks good." The entertainer now casually wrapped the towel around his waist. The tent pole effect was cruder than his nudity.

"When you come out of the closet, Bradley Turner, the sound is going to be heard around the world."

"Bullshit!"

"Come here," Mike growled as he reached for Brad's wrist and pulled him onto the couch.

"Don't get undressed," Brad cautioned.

"I don't have to," Mike assured him.

Mike poured himself a nightcap before going to bed. "Well," he whispered aloud, "it wasn't a box of TNT but it was one hell of a big firecracker."

12

Two days later Mike lost his last lead to the identity of Susan Kennedy.

"You can scratch Symington off your list." Brandt's voice was as foreboding and cold as the bleak winter morning.

"Why?" Mike yawned, looking about for something to wrap around his shivering body.

"He's dead, that's why."

"What?"

"You heard me, Manning, he's dead. Stuart Symington departed this world from a sleazy hotel room on West Forty-Ninth Street. The good Lord is going to think he was one of us common folk." If this was a dream it was the coldest and most realistic dream Mike Manning had ever had.

"Hotel?"

"The Chatham Arms. And wait till you see it. A regular office building for whores."

"Where are you?" Mike asked, just beginning to grasp the full implication of Brandt's news.

"At the hotel."

"I'll be there in half an hour."

The Chatham Arms was located between Ninth and Tenth Avenues. The tenements which had once abutted its east side had been torn down and replaced with nothing. These vacant lots were surrounded by a chain-link fence which had not prevented the area from becoming a dumping ground. Garbage, furniture, toilet seats, pipes coated with rust and the skeletal remains of automobiles had all managed to traverse the barrier and set themselves up as a macabre memorial to the dregs of mankind. An ancient fire escape zig-zagged its way up the hotel's exposed flank like some grotesque vine spawned from the debris below. Its windows were either black with filth or painted over to prevent the sun from interfering with business.

Nowhere did the Chatham Arms identify itself, possibly in deference to its clientele. The only happy note to greet Mike as he exited his cab was the smiling face of patrolman Harold Sadowsky.

"We've got to stop meeting this way," Mike quipped and was sorry almost before the words were out of his mouth. Those were probably the first words he had spoken to another young man wearing a similar uniform and undoubtedly also guarding the way to the scene of a shoddy murder. The hurt, sudden and unexpected, was like a sharp blow to his gut.

"Thanks for the mention, Mr. Manning. You made me a hero in Staten Island."

Mike forced a smile, nodded and opened the door of the Chatham Arms before Sadowsky had the chance to play doorman. The smell of cigarette smoke, worn carpeting, peeling wallpaper, lighting you couldn't read a billboard by and a dozen men in blue all conspired to intensify Mike's painful memories. He spotted Brandt's tweed coat in the dim light, the broad shoulders hunched over, the blond head staring down at a small, balding man seated in the only chair the lobby of the Chatham Arms offered its guests. Brandt looked up as Mike approached.

"The night clerk. He's deaf, dumb and blind." The small man shrugged his shoulders and looked at his wrist watch. Dead bodies were not an uncommon occurrence at his place of business.

"How?" Mike asked.

"Enough Seconal in his drink to kill an elephant He must have gone to sleep in two minutes and died a half hour later."

"Can I go home now, Sergeant?" The clerk started to rise.

"Inspector…and no, you can't go home now." Brandt pushed the man back into the chair.

"I don't get no overtime."

"A man died while you were on duty in this flea bag and we

want some answers."

"I told you everything I know," the man pleaded.

"You didn't tell me dick."

"Because that's what I know, Inspector…dick."

Brandt turned to Mike. "Symington checked in about midnight with another man."

"A hustler," the clerk whined. "He came in with a young stud and a bottle in a brown bag. He paid his money, I gave him a key and they climbed the steps to paradise. That's all I know."

"You hear that?" Brandt sighed. "The guy's a fucking poet. What did the stud look like, Mr. Poet?"

"Who knows? They all look alike an' this bimbo was wearing a heavy coat, collar turned up, dark glasses…the whole bit. Maybe he was a movie star hustler, eh, Inspector."

"Could it have been a woman?" Mike asked.

"Say…ain't you Mike Manning?"

"No, he's Mickey Mouse," Brandt answered.

"Could it have been a woman?"

"Under all that shit it could have been Greta Garbo. But I ain't never seen no hooker dressed like that. You gotta show it, not hide it."

"Did you see him … or her…leave?" Mike questioned again.

"Could have…but I don't remember. You know how many people go in an' out of this place every night? Shit, it's like the subway. I get my money up front an' then I don't care what they do. It ain't my business. Say, you gonna give us some press, Mr. Manning? I'll turn this dump into a disco an' cater to the carriage trade. Girl dancers…boy dancers…"

Two men in white appeared on the dimly lit staircase, each gripping the metal handle of a stretcher. Holding up the other end were two more men in white. What lay on the stretcher was covered with a blanket. As the cortege passed Mike, he noticed Stu Symington's expensive cordovan shoes sticking out beneath the covering.

Mike watched his last hope of solving the riddle of Susan Kennedy pass through the doors of the Chatham Arms on its way to the morgue. Everyone connected with the Kennedy girl seemed to travel the same route. Mike felt as hopeless and depressed as his surroundings. A slightly sick feeling began to invade his stomach and he remembered he hadn't had his morning coffee.

"There's nothing to learn here," he said to Brandt. "I'm going."

"What's the matter, Manning, can't you take it anymore? Where's the cub that used to eat his lunch while he viewed the remains?"

"He grew up, Inspector." Mike headed for the door.

"Hold it," Brandt shouted. "I'll give you a lift across town."

He pointed a finger at the clerk. "You don't go anyplace till my men are finished here."

"Nice meeting you, Inspector."

"Oh, we'll meet again...real soon."

"I'm here every night," the clerk grinned.

"And from tonight on you'll be here alone. The Chatham Arms is closed till further notice." The little man groaned at Brandt's departing back. Patrolman Sadowsky drove the unmarked car and Mike knew better than to acknowledge the rookie, however innocently, in front of Brandt. Oddly enough, Sadowsky knew this too. The city was just starting to come to life as the car moved east. Office workers, shopkeepers and commuters were now briefly mingling with the night people who scurried, like vampires, to flee the harsh light of day.

"How did they discover the body?" Mike finally broke the silence in the back seat.

"The night clerk who wants to change the place to a disco with your endorsement. He checks the rooms every few hours. If they're empty he rents them again."

"What about the key?"

"It gets left in the room. They don't check out, Manning, like at the Waldorf. They do their thing and go…fast."

"It stinks to hell and back," Mike offered.

"His wallet is missing and so is any jewelry he might have been wearing."

"That makes it stink even more."

"Not Symington's style, is it?" Brandt finally agreed.

"That's the understatement of the year. When Stu paid for sex he hired pros. Five-hundred-bucks-a-night boys who look and act like movie stars, or whatever you want them to look and act like. He never took a trick anyplace but to his home. He liked the security and had no secrets from mama or anyone else."

"You think he was taken to the Chatham Arms at gun point? This isn't a movie, Manning."

"I think the hook was baited and Symington bit."

"Who supplied the bait?" Brandt asked. As usual, he appeared to be paying scant attention to the conversation but hung on every word Mike uttered.

"Symington," Mike answered.

"As simple as all that."

"He trapped himself?" Mike nodded.

"In a sense. I think he called someone for help after I spoke to him and that someone arranged the clandestine meeting. Yeah… he baited his own hook and choked on it."

"Who's the someone?"

"A psychopath with a big pair of balls. Anyone who knew Symington would never believe he took a hustler to a glorified whore house. Our clever killer wants us to think he didn't know Symington very well…or at all."

"Why was Symington killed?"

"What is this, twenty questions?" Mike exploded. "He was

killed because he was running scared and the killer couldn't trust him to keep his mouth shut."

"Keep his mouth shut about what?" Brandt continued to question calmly.

Mike sighed. "I don't know. But I do know it has something to do with Susan Kennedy and Stephen Burke."

"Burke was killed by his wife and Susan Kennedy got in the way. You don't think Milly Burke was behind those dark glasses at the Chatham Arms?"

"That would be too much, Inspector, even for a movie. But the girl figures in both cases. If she got in Milly's way then she also got in Symington's way. Who the hell was she?"

"We have two cases," Brandt began as if summing up for a jury, "and two murderers. One confessed to her crime and the other is a question mark. Burke's murder has nothing to do with Symington's murder. The girl is a coincidence. What I have to do is find the question mark."

"Susan Kennedy is the only question mark you should be looking for."

Mike refused to be deterred from this line of thought. "She's the reason Stu was running scared and your only lead in this whole stinking mess."

"Some lead," Brandt moaned.

"How did you get called in on this?" Mike suddenly asked. "It's outside your precinct."

"I don't have a precinct." Brandt sounded insulted. "And I got the call because it's no secret that I'm interested in anything connected with Stuart Symington."

"Are you trying to connect this with the business in Palm Beach?"

"I'm not trying to connect it to anything," Brandt answered. "I'm trying to disconnect it with Burke. Besides, Palm Beach is a dead issue, isn't it? In fact all three men in my little wire photo are dead. You can scratch that one, too, Manning." They had crossed

Fifth Avenue and were moving slowly down Fiftieth Street in the early morning traffic.

"I wouldn't disconnect it with anything if I were you," Mike said shortly. "What's new on Joe Stern?"

"We're still looking. So is Saxman and he wants the doorman more than we do. I wish him luck. Did you know Stern was a big fan of yours?"

"Meaning what?"

"When we searched his apartment we found a collection of your columns, all neatly cut out and stacked. A neighbor told us he saved the ones where you mention people he opened the door for at Burke's apartment building. Poor slob had nothing better to do than keep a running record of all the rich people who breathed on him in passing. Some life, eh, Manning?"

"We're here," Sadowsky spoke his first words as he pulled up to the curb.

"How did you know where I lived?"

"The police know everything, Mr. Manning."

"Smart man," Mike said to Sadowsky's boss.

"Maybe he can solve the Symington case."

"Get out of here, Manning."

"Keep me posted," Mike requested as he climbed out of the car.

"You do the same," Brandt snapped.

The first thing Mike did when he entered his apartment was to pour himself a glass of juice. The cold, acidic liquid hit his belly like a shot of booze. Munching on a hard roll he filled the coffee pot and set it to brew. He undressed as he walked from the kitchen to his bedroom.

A hot shower and a clean shave revived him, but only slightly. It was eight thirty in the morning and already he had visited a low life hotel, watched a corpse being carted away and lost the only clue he had to a puzzle that could determine the fate of Milly

Burke. If this kept up it was going to be one hell of a day.

The hot coffee revived him a bit more. He lit a cigarette, inhaled deeply and decided he could survive another day on the planet Earth. He called his paper and gave them the details of Stuart Symington's death. He couldn't officially link it to Stephen Burke but he stated... 'this is the second murder to hit the Social Register in the past two months. Milly Burke, confessed murderer of husband Stephen, is now awaiting a trial which promises to be as sensational as the circumstances surrounding Symington's death.'

If the killer was as smart as Mike thought he was he would now know that Mike, if no one else, suspected a common link between the two crimes. Feeling less sorry for himself, Mike began feeling something akin to sympathy for Stu Symington. True, he had never liked Symington, but he was a fellow being and no one had the right to play God with another's life. But does the individual have the right to choose between living and dying?

Mike poured himself a second cup of coffee and went back to the telephone. This time he pushed the button to play back any recorded messages. The voice that greeted him immediately obliterated all thoughts of death and dying.

Jack Montgomery was very much alive and "...Staying at the Sands in Vegas. The weather is warm, the pool is cool and there's a movie star under every pillow. This weekend I play Johnny Carson for I forget which worthy charity. It's a sell-out...naturally...but there's a good seat with your name on it. The hotel is also sold out but my suite is big enough for two. I said two, Mike, so leave your society chickens in New York where they belong. You see, I've got spies, too. Come west, Mike...and hurry up."

Mike looked out at the gray winter day as the second message droned on. A press agent was unhappy over something Mike had written about his has-been actor client. The warm sun would be a delight. The tennis match sounded like fun. He hadn't seen Johnny in over a year and...Jack Montgomery was peeking out of the closet door, beckoning. Mike thought about getting an early flight on Friday...

The third message shaded Mike's imaginary sunshine. "Mike? This is Brad. I'm sorry about the other night." Click!

Damn him, Mike thought. That kid is the most mixed up... and what the hell is he sorry about? Does he think he took advantage of me? Oh, shit. He reached for the phone, began to dial then hung up before the connection went through.

"No. He'll apologize again, say he lost his head and want to know when we can get together so he can lose his head again."

Desert sun and tennis matches faded from Mike's mind as it filled with more pressing problems. Bradley Turner wasn't one of them. First, he had to see Milly and tell her about Stu. She had undoubtedly already heard the news but he thought a one-on-one in light of this new development might get her to open up. And he wanted to see Kevin. Feeling masochistic he called the car service and asked for Frank Evans.

The sometime-chauffeur arrived driving a new car that literally sparkled. "The Impala died," Mike said, trying to hide his joy.

"Nope. I traded it in."

"You mean this is yours?"

Frank nodded proudly.

"What do they pay you at that garage?"

"Not enough."

"You hit the lottery."

"No. The numbers. I hit 'em big, Mike."

"Be careful. I hear they sometimes shoot big winners. It keeps the bank plump and the Godfather happy."

"Bullshit and you know it. Winning is good for business. It gives people the itch. They pay cash on the line and no income tax."

"Don't let Uncle Sam hear you. He's itchy, too."

"Then let him go scratch for himself. How do you like it, Mike?"

Mike surveyed the plush interior and nestled into the soft leather seat. "I love it."

Frank smiled happily. "Where to?"

"Milly Burke's."

"Eight Thirty Fifth Avenue," Frank all but shouted.

Mike looked at the driver incredulously. "You didn't?"

"I sure as hell did."

"You played number eight thirty and hit the jackpot?"

"No." Frank looked at his passenger with disgust.

"Don't you know anything about numbers and hunches? It's eight thirty, fifth. Eight, three and five. You've got to encompass the whole hunch, not part of it."

Mike shook his head. "You're a remarkable man, Frank."

"No, just smart. I've been playing it since the first time I took you there. Seemed to me all the people who lived over that number were on easy street so I rolled with the winners."

"Too bad Joe Stern never thought of that."

"Who's Joe Stern?" Frank asked.

"The doorman. The one who beat it, remember?"

"Did you find him?"

"Not a hair, Frank. And in case you haven't heard, Stuart Symington, of Symington Stores, is dead."

Frank turned to look at Mike.

"Watch the road, please. He got it in a hotel room roaches wouldn't patronize."

"Choked on a big, white ..."

"Frank! Show some respect for the deceased. He was slipped a big, fat dose of sleeping powder."

"By who or whom?"

"I think it's whom. By a young stud wearing dark glasses, if you can believe the hotel clerk."

"Symington like 'em young?" Frank asked.

"Symington liked 'em any age he could get 'em. But not in cheap hotels, Frank. He took them home and introduced them to mama in the morning."

"Maybe he answered one of those ads," Frank ventured.

"What ads?"

"Those coded ads some papers run. S, M, Greek, French, cut, B and D."

"Your range of reading material is remarkable."

"I like to keep up," Frank answered thoughtfully. "What kind of ad would lure this Symington?"

"What difference does it make now?"

"We look for an ad that would appeal to his kink and answer it. If it's the same ad he answered, we got the killer."

"I see what you mean. I'll pass it on to the police."

"You know," Frank said as if thinking aloud, "that gives me an idea."

"Don't answer any ads, Frank, until you've figured out the codes," Mike cautioned.

"The doorman. What's his name?"

"Joe Stern."

"Yeah, him. Why don't you advertise?"

"You mean through my column? What the hell do you think I've been doing since he disappeared?"

"You sure he reads the column?"

"Positive. This morning I found out he even saved some of them."

"What did you say to him?"

"If you kept your nose out of the trashy ads and read something literate, you'd know," Mike admonished the driver, then relented. "I told him how important it was for the police to contact him and I stressed the fact that he was the only person who could corroborate Milly's story regarding the timetable on the night of the murders. He liked Milly and I don't know why he's doing this to her."

"'Cause he's scared, that's why."

"I know that," Mike answered, losing patience. "But the police would offer him protection."

"I think he's scared of the police and that's who you're asking him to contact."

"What are you getting at?"

"Run a coded message," Frank advised. "Something only he'll understand. Make it clear that you want to talk to him and that no one, especially the police, will be brought in on it."

Mike gave this some thought, recalling how the doorman had pleaded to be heard on that fateful night. Whatever he had wanted to tell Mike he obviously didn't pass on to Brandt's men, which gave credence to Frank's suspicion. Mike had long regretted not listening to what Joe had to say, but now there was a good possibility he might get a second chance

"I could kiss you, Frank," Mike said, feeling slightly euphoric.

"Forget it. I don't like white boys."

"I'm not a boy."

Mercifully, for Mike, they arrived at the winning address.

13

Thanks to Milly's chainsmoking, a perpetual blue aura enveloped her audience like some mystical harbinger of doom. She looked pale, drawn and nervous to the point of being unable to concentrate on anything except the cigarettes she extinguished and lit in rapid succession.

This study in bereavement was countered by her son who appeared as calm, collected and distractingly handsome as ever. Kevin's somber expression was his sole contribution to the depressing meeting.

The atmosphere in the palatial room was as inviting as the air Milly insisted on polluting. She had obviously taken the news of Stuart Symington's death very badly indeed. In fact, she seemed more perturbed by the demise of her casual acquaintance than at being the cause of the untimely passing of her husband and an innocent stranger.

Five minutes after his arrival Mike was given the distinct impression that he alone was responsible for all this misery.

"We go through life," Milly expounded, "thinking that murder, like disease, is something that happens to other people. People we read about in the newspapers or see on the telly. Then one day we find ourselves starring in the sordid drama and wonder how the hell we got there."

Keen observation, Mike thought while answering, "I'm sorry he's dead, Milly, but I think you're overreacting. As I recall you liked him as little as I did."

"That's not the point," Milly snapped as she lit yet another cigarette and, in the process, seemed to lose her train of thought. The eyes behind the smoke, so patently blank, assured Mike he would never be told what point he had missed. Milly was on more than nicotine.

Mike looked at the woman he had long considered a dear

friend and saw an uncertain ally. The easy camaraderie that had once existed between them had been replaced with a saccharine tolerance since the night of the crime of passion, as the popular press now invariably referred to Milly's solution to her unhappy marital state. He had attributed her withdrawal to nerves, tension, fear…anything but the simple fact that Milly Burke would do anything, including using her attractive son as a pawn, to avoid a confrontation with Mike.

Where was the young woman who had helped a cub reporter succeed at an almost impossible task, who had accepted his rejection with love and understanding and who had been his only comfort in the hour of his greatest loss? This chain-smoker, tranquilized on chemicals, was a total stranger.

"Kevin told me you upset Stuart the night before his death," Milly was now saying. Mike glared at Kevin Lakewood and called upon every ounce of self-restraint he possessed to keep from bolting. Knowing Milly's sentiments for Stuart Symington in his lifetime made her concern over his death almost indecent. Or was this yet another ploy to keep the spectator's eyes on anything but the magician's nimble fingers?

"I asked him a few questions about Susan Kennedy. If that upset him I'd like to know why."

"Now you'll never know, so what did you gain?"

"I wasn't trying to gain anything," Mike responded, his voice beginning to rise with his temper. "I was trying to find out what the girl was doing here. Christ, Milly, I was trying to help you."

"What she was doing here is perfectly clear to me and the police. All you accomplished was frightening Stuart. He probably drank too much as a result and picked up some…"

"Bullshit," Mike shouted, springing to his feet. "You know as well as I do that Symington didn't do any such thing. Just what the hell is going on around here, that's what I want to know. And don't tell me you're prostrate with grief over his death because I'm not buying it."

"Mike, please…" Kevin tried to intercede.

"I came here today," Mike continued, ignoring Kevin as he tried vainly to penetrate Milly's tranquil brain, "to see if I couldn't get you to level with me. Another murder, Milly…another senseless murder over a girl named Susan Kennedy…"

"Mike," Kevin tried again.

"I think it's damn important that we find out just who she was. Mention her name and men drop dead. How many more murders do we write off before someone around here starts talking?"

Milly turned to her son and looked at him pleadingly. The boy put his arm around his mother and gently prodded her to her feet. She turned to Mike, her face a waxy mask, and said,

"I've told you…"

"Not now, mother," Kevin assured her. "You lie down and I'll talk to Mike. I'm going to tell him the truth."

Milly seemed to turn to stone before Mike's startled eyes. The look on her face was pure anguish as she tried to speak but was unable to force her brain to comply. Only her eyes, wide and fearful, expressed the terror her son's words had evoked. Mike took a step forward but Kevin warded him off.

"Please, mother, it's best. You lie down and try to sleep. Let me handle this." He began once again to lead her out of the room and she moved with him like a somnambulist in protective custody.

Mike turned his back on the pathetic scene. He felt like an intruder who had accidently laid bare the closet which contained the family skeletons. Perhaps none of this was any of his business and maybe he was seeing sinister clues where nothing but the obvious existed. Was he, out of some misguided sense of loyalty, committing crimes in the pursuit of justice? In Milly's present condition she was capable of anything, including taking her own life.

Mike sank into a chair and buried his face in his hands.

"I think she'll sleep," Kevin said as he re-entered the room.

"The housekeeper is with her and I'm going to send for a nurse. I don't want her left alone."

"What has she been taking?" Mike asked quietly.

"A sedative. Don't worry, we have a prescription for it. But I know she's been drinking Scotch on the sly. I found a bottle in her room."

Mike winced. "It's so unlike her."

"So is a trio of murders, but it happened to her. Not everyone has your zest for the genre."

"Okay, I deserve it."

Kevin sat on the long couch and rested his head against the flowered upholstery. "I'm sorry, Mike, I didn't mean it the way it sounded."

"That doesn't make me less deserving. And I don't want to know the truth. I've decided to fold up my tent and call it a day."

Kevin sat up, shaking his head at Mike. "Oh no you're not, Mr. Manning. You've probed and prodded and turned over every stone that got in your way…the ones you didn't trip over, that is…and now I'm going to show you what you've been looking for."

"I don't think it's any of my business."

"It isn't. That's what I was trying to tell you the other night when I asked you to lay off Symington. But you made it your business so whether you like it or not I'm dealing you in."

"I could walk out of here," Mike said.

"You could, but you won't. We both know that your newfound sense of propriety will soon wane and then you'll be kicking the tail that's now between your legs and putting your nose back on the scent. Stay, Mike, and like your sex life you can have all the thrills without the commitment."

At any other time Mike would have been delighted with Kevin's assertiveness and hailed it as the boy's entry into manhood, but at the moment this metamorphosis evaded him. "I don't think our personal relationship has anything to do with this so let's leave it for another time and another place."

"I didn't know we had a personal relationship." Kevin had the ball and was determined to run with it. "I'm so young and you're so old and all that shit. Tell me, did you give Brad Turner the same line?"

Riled, Mike decided to stop ducking and fight back. "This town has about as many secrets as the State Department and it's none of your damn business what I told Brad Turner. I'm not married to anyone."

"But my mother was," Kevin began, catching Mike off guard. "To a man who was as loaded with charm as he was bereft of ready cash. Always a lethal combination but with a bastard like Stephen Burke it became something of a plague. What I mean is, it infected whatever it touched."

Like it or not, Mike was going to hear the truth. He sat rigidly still as the tale unfolded — a tale so gross it could be worthy only of its leading characters.

"Stuart Symington had money and kinky tastes. Sooner or later the two were bound to team up for their mutual satisfaction. What they happened to destroy along the way couldn't bother them less. Did you know Symington liked to watch? Men in action, that is. And the man he wanted to watch most was my stepfather. How or when is a moot question, but the two of them came to an agreement. I think Symington propositioned Steve and Steve refused. Why not? He preferred women and their money was as green as Symington's. Then, I suspect, Symington suggested the Peeping Tom alternative and, I'm sure, upped the ante. Knowing Steve, it must have cost Symington a fucking fortune. What they needed, of course, was a girl to take to the party. The women Steve played gigolo to were out for obvious reasons and your run-of-the-mill prostitute was far too mundane for the millionaire and the penniless playboy."

"Enter Susan Kennedy," Mike thought aloud.

"Aren't you clever."

"There's no need to go on, Kevin. I get the general drift."

"I'm sure you do, but not the consequences and that's the whole point of my story."

Mike resigned himself as Kevin continued.

"I don't know if Steve found her or if she was Symington's discovery, but it doesn't really make any difference, does it? She was a girl with ambitions and, like Steve, very little cash, but I think she did it mostly for the chance of being introduced to the right people."

Kevin grimaced. "Some name tag for Symington's crowd, eh, Mike?"

"Did your mother know all this?"

Kevin nodded. "Indeed she did."

"So when she saw the girl and your father…"

"My stepfather," the boy reminded him. "We don't know what she was doing here. Sam Saxman says there's talk that she was getting ready to leave town, so maybe she came for a final payment and Steve decided to give her a little something extra… for the road. And don't start that bullshit about his clothes because I don't know what it means and I don't care. The man my mother was married to had gone from gigolo to a combination of pimp and prostitute, that's what I know. My mother is a very proud lady and comes from a very proud family. Do you know what the newspapers would do with all of this if it came out in the trial? It would kill her," Kevin shouted. "It would kill her."

Mike went to Kevin and took him in his arms. "Okay, okay…I understand."

"It was a crime of passion," Kevin sobbed, "more passion than anyone will ever know, so let it rest there and let Saxman do his job."

"Why didn't you tell me this months ago?" Mike demanded.

"What for? My mother and I decided the fewer people who knew the less chance it had of coming out in the open. Symington would never talk because he had too much to lose."

"He thought I knew," Mike said thoughtfully, "that's why he was so frightened that night. It wasn't the possibility of a scandal that worried him, his life was never anything but scandal. It was the fact that this one ended in murder and Stuart Symington couldn't afford to be implicated in another murder."

"But I told you that," Kevin said, "and you refused to listen. I hinted in every way I knew how but you insisted on going after what was never there. I think Symington went to that hotel to arrange one of his parties. His mother never questioned his male guests but I'm sure that a *ménage a trois* with a woman would be a bit too much even for her. Without Steve to guide him, Symington marched happily to his death with high hopes and a hard-on. It was no secret that he always carried a lot of cash," Kevin concluded.

"If only I had known," Mike said, shaking his head in regret. "If only you had told me the truth."

"The truth," Kevin was shouting again. "You are so fucking interested in the truth. Well, now you know it but I don't see you jumping with joy."

"If I had known the truth I would have kept my nose clean. If the police knew the truth they would be in sympathy with your mother. Deception leads to nothing but more of the same…and suspicion. Did you ever think of that?"

"Yes, I did, but I would rather people suspect whatever the hell pleases them as long as my mother stays alive and reasonably happy. I'm sure Ken Farley would agree with me."

Mike hauled off and slapped the boy so hard the blow almost knocked him off the couch. A moment later he was staring in disbelief, first at his hand and then at the red welt it had left on Kevin's cheek.

"Christ, I'm sorry." He tried to take the boy back into his arms.

"Just go, Mike."

"Please…please…I'm sorry."

"Just go," Kevin repeated.

"Not now and not with this between us. What you said…"

"Was unfair and I'm sorry I said it. Now we're even, the perfect climate for a truce…remember? Now get the fuck out of here."

14

When Kenneth Farley committed suicide Mike's initial reaction had been rage. An all-consuming rage focused on the world in general and everyone in it in particular. Among Kenny's possessions was that cold piece of steel which had so quickly and efficiently severed all of Mike's hopes and dreams for the future. Night after night Mike had sat holding the gun in his hands, the last thing on this earth Kenny had touched, and contemplated loading it and using it to atone for his lover's death. Andrew Brandt headed a list which was followed by every bigot and keeper of the moral flame who had ever questioned a human being's right to keep his own counsel and live in peace.

The rage was followed by depression. Mike had gone about the business of living in a daze. As if by some magical trick, he was able to stand aside and watch the world, himself included, go by. When this, too, passed and he was able to feel again all he felt was hurt and longing. He was sexually dead except for those occasions when liquor made it possible for him to blot out the past and imagine Kenny alive and near...so near he could feel the texture of Kenny's skin and smell the odor of the expensive cologne Kenny always wore and Mike ridiculed as pretentious.

Mike would then make love to himself and feel a satisfaction particular to that ancient ritual, falling asleep believing that this was as much as he could ever hope for and, perhaps, more than he deserved. Opportunities for sex abounded. Mike didn't shun them, he simply had no desire to pursue them. Then, on a stormy winter night, he had gone out to rescue Milly's son and in the process resurrected himself. He had touched Kevin that first night with more wonder and awe than passion. He had taken him gently, more gently than his need demanded, because he feared shattering the fragile vessel of his rebirth.

"I'm not made of glass."

"No, you're flesh and blood and warm...so warm..."

That warmth had nurtured Mike's recovery from sexual apathy to desire. There would never be another Kenneth Farley but the human heart is big...all one had to do is make room. And today, a day which began with a corpse in a sleazy hotel, he had abused his savior.

Mike moped about the apartment, his thoughts alternating between rightful indignation..."The kid deserved it..." to shameful despair... "I let him down in every respect and hit him for good measure."

Kevin had dared utter the words Mike refused to believe were true, regardless of the evidence in their favor. And then the question, like a phonograph needle stuck in the groove of an old record...Would Kenny be alive today if Mike had not insisted they go public? If Mike could prove this wasn't true he could make his own peace with Kenny's death and go on to...what?

He walked to the window. The gray day had finally surrendered to a black, starless night. He wondered if the sun was still shining in Las Vegas. No, Las Vegas was out of the question. He had to square things with Kevin. If he left town before doing that he would lose the boy forever. Or would he rather be with Kevin than in Las Vegas? So many questions and no one to come up with even one clever answer.

He could call the charming Inspector Brandt, his partner in crime-smashing, and announce, "Scratch everything, Andy, we're out of business."

Mike gave up resisting and poured himself a big bourbon over a little ice. It wasn't what he needed but it was a comforting substitute.

He raised his glass and drank to himself.

"The perfect horse's ass." All those interviews, all those leads, all those wrong conclusions and what the hell for? Just what had he been trying to prove? Suddenly it all escaped him. Milly knew what the girl and Steve were up to, saw them in her bedroom and did them in. Who could blame her? And naturally Milly didn't want anyone to know her husband's relationship to Susan

Kennedy. It wasn't just humiliating, it was depraved.

Steve's clothes? As Kevin said, who knows and who cares? The answer, of course, was that Steve stowed them all neatly away, just like everyone refused to believe he would do. Ms. Kennedy's luggage? Undoubtedly left with the guy she was leaving town with and who was now scared to death to come forward. Mike strongly suspected the guy in question was a stud Steve had lined up with Susan for Symington's amusement.

Poor girl...hell bent on getting it on with the right people and then falling for a joy stick attached to a man who knew how to use it. Who said broads were dumb? And poor Stuart Symington. Surrounded with dead bodies he didn't know shit about. All the poor bastard wanted to do was play nice with himself while the live puppets danced to his music. The kid in Palm Beach went on a spree and terminated his own existence and how was Stuart to know Milly would walk in when the Kennedy girl came calling for her paycheck, or that Steve, true to form, would decide to give his protégé one for the road as a dividend.

Mike didn't know if Susan's initial contact was with Burke and Symington, but he was fairly certain Symington arranged for the girl's employment at the ad agency. When Stuart Symington played fairy godfather he went all the way. Besides, it lent a note of respectability to Susan's existence.

That left Joe Stern. It was better than an educated guess that all Joe had to say was that he knew Susan Kennedy. Knew her because Burke had taken her and Symington to the Fifth Avenue apartment, probably on more than one occasion. Milly was away a lot, thanks to her happy marriage, and Burke was using the place for his play-for-pay operation. When Joe's name popped up in connection with the crime of passion, Symington got to him and sent the doorman packing. Stuart Symington wasn't taking any chances.

Well, good for Joe. Mike hoped he had squeezed enough cash out of Symington to live happily ever after in cough-free Arizona. All the pieces locked into place and the picture which emerged was the craziest of all possible worlds. Considering the two artists responsible for the creation, Mike should have expected nothing less.

"And that was my first mistake," he thought. "Looking for a thread of sanity or some logic to the whole bloody mess, when I should have closed my eyes, opened my fly, and read the writing on the outhouse wall."

The house intercom buzzed. Mike ran down an imaginary list of prospective callers as he went to answer the summons. Andrew Brandt? No, he never made house calls unless it was official business. Brad Turner, calling for an encore? Theresa Allen coming to collect her expensive dinner? He made a mental note to pay that debt as soon as possible.

"Yeah," Mike said, picking up the receiver.

"Mr. Lakewood's in the lobby. Are you home?"

Mike heard the roller coaster gearing up for another run. Would this lousy day never end? He had composed his copy on Stuart Symington's murder, lamented his stupidity and licked his wounds. He could think of nothing worse than to have to face Kevin at this moment. Tonight was for getting drunk and crying in his beer. Tomorrow was for making up. Didn't the young know anything?

"I'm home. Send him up." Mike thought of several opening lines, rejected them all and consequently said nothing when he opened the door to admit Kevin Lakewood.

"Am I intruding?" Kevin asked somewhat formally.

"Not at all," Mike answered.

"Come on in." Mike led the way.

"How's Milly?"

"Better. Much better, in fact. She slept most of the day and woke up hungry and...more composed, I'd guess you'd call it. I did get a nurse and when I left they were playing bridge." Kevin sat stiffly in his chair. Mike got the impression of a student calling on his headmaster.

"Were you working?"

"No. I laid Stuart Symington to rest a few hours ago. I'm putting off the follow-up till I see what develops." Mike reached for his drink.

"Are you going to offer me one or do you want to knock me around a little first."

Mike looked startled and Kevin began to laugh. A moment later Mike joined in and the tension was broken.

"It's bourbon," Mike said a little self-consciously, "and it's all I have in the house."

"I've acquired a taste for it, thanks to you. It must have something to do with my latent masochism."

"Also thanks to me?"

"You said it, I didn't." On his way to the kitchen Mike paused before Kevin and gently stroked the boy's cheek with one finger. Kevin looked up and smiled. Words were unnecessary. The incident was forgotten.

"That was some scene you walked into this morning," Kevin said when Mike returned.

"It was my day for scenes. Which one are you referring to?"

"Mother's lament over the death of the dearly-detested." Kevin drank the bourbon as if he liked it or needed it.

"I was a little surprised," Mike nodded.

"You were shocked. We heard about it on the morning news," Kevin began to explain, "and mother went into hysterics. Mike, she's almost paranoid about someone finding out what Symington and Steve were up to. The trial is going to be bad enough with the facts as they are, but if the true relationship between Steve and the girl ever came to light it would go no place but downhill. When we got the news on Symington, she thought he was staging a party at that hotel and an investigation would come to roost on Steve's doorstep."

"Not to mention the fact that Milly's plea of temporary insanity would go up in smoke."

Kevin looked at Mike questioningly.

"Come on, Kevin, you know what I mean. Milly's whole case rests on the fact that she walked into her bedroom and found her husband, naked, about to make it with a stranger. If it were known that your mother knew who Susan Kennedy was and had a vendetta against her and Steve, the D.A. would scream premeditation and probably win."

"We never thought of that," Kevin responded, shaking his head slowly. "Believe me, Mike, we never did."

"Oh, I'm ready to believe anything. Does Saxman know who the Kennedy girl was?"

"No. My mother and I, Symington and now you are the only ones as far as we know."

"I should be happy I'm still alive," Mike grinned.

"That's not funny."

"There's nothing funny about any of this, young man. May I ask how Milly became privy to the goings on?" Kevin turned his head as he answered.

"Steve told her."

"Christ. Okay, I don't want to hear any more."

"They were arguing about money," Kevin continued as if Mike hadn't spoken. "They were always arguing about money. Steve wanted a bigger allowance and mother told him to get it from the ladies he serviced. Steve didn't like that so he told her he was getting it from Symington and why. He mentioned Susan Kennedy specifically and reminded mother that she had met her. He made it sound as if it were mother's fault that he had to stoop to this to get his hands on some ready cash."

The tabloids would not only have a field day with this but Mike had visions of some smart young writer turning out a best seller which began "any resemblance to persons living or dead is strictly coincidental."

"She wanted to divorce him," Kevin was saying, "but he wanted half her fortune to get out. If she tried for a lesser settlement he threatened to sell his life story to the highest bidder. It wouldn't have only hurt my mother, but also a hell of a lot of women whose only crime was that they fell for Stephen Burke."

"Life among the gentry," Mike sighed. "And let me tell you something just in case the you-know-what hits the fan. If I know your stepfather's appetite for money and Symington's appetite for sex I would say we aren't the only ones who know what those two were up to. It's my guess that Steve hired other studs to pleasure Ms. Kennedy and Stuart Symington and by now they sure as hell know they weren't performing for a stroke club."

"Do you think one of them was the guy Symington went to the hotel with?" Kevin said quickly. "There could have been a girl waiting upstairs."

"In that place there could have been anything waiting upstairs," Mike answered, remembering the Chatham Arms.

"Mike, you aren't going to say anything to your policeman friend about this, are you?"

Mike pretended to mull this over. "No, Kevin, I'm not. I think everyone involved, except Milly, got what they deserved. And I'm not being judgmental about the sexual aspect of all this. What Stuart Symington and Stephen did was their own business and no one else's. It's the fact that they implicated others, not always consenting, that makes them first class shits. Susan Kennedy, thanks to a misguided sense of achievement, wanted to get into what she thought was society. Symington, or Burke, opened the door and she was willing to pay the price which was usurious to say the least. They involved your mother by association and Steve was literally blackmailing her to keep his ass in the butter tub. No, I would say justice was done and only regret that the innocent party has to stand trial for rendering the service. And God only knows what Symington was up to when he got his, but you can be sure it was no good."

"Thanks, Mike."

"For nothing. Look, I'm not trying to rationalize my way out of this. If I didn't believe what I just said I would have been on the phone to Brandt ten minutes after you tossed me out of your home."

"I didn't toss you out," Kevin protested.

"You gave one hell of a damn good imitation." Kevin went to Mike and kissed him, then he very gracefully sank to the floor and rested his head against Mike's knee.

"And forget that I mentioned Brad," Kevin said softly. It was forgotten…until now. Clever boy, Mike thought, very clever boy.

"How did you know I had seen Brad? Did he tell you?"

"No. I know one of the girls in the show. She called me, all excited because Mike Manning had attended a performance. Thought you were going to carry them all to Broadway with twenty-five words or less in your column. By the way, the show closed a few nights ago."

"May it rest in peace," Mike answered, aware of the pressure of Kevin's head. "Why didn't you tell me Brad was interested in the theater?"

"Because I didn't want him to appear more exciting than you already thought he was."

Mike's hand caressed Kevin's head. The soft curls felt like threads of fine silk. "Is there something going on between you and Brad?"

"You asked me that once before," Kevin reminded him.

"I know, and I never got an answer."

"In prep school. Christ, we were fourteen and you know that scene. After that he was jock all the way."

"I think after that you lost interest because I can't imagine anyone, jock or not, escaping your net if you set your cap for them."

Kevin giggled. "That's the nicest thing you ever said to me."

"It wasn't meant as a compliment and take your hand away from there."

"Why? It feels like it wants company."

"It wants to go to bed."

"I can't spend the night," Kevin lamented. "I don't want to leave mother alone that long."

"It wants to go to bed alone. It's been a long, tough day."

"Is that what you said to Brad?"

"No, I asked him if he thought it was going to snow," Mike answered, knowing Kevin couldn't see the grin which accompanied the line.

"Okay, don't tell me," Kevin said. "I don't give a shit anyway."

Always tell the truth and no one will believe you. It was a maxim Mike had long adhered to and it almost never failed to work.

"I think we should cool it, Kevin." Mike's fingers moved through Kevin's hair methodically, as if he were trying to commit to memory the delicate flow of each individual strand.

"We've both been through a lot these past few months and I think we were looking for a little solace in the storm."

"I found it," Kevin said hopefully, "and I thought you did, too."

"I did," Mike assured him. "And I found something else. Something you wouldn't understand just yet and I'm not ready to talk about. What happened between us happened at the right time and it was good. No…it was more than good. But what happens when we have nothing left to commiserate?"

"You mean the trial."

"I mean the trial. I'm sure Milly will walk away clean and to celebrate we announce…"

"I love you, Mike," Kevin cut in abruptly.

"And I love you, but that word doesn't always have to lead to the sack."

"I'm getting the gate."

Mike bent and kissed the top of Kevin's head. "No. But I

think we should stay away from the hot and heavy stuff till after the trial and then see what's there. We also have to think about Milly. You're not a child anymore and God knows I'm not. Let's wait it out, Kev. Jesus, we don't even know each other very well." They sat quietly for a long time, Kevin's head still on Mike's knee and Mike's hand resting gently on the boy's head.

"Okay," Kevin finally offered.

"You agree with me?" Mike wondered if he sounded disappointed.

"No, but do I have a choice?"

"You could give Brad another chance," Mike said jokingly. "I think he's longing to be led astray. You can also make us another drink."

Kevin stood up and bowed to Mike. "At your service. Anything edible in the pantry?"

"Potato chips, I think," Mike answered as Kevin headed for the kitchen. Mike watched the tight little behind in retreat and felt like kicking himself. Was there such a thing as being too good? There most certainly was.

"Stale," Kevin announced with his mouth full.

"Don't you ever eat at home?"

"Not if I can help it."

He took his drink from Kevin. "Thank you. It looks strong."

"It is. I'm trying to put a little lead in your pencil, as we used to say in school."

Kevin picked up his parka and unzipped the chest pocket. "I want to show you something."

"Non-sexual, I hope."

"That depends on the beholder." Kevin handed Mike a photograph. It was a snap of himself on the tennis court, probably taken at college. Kevin waited while Mike inspected the picture.

"Well," he said, "better than Jack Montgomery?"

Mike shook his head. "Nope."

"As good as Jack Montgomery?"

Mike was still shaking his head. "Nope."

"What do you think?" Kevin asked, reaching for the photo. Mike continued to contemplate. Mike relinquished the picture but grabbed Kevin's hand and pulled the boy down until he was kneeling before Mike.

"I think Jack Montgomery is three thousand miles away and you're right here."

"What about your sermon?"

Mike cupped Kevin's face between the palms of his hands. "No preacher has ever been confronted with the likes of you."

It was close to midnight when Kevin left. Mike was physically exhausted and morally dejected. The spark of passion had been rekindled but, he was just beginning to realize, a fire needed a constant supply of fuel. He was too tired to think about that or anything else. All he wanted to do was to sleep and pull the covers over this godforsaken day. When the phone rang he was tempted not to answer it, but it was his private line and that could mean work. He picked it up on the third ring and prayed for a wrong number.

"Mike Manning here."

"Mike? Frankie Russo."

"The name drew a blank and then Mike remembered. The stringer in Palm Beach.

"I hope I didn't wake you," Russo continued, "but I'm leaving for a short vacation tomorrow and I want to wrap up everything I had pending."

"Have a good time," Mike answered, "and if this is about Pasternak you could have saved yourself the trouble. It's a dead issue."

"Good, because I have nothing to report. I talked to a

neighbor, an old codger who used to play chess with Pasternak. He said Pasternak had a niece who lived in New York, his sister's daughter like you thought, and she was pretty attentive to the old man. Called at least once a week, but that's all he knew."

"Good. I don't think an old chess player would have been thrilled with the life and times of Pasternak's niece."

"You sound tired," Russo answered.

"That's because I am tired. Have a nice vacation, Frankie, and thanks for the help."

"Just one more thing for the record, Mike. Her name wasn't Kennedy. She must have changed it for professional reasons." In her profession, Mike thought, what the hell difference did it make.

"I thought as much. Have fun, Frankie."

"Her real name was Susan Burkowski."

15

The *Ledger* owned and occupied a skyscraper in mid-town Manhattan. The glass and steel structure stood on the site of the original daily, founded at the turn of the century, which had grown from a sensational tabloid to the most widely read newspaper in America. Like a giant octopus its tentacles now circled every area of communications from wire services to satellite television. A corner office in the tower of this megacomplex had Mike Manning's name on the door. Mike seldom visited his home office and when he did it was the cause of great speculation among the secretaries, proof readers, editors and clerks who occupied the floor Mike had not set foot on since Hollywood pipe dreams had replaced peanut politics in Washington. The fact that he had arrived at his office before nine on this windy March day had the rumor mill grinding in exceptionally high gear.

"The President is dead" was whispered repeatedly and seconded only by "Jackie O. is going to marry Robert Redford." The party atmosphere which prevailed and upset the usual office routine did not extend into the inner sanctum. The award-winning columnist wasn't pounding away at his typewriter, ready to shout "stop the presses" a second after pulling his copy from the machine. What he was doing was sitting at his desk, staring at a slim dossier on Stephen Burke taken from the paper's morgue and sipping from a cardboard container of now cold, black coffee.

He had come here after a long, sleepless night because he was certain it was the one place no one would think to find him and because what he had to do could only be accomplished through the vast resources of the *Ledger*. Her real name was Susan Burkowski. Those words had been echoing in Mike's head since Frankie Russo had uttered them some ten hours ago. A case Mike thought firmly closed had suddenly opened, only he had no idea what was going to pop out of its guts. The possibilities were as limitless as Susan Burkowski's relationship to Stephen Burke, née

Steven Burkowski, was limited.

Mike had closed his mind to everything connected with the murders except this relationship knowing, as he had always known, that solving the riddle of the girl called Susan Kennedy was tantamount to solving the mystery of the New Year's Eve massacre. She could have been Steve's niece or cousin. Former wife was impossible because Steve had been married to Milly for ten years and prior to that Susan would have been a child. Sister or sister-in- law was out because of the vast age difference between Steve and the girl.

Mike refused to accept the possibility that there was no relationship, only a chance coincidence. The name wasn't uncommon in ethnic neighborhoods but Mike had pondered over just how the initial contact between the girl and Steve, or Symington, had been made and now he knew. When Susan hit town the first thing she did was contact her long-lost relative, Steve Burkowski.

There was one other possibility that Mike didn't even want to contemplate. She could have been Steve's daughter. If he had married and divorced prior to his marriage to Milly, Susan could very well be Steve's daughter...and Milly's stepdaughter. Remembering those nude bodies and Milly's confession made Mike shudder and turn from this line of reasoning. Knowing how Steve and Symington were using the girl seemed to justify Mike's ruling out a father-daughter relationship. No one he knew, Mike prayed, could use their own daughter for sexual pleasure and profit. Stephen Burke had been many things, all bad, but certainly none as bad as that.

On the other hand, could Steve's actions be measured on a sliding scale? Was a cousin less offensive than a niece and a niece less horrendous than a daughter? Or was the scene even kinkier than poor Milly suspected? If Symington knew Steve was related to the girl, he was killed for that knowledge. But by whom...and why? Steve and the girl were already dead. Who was desperate enough to kill to keep the relationship a secret? Milly Burke, that's who. If Steve's partnership with Susan came to light it would cause a furor at the trial. If it were known that she was related to Steve the resulting coverage would make Watergate look like a dull Sunday tea party.

"Could it have been a woman?" Mike asked.

"Under all that shit it could have been Greta Garbo. But I ain't never seen no hooker dressed like that. You gotta show it, not hide it." A hooker didn't hide it and a man wore pants. At the Chatham Arms no one would look any closer than that to distinguish one sex from the other.

Mike shoved aside the dossier. It had proven useless, being filled with fact and fancy regarding Stephen Burke, most of it culled from Mike Manning's New York. Stephen Burke had been a pop celebrity who was born the day he eloped with Milly and died the night she did him in. No one had ever written one line about Steven Burkowski and that's whose biography Mike desperately sought. There was a light knock on the office door and when Mike shouted "Come in," a small, gray haired woman timidly entered.

"You wanted to see someone from Research."

"I said I wanted the best researcher we employ," Mike snapped.

"You've got her," the woman snapped back. It was instant love.

"I'm Mike Manning."

The woman nodded. "I read the name on the door. I'm Elizabeth Sherman."

"Do they call you Liz?"

"They might have if I were twenty years younger. Beth was my generation's speed."

"How old are you?"

"That's none of your damn business."

"I'd say five years from retirement, give or take a year."

"And you'd be wrong…give or take ten years."

Mike laughed. "Now that we've introduced ourselves, let's

get down to business. Have a seat, please." The woman sat and looked at Mike expectantly.

"Don't you want to know how old I am?" he asked.

"I know how old you are," she answered.

"Does it show?"

"Hardly. I looked over your bio before I came up here." That's what Mike wanted to hear and Elizabeth Sherman knew it. A researcher who instinctively checked the facts before pursuing the unknown. He opened the dossier and showed her a picture of Stephen Burke.

"Know him?"

"The chauffeur who married the limousine."

"Not bad, Liz."

"I got it from your column."

"That makes it even better. He used to be Steven Burkowski, the correct spelling is in here, and I think he was born in Queens. I said think...I don't really know. I want to know everything about the guy, especially family relations, from the day he was born until the day he married the limousine."

"Is this for the trial?" she asked.

"This could..." Mike hesitated. "This could change the nature of the trial."

"Sounds interesting. All hush-hush?"

"Not a word to anyone, especially around this place. Take your time, spare no expense and make your own hours. It's all been cleared with your boss."

"Is there a deadline?" she asked, beginning to rise.

"Not in the newspaper sense of the word, but the quicker the better. Where are you going to start?"

"Backwards," she quickly answered, "from the day he married Milly Lakewood. The marriage certificate will contain the date and place of his birth. From there I'll start from the beginning."

"You're a genius, Liz," Mike said happily.

"That's not genius, Mr. Manning, it's elementary."

"Call me Mike."

"I will…if you call me Beth."

Now all Mike had to do was wait and while he waited he was going to carry on as if he had never received Frank Russo's call. From day one he had shared his thoughts and information with anyone who would listen and someone had led him up the garden path. That someone could be anyone. Now, he was resolved to consider everyone an enemy, including Andrew Brandt…or maybe especially Andrew Brandt. It would be business as usual with the Burke case closed until the start of Milly's trial and the investigation into Stuart Symington's death entirely in the capable hands of the police.

When the phone on his desk rang, Mike looked at it as if it were malfunctioning. When he picked it up he was surprised to hear a familiar voice.

"Mr. Manning? This is Nick. I heard you were in the building and thought I'd pass something on that might be important." Nick was a young man on the staff of the *Ledger* who sorted Mike's mail and phone messages. His routine was to forward the former, carefully separating the significant from the adverts and cranks, and transmit the latter on Mike's recording machine.

"You got a call from a guy named Moe Jacobs."

"And you think that's important?" Mike asked, wondering, as he always did, what Nick looked like. The voice was pleasant and the attitude accommodating. Mike imagined an ambitious nineteen- year-old who was studying journalism at night school.

"He said he worked at the Chatham Arms. That's the hotel where…"

"I know the Chatham Arms, Nicky. What's the message?"

"He said he had some information you might be interested in and you could catch him at the hotel tonight."

"Thanks, kid, it might be something," Mike answered with

little conviction. "Can I buy you a cup of coffee?"

"Shit, yeah…I mean sure."

"I'm on my way to the lobby, meet me in the coffee shop." Nick was nineteen, ambitious and studying journalism at night school. He was also tall, blond and sexy. The coffee break was just what Mike needed to perk up his spirits.

That night Mike attended two cocktail parties. At the first, all the talk was of Stuart Symington who had managed, for the moment, to put Milly Burke in second place on the cocktail party conversation agenda.

"Do you remember the night he…Once he walked into El Morocco with…He used to charter a small sea plane to take him to Fire Island…" And so it went for the better part of an hour. Mike left, never wanting to hear the name Stuart Symington again. At the second gathering he encountered Sam Saxman. Both men tried, gently, to probe each other for information. The result was a stand-off.

"I've got half the private detective agencies in Arizona looking for Joe Stern." Saxman offered. "So far, they've come up with nothing."

"There are other states in the sun-belt," Mike reminded the lawyer.

"But Arizona is my only lead. Christ, we can't comb the entire southwest. Do you think he's dead, Mike?"

Mike raised an eyebrow. "Murdered and dumped? Who do you suspect, Sam?"

"The guy I thought gave Stern the money to blow town."

So Saxman had that figured out, Mike thought, not overly surprised. But had he made the Symington connection yet? "Who do you think wanted the doorman out of the way?" Mike asked.

"Someone who's out to get Milly, obviously. My guess is it's a friend of the girl, Susan Kennedy." Too warm to be a guess, Mike concluded from that. Either Milly had decided to confide in her lawyer, which would be a smart move, or Saxman was even smarter than Mike suspected.

"What do you make of the Symington murder?" Mike asked, following through with the invisible line of connections both were carefully courting.

"I think he went to that hotel like I eat at McDonald's every day. I also think it comes suspiciously close to Burke's death. Those two were closer than most people suspected. You have any idea?"

"A few, but too speculative for publication." The two men looked at each other and silently agreed that both had said as much as they were going to at this juncture.

Then Sam Saxman verbally ended the conversation. "Keep me posted, Mike."

"I'll do that," Mike nodded. As Saxman moved away Mike recalled a time when the lawyer couldn't care less if Joe Stern was ever found…dead or alive. But that was when Saxman thought he had a cut and dried case amounting to an easy win. Now Saxman realized that nothing was what it seemed and, Mike guessed, was doing a little investigating to cover himself.

One thing Mike knew for certain was that the man wisely was not about to impart what he knew…or didn't know. It was a course Mike should have followed three months ago. Mike also suspected that Sam Saxman had never bought Milly's story but was willing to go along with it as long as no complications arose to cloud his defense. Steve's neatly stored clothes, the girl's missing luggage and untraceable past had started him worrying and Symington's murder had turned the worry to fear.

If Sam Saxman had to choose between defending Milly and saving his own face, Mike knew exactly which path the lawyer would take. Mike had to talk some sense into Milly and her son in the very near future.

Mike's next stop was the latest disco factory on the west side of town. He still hadn't decided if he would pay a call at the Chatham Arms but he seemed to be unconsciously ambling toward the hotel. A huge crowd waited outside the disco but the keeper of the sacred gate led Mike past them and into the converted theater.

"Many are called, but few are chosen," Mike quipped. There were as many people inside as the law would allow, all of them in frenzied motion. The music was a decibel lower than the intensity needed to pulverize the human brain. The light show was spectacular and the air contained more smoke than oxygen. It was the paradise of the eighties for the chosen few.

"Liza Minnelli just left," the disco's owner, or the guy who fronted for the real owners, greeted Mike.

"Smart girl," Mike thought as he shook the extended hand.

"But most of the Hollywood brats are here. Cruise, Atkins, Hutton ..."

"I'll just wander around," Mike answered and began to shove his way to the bar. He ordered a drink and the bartender told him his bill had been taken care of. He drank with more guilt than pleasure as he watched the suckers on his right and left fork over five bucks for an ounce of cheap booze.

"You just missed Liza Minnelli."

Mike turned slowly at the sound of the familiar voice and found himself face to face with Brad Turner.

"You could have called and left that startling bit of information on my machine. You do that very well."

"I said I was sorry, what the hell is wrong with that?"

"Nothing," Mike answered, "except I don't know what you're sorry about ... your performance or mine."

"Look, we both acted a little foolish..."

"I didn't," Mike broke in, "and if you think you did, that's your problem."

"I'm going through hard times, Mike."

"So is the rest of the world."

"Before ... with guys, I mean...it was always them who started.

I never did anything."

"Except tease, which you do very well." The lights played over their heads. Red, purple, blue, black. The eyes Mike looked into flashed with fire and then went dead.

"The show closed," Brad said, abruptly changing the subject.

"It never should have opened."

"What do you think of Symington?" Brad tried again.

"I think he's dead. What's your opinion?"

"I think he offered the wrong guy a leading role in the next Symington commercial."

The music, constant and pulsating, began to throb a steady beat inside Mike's head. "Could be, especially if we remember that not everyone is as tolerant as Bradley Turner."

Brad shrugged his shoulders hopelessly. "Can I talk to you when you're in a better mood?"

"Any time you want to talk sense, I'll be all ears and sympathy."

"I've got people waiting."

"Don't keep them on my account."

"Call me." Brad turned and melted into the music, the lights and a thousand arms jerking spasmodically to a disco beat.

Mike shoved his way to the exit. Outside, he gulped the fresh, cold air like a drowning man offered a reprieve. The pain in his chest felt terminal, but he knew loneliness was a lingering disease. He wanted Kenny, now, more than he had ever wanted anything in his life. That relationship had never known a moment's uncertainty because it had thrived on instinct, not learned responses.

He arrived at the Chatham Arms before he knew he was headed there. Moe was behind his old stand reading a newspaper.

"Business as usual," Mike said from the center of the small, dark lobby. Moe looked up and squinted.

"Manning? You're here."

"You seem surprised, or wasn't that you who called the paper."

"It was me."

"And what you have to tell me had better be good or you'll be out of business again."

The clerk laughed. "Your friend, the Inspector, shut us down for twelve hours. We got lawyers, Manning."

"I know all about your lawyers. What do you have for me and why didn't you call the police?"

"Because the police make mountains out of molehills an' my job ain't to finger customers. It's bad for business."

"Why me?"

"You can't arrest anyone for questioning."

"But I could go to the police," Mike reminded him.

"So go," Moe answered, "but I didn't finger no one...you did."

"You have some sense of honor, Moe."

"You wanna know, or don't you?"

"Like you said, Moe...I'm here." The clerk pulled a copy of a show business weekly from under his counter. He thumbed through it, found what he was looking for and turned it toward Mike.

"He was here the night Symington died." Mike was looking at a photo of the cast and crew of a play he had recently seen. They all wore t-shirts that advertised the show's title. Moe's dirty finger nail was pressed under the chin of a smiling Bradley Turner.

16

Another sleepless night. More adding and subtracting and coming to a dozen different conclusions, all logically possible but none even remotely plausible. Bradley Turner was a mixed-up young man but that didn't make him a murderer. Then what the hell was he doing at the Chatham Arms hotel the night Stuart Symington was killed? Moe Jacobs's information, except for identifying Brad, was less than useless. He didn't know when Brad had arrived, if he checked in or was visiting or how long he had stayed. The only reason he knew that Brad was in the hotel that night was because when Brad left he asked the clerk to call him a cab.

"Around this joint," Moe had added, "you remember something like that." The hotel's registry was a joke unless one was willing to believe all the guests were named Joe Smith. So the field was wide open. Was Brad the youth behind the dark glasses who arrived with Symington? Is that why Moe didn't remember Brad's arrival?

But the clerk had insisted to Mike…"I told you an' I told the Inspector, I don't see faces. They're all alike to me. I remember this one because of the cab business an' that's the fucking truth." Symington was into watching and Brad was something of an exhibitionist. Brad had admitted that he had been propositioned by Symington. Had Brad, like Stephen Burke, refused one offer and accepted another? Or had Steve recruited Brad, his stepson's friend?

Mike twisted and turned, fell asleep for what seemed like a brief moment and then awoke to ask himself the same questions, each of which called to mind a variety of answers. But he still didn't have even one answer to the first question he had ever asked regarding the double murders.

"Why the girl, Milly?" The next day, with an urgency he couldn't account for, Mike composed his cryptic message to Joe Stern.

Through his column he had sometimes done investigative work and he decided to use this ploy to reach the doorman.

"Some New Yorkers have bought real estate in Arizona through advertisements and mail order solicitations. Many have been duped and now own plots of uninhabitable, barren desert land. I urge readers who feel they've been the victims of unscrupulous misrepresentation to contact this column. Confidentiality guaranteed."

Sam Saxman and Andrew Brandt would know exactly what he was up to and wish him luck. Now he could only hope that Joe Stern was clever enough to read between the lines. He also hoped Joe Stern was still alive. He called Nick at the *Ledger* and told him to expect a flood of calls and letters from unhappy land owners in Arizona.

"The only one I'm interested in is from a guy named Joe Stern," Mike explained.

"I got it, Mike...and thanks again for the coffee."

"My pleasure. We have to do it again sometime."

"I'm available on two minutes' notice."

"I'll remember that." Mike knew the next thing he should do was pay a call on Andrew Brandt and explain what he knew. He decided, instead, to give himself twenty-four hours to make some sense out of the facts that Susan Kennedy was Susan Burkowski and Brad Turner was at the Chatham Arms the night Symington was murdered. If Brandt's men pulled the boy in now the ensuing headlines, innocent or guilty, would haunt Brad Turner for the rest of his life. Mike thought of that comfortable home in Sands Point and Brad's parents whom he had talked to on New Year's Eve. Certainly they all deserved a chance.

Mike ruled out contacting the boy before paying him a surprise visit. He called the car service and arranged with Frank Evans to be driven to Sands Point. After last night the last person Brad would be expecting was Mike Manning.

"You know a lot of rich folks," Frank said as they pulled into the driveway leading to the Turner home.

"And right now you're one of them. How much did you win?"

Frank pretended not to hear the question as his eyes scanned the Turner's front door. "What's the address of this place?"

"Not again, Frank. Believe me, it won't work a second time."

Mike pressed the door buzzer and waited. There wasn't a sign of life around the place which led him to believe the Turners were still in Palm Beach. He pressed the buzzer again, long and hard, remembering that Brad's room was on the third floor of the house. A minute later he was rewarded with the sound of the door bolt being retracted. When the door finally opened a very surprised Bradley Turner said, "Mike!" and took a step backward.

"You said you wanted to talk." Brad pulled himself together and smiled amiably.

"I said when you were in a better mood. Come on in." As Brad stepped aside to let Mike enter he spotted the car in the driveway.

"Who's with you?"

"My driver."

"Tell him to come in, it's a long drive from the city."

Mike motioned to Frank and the driver got out of the car and came up to the front door.

"I'm Brad Turner," Brad said. "Make yourself comfortable. The kitchen is that way and so is the bath. Help yourself."

"Thank you, Mr. Turner," Frank said with a smile.

Brad turned to Mike. "You want to go upstairs?"

"That would be nice," Mike answered as he once again began to follow Brad up the flight of carpeted steps.

"Say, Mr. Turner," Frank called.

Brad stopped and turned. "Yes?"

"What's the address of this place?"

"Seven Forty-two Linden…"

"Thank you kindly," Frank waved with a grin.

"What was that all about?" Brad asked over his shoulder.

"He's into numerology," Mike answered, shaking his fist at Frank.

"I think he's into bookmakers."

When they got to Brad's apartment he offered Mike a beer. Mike accepted and when they had settled down he asked Brad if he had another job lined up.

"An interview with Jonathan Prince," Brad said. "He's looking for an assistant."

Mike nodded. "Very good. He's the hottest producer in town."

"Do you know him?"

"We've met," Mike said. "And what were you doing at the Chatham Arms hotel the night Stuart Symington checked in and out, so to speak?"

Brad's blue eyes opened wide. "I didn't know the place had a name."

"You know it now and you knew it when you read the papers the next day."

"I don't know anything about Stuart Symington, I swear it, Mike." Brad was scared and couldn't hide the fact even if he had tried.

"I want the truth," Mike said. "The police won't interview you in your third floor suite while you serve them beer. They've shaken down every whore and hustler who keeps a room at that flea bag but they can't get their hands on one transient who was there that night. You're it, my boy."

"How do you know I was there?"

"The clerk identified you. He told me but not the police. Seems he has a sense of loyalty to his clientele. You made the mistake of asking him to get you a cab when you left. Christ, at a place like that it's like asking for room service. I suspect you also tipped him five bucks and that's really why he remembers you. He linked you to your pretty picture in Back Stage."

"I went there to get laid," Brad said, looking at his sneakers.

"You what?"

"I've been there before. You can check with a girl named Karen on the second floor."

"Now that's a statement if I ever heard one. A girl named Karen on the second floor of the Chatham Arms hotel. Some alibi you got, baby. She would swear the Pope screwed her if you paid her enough."

"It's the truth," Brad shouted, jumping out of his chair.

"Why did you go to a place like that to get laid?"

"I like to pay for it," Brad said, looking at his sneakers again. "After that night with you..."

"Oh, shit," Mike snapped his fingers in the air. "After me you had to prove you could still do the trick with a woman. Do you do that every time you make it with a guy?"

"Okay...yes...I do." Brad forgot his embarrassment as he continued. "If the police question me, Mike, my parents will know...and my friends. Please believe me. Shit, you've got to believe me. It's the truth."

Mike wondered what was more important to Bradley Turner, his parents or his peers. "This is just crazy enough to be true," Mike thought aloud.

"It is true," Brad pleaded.

"Sit down," Mike ordered and Brad obeyed reluctantly.

"And look at me. Now...what about you and Kevin?"

"What about me and Kevin?"

"You know what I mean and I'm not looking for a vicarious thrill. This is serious business, Brad, and I want honest answers."

"We used to fool around when we were kids."

"And later on?" Mike probed.

"He got interested in someone else."

"And what did you do?"

"I was never that into it," Brad answered.

"I don't give a shit what you were into or not into. Just the facts, Brad...come on, give."

"I played both sides of the fence."

"Always with prostitutes," Mike stated.

"Most of the time." Brad looked thoroughly miserable.

"Why?"

"I don't know why," the boy said, shifting his position.

"Because you were afraid," Mike told him. "Because if you couldn't do it they wouldn't laugh or spread the word around."

"You ask a lot of questions for a guy who knows all the answers."

"Don't get smart. And remember, I'm holding all the aces. Did you ever make it with Kevin again? I mean after the prep school circle jerks."

Brad shook his head.

"But you knew Kevin was gay."

"I knew."

"So what was all that crap about the night we met? Those two roommates you had set up for you and Kevin."

Brad shrugged. "It was a game. Pretend you tried to score but couldn't and then get it on with your buddy. Shit, didn't you go to college?"

"I went...but I never pretended anything of the sort," Mike said, not very kindly. "Are you saying that you expected to get it on with Kevin that night?"

"I thought about it."

"Why, after all that time, did you think Kevin would be interested?"

"Because we had become very close again."

"And when did that start?" Mike asked.

"I don't know. About a year ago…"

The word hit Mike like a cannon ball. Year…year…year. He took his frustration out on Bradley Turner. "Have you and Kevin resumed what I interrupted that night?" he asked crudely.

"I don't think that has anything to do with Stuart Symington."

No, it didn't, but it had a lot to do with Kevin Lakewood's honesty.

"You're in no position to argue," Mike answered, "just tell me what I want to know or tell it to the police."

"I don't like being blackmailed and the police aren't going to ask me about my sex life."

Mike laughed mockingly. "Climb out of your ivory tower, kid. You're a frequenter of the Chatham Arms…your sex life is *all* they're going to ask you about."

"I haven't even seen him since that night. We've talked on the phone but that's all." Brad looked squarely at Mike as he added, "Besides, I think he's found another new interest. Kevin is partial to father figures."

Now Mike laughed. "You've got spunk, kid. There you sit, scared out of your wits, but that doesn't stop you from taking a jab at the competition."

"I don't compete for boys, Mr. Manning. One blow job is very much like another."

"My, my. And I thought I had a special place in your heart."

"You do," Brad shouted, jumping out of his chair again. "That's why I was sorry that happened between us the way it did. It's what I wanted to talk to you about." He turned from Mike and walked to a window.

"With you I was ready…" His voice trailed off.

"To lose your virginity?" Mike continued to needle.

"Call the police," Brad said, looking out at Long Island Sound. "Do whatever the fuck you want, but just leave me alone."

Mike got up and went to him He put his hands on Brad's

shoulders and very gently pressed his chest against the boy's back. "I'm sorry," he whispered into Brad's ear. "Three people are dead. All murdered. Kevin's mother, my very good friend, is responsible for two of them. I'm trying to make some sense out of all this useless taking of lives and...and to prevent more of the same. You happened to walk into the middle of the whole damn mess."

Brad shook his head. "I don't know anything about it. I didn't know Stephen Burke very well and I knew Stuart Symington even less. All I know is that Kevin is going through one bitch of a time right now. I think he feels it's all his fault."

"We all feel that way when something happens to people we love, but the truth is we aren't our brother's keepers. For a while I thought Milly's predicament was my fault."

"Why?"

"It's a long story with an unhappy ending." He turned Brad around, still holding him, and looked straight into those startlingly blue eyes. "Are you telling me the truth...about the Chatham Arms?"

"Everything I told you is the truth, Mike." They looked at each other for a long time, their faces inches apart. Mike's finger traced a line across Brad's jaw. He could feel the boy's beard already beginning to break through his morning shave.

"When all this is past history," Mike said, "we'll talk. I never meant to make fun of your feelings. I've always been very sure of myself and sometimes forget that others aren't as lucky."

"I never kissed a man," Brad said.

Mike bent his head and their lips touched for a brief moment. "Another hurdle traversed, Bradley."

"Stay for a while, Mike."

"I can't...for your sake as well as mine."

"I know what I want now," Brad insisted.

"You might know what you want, Brad, but you don't know who you want."

Mike sulked as Frank Evans raced back to the city. "The bookie won't take any bets after four," he explained when Mike told him to slow down.

"And if you're dead you can't place a bet either."

"Every time you see one of your white chickens you turn mean," Frank answered, pushing harder on the gas pedal. Mike moaned. He should have driven himself to Sands Point. "If you hit with seven forty-two I want half your winnings."

"Mean," Frank mumbled, "real mean."

Mike thought he might live to regret it but he decided to believe Brad Turner. He had to start narrowing down the field of suspects sometime so why not start with the least likely candidate — or did he mean one of the most attractive candidates? When he got back to his apartment Mike checked his answering machine. Nothing from Elizabeth Sherman and it was too early to expect anything from Joe Stern. He showered and dressed for the evening, determined to stick to his business-as-usual routine. Twelve of his twenty-four hours were down the tube. Tomorrow he would have to see Brandt. In his bedroom he picked up the picture of Kevin on the tennis court at school.

"I lied," he said to the photograph. "You're better than Jack Montgomery." Then, like a doting parent, he thought what a good match Kevin Lakewood and Bradley Turner would make. Still looking at the photograph he imagined those perfect legs propped up on his living room coffee table, the blue robe parting…The doting parent succumbed to the jackrabbit. He picked up the phone and dialed the Fifth Avenue apartment.

"Hello," Kevin answered.

"I just wanted to touch base," Mike said.

"You could do that much better in person."

17

The next morning a messenger delivered Elizabeth Sherman's report to Mike's apartment. The writing was as clear and concise as the writer. Fact after fact was stated and footnoted with its source. Steven Burkowski, at age twenty, had married Natasha Pasternak who was then eighteen and pregnant. Six months later she gave birth to a girl who was christened Susan. The Burkowskis stayed married until Steve went to work for the limo service. A year later he divorced Natasha and two years later he married Mildred Hamilton Lakewood.

Mike's worst fear was now a reality. The story was typical of the Stephen Burke that Mike had known. A shot-gun wedding and a simple wife who undoubtedly allowed him to indulge his fancy with every skirt who caught his eye. When Steve went to work for the limo service his horizons broadened. He met women who were not only pretty and receptive, they were also rich. To expand he had to lighten his load — so it was goodbye to Natasha and Susan. Then Steve caught the brass ring, but his turned out to be solid gold. Mother and daughter moved in with Uncle Vladimir and two years ago Mrs. Burkowski died. Susan disappeared into the sunset.

Mike tossed the carefully typed sheets of paper aside. Every fact raised more questions than it answered. No way would Mike believe that Steve was using his own daughter for fun and profit. Then why did he tell that outrageous lie to Milly? And if Steve hadn't...why did Milly lie to Kevin? That he could answer. She would lie to turn cold-blooded murder into a crime of passion. Milly didn't know who Susan was and simply assumed, from experience, that the girl was sleeping with Steve. But they were both naked...

"Jesus H. Christ!" Mike shouted. "Steve's clothes. He was undressed after he was shot."

Mike tried to imagine Milly arranging the murder scene

like a set designer but the picture refused to form in his mind. Milly was the most genteel, compassionate person he knew. She just couldn't do it. Frustrated, he began to pace the room. The thought that he was missing something that was right under his nose returned to haunt him like a bad dream. He knew he would walk his feet off before he came up with the single fact that would bring everything into focus, so he did what he had to do. He called Andrew Brandt.

The desk sergeant on duty told Mike, "Inspector Brandt is in Philadelphia on business. We don't expect him back today."

Mike got himself another twenty-four hours. He couldn't call Sam Saxman until he had spoken to Brandt so he called Kevin Lakewood. If Mike couldn't talk some sense into Milly, maybe her son could.

Then he wrote his release on Susan Burkowski. The *Ledger* would get it five minutes after Andrew Brandt. Kevin had promised to be at Mike's apartment at eight. It was close to ten when he arrived.

"Saxman came to see us," he said. "I couldn't leave until he did. I think he's backing out on the case, Mike." The boy looked as distraught as he sounded.

"I don't blame him," Mike answered. Kevin took off his jacket and tossed it over the back of a chair.

"Thanks."

"I told you once, if you want sympathetic bullshit you've come to the wrong place."

"I didn't believe you then and I don't now." Kevin said.

"I got sidetracked but the party's over, Kevin."

"What is this, Mike? First Saxman puts me through the third degree and now you're starting on me."

"Saxman is trying to get the truth out of your mother because he knows the story she's telling is pure crap. The man isn't going to walk into that courtroom and come out with egg on his face. I want you to tell Milly to open up. Her life may depend on it."

"But she *is* telling the truth, how many times do I have to repeat that? All she's leaving out is the business between Steve and Symington. I told her she should…"

"Susan Kennedy was Steve's daughter," Mike stated bluntly.

Kevin stared at Mike with his mouth open and then made a sound that was halfway between a giggle and a moan. "You're crazy," he finally responded.

"I might be, but that doesn't change Susan Kennedy's real name. It was Susan Burkowski." Mike waited for Kevin to digest the news and offer an explanation but when the boy finally spoke he asked Mike if he could have a drink. Mike went to the kitchen and came back carrying the bottle and two glasses. He poured out two generous shots and handed one to Kevin.

"This won't change her name either," Mike offered along with the drink. In a gesture of sympathy he just denied possessing, Mike put his hand on Kevin's shoulder and squeezed. Kevin covered Mike's hand with his own.

"Milly's in trouble," Mike whispered, "and only the truth can help her. She's got to level with Saxman."

Kevin nodded and looked at the shot glass of bourbon Mike had given him.

"Go on, drink it," Mike urged. "It might help."

"But it won't change her name," Kevin answered.

"You're not going to freak out on me, Kev."

"No…but I don't know what I should do."

Mike took the glass, still untouched, from Kevin and sat on the floor next to Kevin's chair. "Talk to your mother," he began slowly, as if instructing a student, "and tell her the facts. That's all you can do. The rest is up to her."

"Mike, you don't think my mother knew who the girl was?"

"No. I'm sure she didn't. But I think Stuart Symington knew and he's dead. I also think your doorman, Joe Stern, knew something and he disappeared. Symington must have got to the doorman, but who the hell got to Symington?"

"Why did Steve tell my mother that story?" Kevin asked.

"I don't think he did, Kevin."

"Are you saying my mother made it up? No, Mike, no…I won't believe that."

"Then come up with a better answer."

"It's what Steve told her," Kevin said, more animated than he had been since his arrival. "He was a diabolical bastard who didn't give a shit about anyone or anything except himself. He said it to upset my mother."

"Then why did the very mention of the girl's name upset Symington?"

"Because maybe it was true," Kevin answered. Mike shook his head.

"I'm not buying that and once you've cooled off neither will you."

"But they were naked," Kevin protested. "He was going to…"

"No one knows what they were going to do and anyone can undress a corpse." Mike countered.

"You think my mother…"

"I'm giving you the facts," Mike said adamantly, "and from now on that's all Saxman and the D.A. are going to be dealing with. I know it's not easy, Kevin, but we have to face it. Milly's got to level with us. It's her only chance at beating this." Kevin made a motion to reach for his drink and Mike handed it to him. He downed it in one gulp.

"Are the police trying to connect Steve's death to Symington's?"

"No," Mike said. "Right now I'm the only one who suspects a tie-in but I think Sam Saxman is right on my heels. No one believes Symington went to that hotel for a party."

"Don't be too sure," Kevin told him. "We all have our secrets…our little sexual quirks no one knows anything about until we get caught."

That's a fact, Mike thought, recalling Brad Turner. "The Chatham Arms is a virtual Pandora's Box," Mike added aloud.

"A lot of respectable people go to places like that, Mike, including Brad Turner."

For a moment Mike was thrown off center by what appeared to be Kevin's ability to read minds. He tried to sound disinterested as he asked Kevin how he knew this.

"Brad likes whore houses," Kevin answered with a shrug. "The old macho routine. He frequented one at school that was the pits of this world and he mentioned one he had visited here in the city. Christ, he wanted to take me there."

"Did he specifically mention the Chatham Arms?" Mike asked.

Kevin shook his head. "If he did I don't recall and what difference does it make? I'm just trying to tell you that a lot of people go to those places and Stuart Symington could have been one of them. I don't see any connection between Steve and Stuart."

Mike hardly heard what Kevin was saying. Instead, he tried to quickly calculate how much it was necessary for Kevin to know to save Brad's skin.

"Do me a favor, Kev, and don't mention this to anyone."

"Don't mention what?"

"That Brad gets serviced at places like the Chatham Arms," Mike responded.

Kevin thought about this for a moment and then nodded knowingly. "So the Chatham Arms was Brad's haunt. Interesting... and how did you find this out?"

"How I found out isn't important, but I went to see Brad today and I'm convinced he's clean. If the police get wind of it they'll drag Brad in and he'll never be able to live it down. Let's keep this in the family, okay."

"Very generous of you, Mike," Kevin said, "to go out on a limb to protect poor Brad. You two have become as thick as thieves…no pun intended, naturally. May I ask what else you and Brad discussed, besides Brad's mixed-up sex life?"

"You," Mike answered honestly. If Kevin was surprised he didn't show it. "And why not, it's all in the family." Then he turned nasty. "This relationship is getting a little crowded, or is that how you like it? Tell me, do you intend to sleep in the middle or do we rotate positions?"

Good, he's jealous, Mike was thinking. That should keep his mind off more serious matters like asking if Brad was at the hotel the night Symington was killed.

"I think Brad's in love with you," Mike answered to reinforce this line of thought.

"Is that why I haven't seen him in months and why he keeps popping up under your protective wing? If that's being loved I'll pass, thank you."

"He told me he's worried about you, Kev."

"I think he should be worried about himself. He's the boy wonder of the Chatham Arms, not me."

Mike sighed. "Let's drop it for now. Just promise me you won't say anything about Brad frequenting that hotel."

"My lips are sealed and I don't give a shit where Bradley dips his wick. Do you know when we were kids he used to let it hang outside his jockeys so it looked bigger under his jeans and…"

"I don't think I want to hear this," Mike broke in, grinning in spite of himself.

"Neither do I, as a matter of fact."

Kevin reached behind his chair for his jacket. "It's been a pleasure, we have to do it again real soon."

Mike put a restraining hand on Kevin's knee. "You stay right where you are until we finish our business."

"Namely?"

"Your mother," Mike answered curtly. Those two words brought into focus the pettiness of their little quarrel. Kevin looked shame-faced and Mike felt like a cad.

"Is that nurse you hired still with Milly?"

"Yes," Kevin said. "My mother is better but they get along and I didn't see any reason to let her go just yet."

"Good. I want her with Milly when you tell her about Susan."

"Will you tell her?" Kevin asked hopefully.

"No," Mike said quickly. "I want this to be between you and Milly. If she opens up to anyone it'll be you."

"What do you expect her to say?" Kevin sounded on the brink of tears.

Mike shook his head without speaking.

"You're thinking the worst, aren't you, Mike?"

Mike looked up at the boy.

"Yes," he answered simply. Kevin moved slowly from his chair to the floor and heaved himself into Mike's arms. "Sometimes people we know… change," Mike whispered, stroking the soft curls which had become almost an obsession with him. "Things happen in their lives and they act without thinking. We all have a breaking point…" Mike ambled on, holding Kevin tightly and making little sense.

When he finally worked up the courage to drop the metaphors and speak directly he felt like a murderer. "I want you to be careful, Kevin."

"She would never hurt me," Kevin sobbed. "Never… never…"

"And Kenny never meant to hurt me."

It was close to midnight when Kevin left. Mike was mentally drained and could hardly keep his eyes opened. When his private line rang he picked it up more out of habit than desire to answer the call.

"Nice try at contacting the doorman," Brandt began, as

usual without the preliminary amenities of polite telephone conversation. "But you could have saved yourself the trouble. Dead men can't read...not even your column, Manning."

"Oh, no," was as much of a response as Mike could offer.

"Not murder, Manning. Not this time. He packed it in like respectable folk...in a ward at the General Hospital in Philadelphia. The poor slob was probably trying to make it to Arizona and got as far as Philly when he got sick. We figure he took a furnished room or a hotel to rest up before he made the big push to the promised land. Three months later he was still resting. The idiot never called a doctor...probably too scared. He went to the emergency room of the hospital a couple of days ago and died yesterday. Are you still there, Manning?"

"I'm here," Mike answered. "How did they get you in on it?"

"Seems Joe carried an overnight bag to the hospital. When he died they opened it expecting to find a comb and toothbrush and guess what they came up with instead? Twenty-five thousand bucks in tens and twenties. The hospital called the police and they checked Joe's I.D. to the All Points Bulletin file. I got the call."

"Did he say anything before he died?" Mike asked, knowing the answer.

"Are you kidding? At that point he didn't even have the energy to cough. But he didn't have to say anything. He was toting the D.A.'s entire case in the trunk of his car. Two suitcases of clothes Joe would never wear unless he was going to turn drag queen in Tucson...which I seriously doubt. Among the finery was a man's shirt with a hole right over the part that once covered Stephen Burke's heart. The blood stains are dry but identifiable." Mike felt like an actor in a horror film, moving rapidly from one nightmare to another.

"Someone paid him to dump the girl's clothes and..."

"Someone?" Brandt laughed. "Wake up, Manning, it's all over. We checked with Milly Burke's bank. The lady withdrew twenty-five thousand in tens and twenties on January three, the day after she was released on bail." The room began to spin around him and Mike sank to the couch before the floor came up to meet his head.

"But he didn't disappear until almost two weeks later," Mike managed to get out.

"He called in sick, remember? We thought he was home nursing himself and didn't know he had beat it till we tried to contact him. I figure he was told he was helping Milly cover for one of Steve's indiscretions. When he learned the true story he turned to jelly, was given the bag full of money and told to scram or be implicated. She must have gotten to him a day or two after Saxman got her out on bail."

"What happens next?" Mike asked because there was nothing left to say.

"The D.A. is going to request the bail bond be revoked. He wants Milly under lock and key now." Mike placed the phone in its cradle, not knowing or caring if Brandt were still talking. He stretched out on the couch and covered his face with his right arm. His mind refused to function and all he desired was the peaceful oblivion of sleep.

18

The sky was streaked with light. His body ached and it took some time before he was oriented as to time and place. Once, he and Kenny had fallen asleep on this very same couch while watching a late, late movie on the telly. He wondered if everything that had happened in the past three months was the plot of that long-forgotten film. If he moved his arm would he feel Kenny sleeping placidly next to him?

He reached out but all he felt was pain from his cramped muscles. Would things be different now if Kenny were still with him? Perhaps not for Milly but Mike certainly wouldn't be involved with two boys who were still learning the difference between love and sex.

He sat up rubbing the back of his neck and squinting at the early morning light. Was it possible that a little over a year ago he was living in monogamous bliss? It didn't come to him in a sudden burst of cognizance but rather like the cascade of a gentle tide lapping at the fringes of his mind. Still more asleep then awake he heard Bradley Turner's voice as if it came from a radio set to herald in a new day.

"Because we became very close again…about a year ago." He moved his feet to the floor and other voices, as if someone were toying with the radio's dial, floated in the air.

Kevin Lakewood: *"Susan Kennedy…I met her about a year ago…"*

Theresa Allen: *"And then about a year ago she meets this guy…"*

Andrew Brandt: *"I've been trying to nail that bastard for a year…"*

His eyes came to rest on the powder like ashes in the fireplace and he heard his own voice. *"Just about a year ago…he took his service revolver, loaded it and blew his brains out ."*

He giggled, like a child in possession of something awesome and beyond his ken. It seemed impossible but it had to be the answer. He was the link…the common denominator. The mysterious something that was right under his nose was his own self. He stood up feeling like a stranger in his own home. Suddenly nothing was what it seemed but he needed one piece of information to make the impossible a reality.

He went to his desk and began leafing through his index of phone numbers. He found Jerry Hagen's and dialed the Westchester number. He listened to it ring ten times before he realized the Hagen household was probably still fast asleep. A very young boy finally answered with a timid hello.

"Is your father there?"

"They're sleeping."

"Wake him, son, please. Tell him it's Mike Manning and it's very important."

It seemed like hours before Jerry picked up the phone. "Mike? Do you know what time it is?"

"I wouldn't be doing this unless I had to, Jerry. I want to know when Susan Kennedy came to work for the agency."

"Christ," Jerry yawned, "I don't remember."

"Try. Give me an estimate," Mike begged.

"Ask the police or call the agency after nine," Jerry reminded him

"By then it might be too late."

"For what?" Jerry asked, annoyed.

"It doesn't have to be exact, Jerry. Even a guess would do." There was a short pause and then Mike began to mouth the words as Jerry Hagen spoke them.

"About a year ago..."

"Thanks, Jerry. I owe you."

Susan had come to New York two years ago but didn't go to work for the Symington Company's ad agency until a year later. Everyone's life had changed "about a year ago," including Mike Manning's. No...especially Mike Manning's.

What had seemed crystal clear to his sleepy brain was now a jumble of facts, like a mathematical equation, to his wide-awake mind. Nature intervened and he went to the bathroom to relieve himself and splash cold water on his face. In the kitchen he began brewing a pot of coffee, unaware that he was still dressed in the pants and shirt he had slept in. Everyone's life had changed, for better or worse, a little over a year ago. Mike had lost Kenny. Brad had gained Kevin. Susan gained a job and introductions to the "right people."

She also, suddenly, gained a father. It had to be Steve behind Susan's sudden appearance on the social scene, but who was paying her bills? The same guy who arranged for her job ... Stuart Symington. The mathematical equation appeared to be strictly one-sided. Everyone was a winner except Mike.

He burned his mouth on the scalding hot black coffee. He waited for it to cool and went back to his equation but it played the same way. Everyone appeared to be on a roll "about a year ago" except him and Ken Farley.

He sipped his coffee without tasting it. None of it meant anything. He felt like the fool Jerry Hagen insinuated he was and went in search of a pack of cigarettes. He found them on his desk, on top of the wire photo from Palm Beach that Brandt had given him. He picked up the photo and forgot his cigarette.

Mike wasn't the only loser a year ago. A boy named Robert Cimino had lost his life. He sat at his desk staring at the fuzzy black and white photograph. It had to mean something. A boy dies in Palm Beach and a girl gets a job in New York. The suspected murderer becomes a benefactor.

A boy dies in Palm Beach and a man suddenly remembers he has a daughter. A boy dies in Palm Beach and a young man begins seeing an old friend.

Those two bodies on Milly's bedroom floor and the one carried out of the Chatham Arms hotel were the end of a story that began a little over a year ago in Palm Beach. Steve Burke was blackmailing Stuart Symington.

Mike laughed aloud at the simplicity of the solution. Again he looked at the photograph and laughed louder. Steve couldn't help his daughter when she arrived in the city because he didn't have the means. Robert Cimino's death gave him the means. It sounded like the old give and take game. Steve must have finally hit Symington for a fortune and was pulling out with his daughter when Milly walked in on them.

Mike remembered his cigarette and lit it. So why did Milly kill them? She would have been the happiest person on earth to see Steve go...especially if he wasn't taking any of her money with him. And who killed Stuart Symington? A two-bit hustler? He began to unbutton his shirt. What he needed was a shower and shave and a one-way ticket off cloud nine.

A lot of things happened to a lot of people about a year ago and most of them didn't even know Palm Beach existed. So the link he thought would solve the riddle was nothing more than his conscience reminding him of Kenny when he had begun to indulge himself physically.

The human mind is a wondrous, if not always helpful, mechanism. He went to his bedroom to undress, wondering how Milly's conscience would react to the news that she had murdered Steve's daughter. She had reached her breaking point once before...when she saw Steve and the girl in her bedroom. But to rearrange the scene and implicate the doorman, not to mention the story she composed about Steve and Symington, convinced Mike that there was indeed such a thing as temporary insanity. He hoped, for Milly's sake, it didn't now become a permanent condition.

It also occurred to Mike that Milly must have known or suspected that Symington was helping the girl and that kernel of knowledge led to the tale she told Kevin. As he reached for his robe he noticed the other two, one blue and one white, hanging side by side in his closet.

"Give and take," he thought sadly. "What did Kevin give a year ago when he started his campaign to take Brad back?" Some varsity football player most likely...no, a swimming star would be more to Kevin's taste. Or was it that other person Brad mentioned? The one Kevin got interested in when he stopped fooling around with Brad? If it was, it had lasted a long time. Kevin and Brad must have been fourteen or fifteen when their little romance ended.

"And weren't those the years Kevin was supposed to be nursing a crush on me? You tell a pretty good story yourself, kid." Mike smiled at the incongruous image of Kevin Lakewood pining away with love for someone almost old enough to be his father.

Mike underlined the word almost...

"Jesus Christ, no!" He dropped his robe and ran back to his desk. He picked up the wire photo and saw it animate, like a nickelodeon, before his startled eyes. The two men and the young boy; smiling, shaking hands, parting. Parting like a curtain to reveal the owner of those perfect masculine legs they had so conveniently obscured. In a sudden fit of rage Mike tore the photo to shreds. If this were possible then anything was possible, including his connection to the events of a year ago. But he had nothing to do with the Palm Beach affair, it was strictly a police matter.

He stood as still as a statue, his brain short-circuited by the flow of information pouring into it. Strictly a police matter... Below his window he could hear the sounds of the city preparing to greet a new day. People were beginning to move about as he stood, rigid, his eyes fixed on the scraps of paper which now littered his desk. The symphony of moving cars, horns and squealing brakes grew louder. The expressway would soon be bumper to bumper with people on the move. He concentrated on this one thought as his fingers moved his Rolodex like a mouse on a treadmill. Brandt picked up on the first ring.

"You've been jerking me off for weeks," Mike said, surprised at the steadiness of his voice.

"Manning? What the hell is this?"

"And now you're going to do exactly what I tell you to do."

"What do you know, Manning?"

"What you should have told me when you started using me as your undercover man. You're a fucking bastard," Mike cried.

"Take it easy. I can explain…"

"Explain what? That you used Kenny to bait your fag and then stuck me on the same hook. You stink, Brandt, you stink like a sewer rat."

"You've got it all wrong, Mike."

"For the first time I've got it all right. You've been playing me for a patsy…"

"Will you shut up and listen to me," Brandt shouted back. The sound of traffic outside his window intensified. Time… time was running out and he didn't have ten seconds to spare for Andrew Brandt.

"No, Brandt, you listen to me and listen good. Call the police in Sands Point and tell them to go to the Turner house and arrest Bradley Turner. You hear me, Brandt? Now…do it right now."

"Turner? Who is he? Why should I arrest him?"

"Because if you don't you'll be investigating another murder… and the one after that will be your own." Mike slammed down the phone and sank into a chair. He laid his head on the desk and closed his eyes in a futile effort to stop the burning pressure which threatened to burst like a ruptured dam

"… and I made love to him…"

Then he let go and sobbed into the pieces of paper that comprised the jigsaw puzzle he had been trying to mount for over a year.

19

Andrew Brandt was sitting in his office when Mike arrived dressed in the pants and shirt he had slept in. The reporter was unwashed, unshaved and uncombed; his eyes were red and slightly swollen.

"You look like hell," Brandt said without a trace of malice.

"It's been one of those mornings, Inspector. Did you get the boy?"

Brandt nodded. "They're bringing him in. Now will you tell me what I'm risking a potential harassment suit for ... Palm Beach, Fifth Avenue or the Chatham Arms?"

Mike eased himself into the chair opposite Brandt's desk. "What was Kenny working on when he died?"

"I thought you knew."

"I want to hear you say it."

"He was assigned to the Palm Beach case," Brandt sighed, turning to avoid Mike's steady gaze.

"Why didn't you tell me?" Mike asked, continuing to stare, his voice a monotone.

"First tell me who Bradley Turner is and why I'm having him brought here."

"I'm not telling you shit, Inspector." Mike spit out the words, his mouth twisted in an ugly curve. "Why didn't you tell me?" he repeated.

"Can't we talk about it when you've calmed down and I know what's going on? I don't like being in the dark, Mike."

"Neither do I but that's where you've had me for over a year." Mike let out a short, hysterical laugh... "Over a year, Inspector, that's the bottom line and I don't want to talk about it later. I want to talk about it now."

"Let me get us some coffee ..."

"I've had my coffee and a good cry. I hope that doesn't upset your manly sensibility but then I don't give a fuck about you or your sensibility so let's get on with it. Why, Inspector...why?"

Brandt opened his arms in a gesture of despair. "Ken Farley was assigned to the case. I thought Stuart Symington was guilty and I still do. Then Kenny...you know what happened to Kenny. I smelled a rat and from the day Kenny died I made Symington my personal vendetta. I checked and rechecked with the police in Palm Beach. I had men shadow Symington around the clock until the Commissioner ordered me to stop and officially close the case. I continued on my own, checking and rechecking, following his every move, mostly through your column, and came up with a big, fat zero on every count.

"I was too close to it and I knew it," Brandt continued. "Everything he did took on a sinister air, every affair he had... and I gave up counting them...looked suspect. I told you I thought he was chummy with Stephen Burke but you didn't buy it. Well, he was. The men I had tailing him reported that he and Burke met on more than one occasion in that piss-elegant hustler bar in your fancy neighborhood."

Mike's eyes opening with surprise was his first reaction to Brandt's story.

"I had just about given up when Burke turned up dead. But I needed a new pair of eyes and a clear head. I wanted someone who knew nothing and suspected nothing to begin at square one and come up with something or nothing and I was ready to accept either conclusion."

"You knew I would try to help Milly and you picked me for your patsy," Mike said, shading in the detail to Brandt's rough outline.

"Not a patsy ..."

"A patsy, Inspector. First you suggested the tie-in between Burke and Symington, then you brought up the Palm Beach case and handed me that wire photo while I paid for lunch. I was the guinea pig you placed in the maze to see which way I would run."

"But you found your way out," Brandt said, pointing a finger at Mike. "Now tell me how you did it and what you know."

Mike shook his head. "Tell me why, Inspector, tell me why."

"I just told you. I needed an objective point of view."

"You didn't need an objective point of view a year ago. You needed help."

"Because I only suspected. Suppose I was wrong…"

"You're leaving something out that I have a right to know." Mike's eyes never left Andrew Brandt's face as he spoke. "Tell me or we'll sit here till hell freezes over."

Brandt's tone reflected a mixture of relief and fear. "When Ken was a rookie, a good year before you knew him — " he raised his head and looked at Mike — "he went out with Stuart Symington."

Mike covered his mouth with his hand but not before a groan, like a cry for help, escaped his lips.

"Kenny was young and naive, he thought New York was Babylon reborn and he wanted it all." The confession began to take on the air of a sermon. "What he was was an overgrown teenager still wet behind the ears."

"How do you know?" Mike asked.

"I saw him get into Symington's car one night after he got off duty."

"How did Symington get to him?"

"How did he get to all of them? Money, that's how. My men make shit and when they get offered a hundred bucks to lie on their backs and look at the ceiling they find it hard to turn down."

Mike shook his head. "Kenny would never do it for money."

"Not Kenny. He did it for the glamour and excitement. He must have read about Stuart Symington for years and thought he was being asked to join the charmed circle."

Mike remembered a young man who went to a fancy barber and wore expensive cologne. A young man with ears too big and a body so slim he could never get a suit to fit. A young man who wanted to be everything he wasn't until Mike showed him he was loved for just being himself. And Stuart Symington had dared...

"It was just once," Brandt was saying. "Kenny was young and naive but he was smart and decent. He must have spotted Symington for the phony he was and never looked at him twice again."

Mike looked bewildered and tried to focus his attention as he asked Brandt why he had assigned Kenny to the case.

"I didn't," Brandt answered as if Mike should know better. "I was on holiday when the case came in. It was pot luck and Ken Farley drew the short straw."

He leaned forward as he continued. "When I found out what was going on I asked Kenny if he wanted off the case."

Mike held up one hand. "How did Kenny know you knew about him and Symington?"

"He didn't. But this was just about the time you were on your big crusade and Kenny laid it all out in the open for me. He told me you two were lovers...as if I didn't know already, along with every man in the precinct...and said you were going public. He thought I wanted him off the case because it involved a gay man and a boy."

"What did Kenny say?"

"He said he was a policeman and knew how to do his job."

Kenneth Farley knew how to do his job. What he didn't know was that a fancy barber and expensive cologne couldn't change him into the man he had never accepted as himself. When he came to the big city he took with him the small town prejudices he had been taught were irrefutable truisms. His relationship with Mike was his first step toward independence and fulfillment but even that he conducted like a school boy doing it in a darkened locker room.

When Mike asked him to step out into the light he hesitated, sought reassurance and got it from his lover. Just when he was about to take the giant step and become his own person Stuart Symington re-entered his life. Symington threatened to denounce as filth what Ken was now ready to announce with pride. His alternative was to give Symington a clean bill of health without a proper investigation and lose forever the pride he took in the uniform he wore.

What Mike had strove to make clear now seemed muddy. Pressure combined with confusion and years of self-righteous indoctrination culminated in depression. Kenneth Farley couldn't come up with a winning hand so he turned over his cards and got out of the game. As the facts became clear to Mike he looked at Brandt and with a note of amazement announced,

"Kenny didn't kill himself because of me."

"Are you crazy? He would have killed for you, but not himself."

Mike nodded a thank you and Andrew Brandt, slightly embarrassed, expressed his belated sympathy without saying a word.

"If Stuart Symington were alive now I would kill him," Mike stated.

"I know. And that's the answer to your Why. I didn't tell you because you would have killed Symington and what good would that have done anyone? I didn't have one fact. Had I been wrong all I would have accomplished was telling you what Kenny gave his life to protect you from learning."

"How could I have been so blind?"

"You were hurt. I never saw a man hurt so much and go on living."

"Then why did you keep sticking it to me?" Mike exclaimed. "Why didn't you ever let me forget that Kenny had killed himself and maybe I was to blame?"

"I was trying to light a fire under you," Brandt explained. "I wanted you to see what I suspected. I wanted to shake you until you realized that Ken Farley might have given his life to uphold his honor but never to hide what he was and who he loved. If you thought he was ashamed of your relationship the sin was yours, not his."

"And I betrayed him," Mike thought aloud.

"You betrayed yourself." There was a knock on the door before it opened to reveal Harold Sadowsky's boyish face.

"They just brought Turner in, sir. We're got him in the holding room."

"Thanks," Brandt nodded. Sadowsky glanced at Mike as if he weren't sure who he was looking at before withdrawing his head from the closing door.

"We play the final hand," Brandt said with a note of uncharacteristic melodrama, "and it's your move. How did you find out Kenny was working on the Palm Beach case? Who is Bradley Turner and why is he here? Is it Burke and the girl or Symington?"

"They're all the same," Mike said, getting slowly to his feet.

"So it is one piece of cloth," Brandt nodded knowingly.

"We had a deal." Mike laid his hands on Brandt's desk and bent toward the Inspector. "I investigate without interference from you and pass on what I learn before I write it. I'm holding you to that."

Brandt shook his head. "I'm holding someone for no reason. When he screams for a lawyer I lose my pension."

"Give me ten minutes alone with Bradley Turner. He won't call his lawyer or anyone else."

"Can I trust you?" Brandt asked, seeming to weigh Mike's offer.

"I promise you you'll close the book on three murders before the day is over."

"But can I trust you," Brandt said again.

"No…but you can't stop me either."

Brandt hesitated a moment, then stood and went to the door. He called Sadowsky's name and the young policeman seemed to materialize from thin air.

"Take Manning to holding and give him ten minutes with whoever the hell's in there." Mike followed Sadowsky down the hall until they came to another officer seated in a chair, chewing gum and reading a newspaper.

"He's got ten minutes." Sadowsky nodded at the door the cop was obviously guarding He put down his newspaper, glanced at his watch and opened the door for Mike. Bradley Turner's face was ashen under his heavy growth of morning beard.

"You told them," he shouted as Mike came into the room.

"I didn't tell them anything."

"Then why am I here?"

"I have ten minutes alone with you," Mike told him.

"Then what happens?"

"That depends on what you tell me."

"I told you everything you wanted to know," Brad all but sobbed. "What the hell more do you want?"

"You answered my questions, but I didn't ask the right ones." Mike pushed the hair from his forehead as he spoke. Brad looked at Mike as if seeing him for the first time.

"You look like hell."

"Thanks. You don't look too swift yourself."

"What's going on, Mike?" Brad pleaded.

"You said two things to me yesterday," Mike began. "One. You thought Kevin felt responsible for his mother's crime. Two. You said Kevin is partial to father figures. You weren't taking a poke at me. Those two statements are related and I want to know how."

For an answer Brad turned his back on Mike.

"Do you know where Kevin is now?" Mike asked.

"How could I? I've had a busy morning, Mr. Manning."

"I'll give any odds you name that Kevin Lakewood is burning rubber on the expressway." Mike raised his voice as he added, "On his way to Sands Point...to kill you."

Brad swung around.

"Either I'm still asleep and dreaming or the whole fucking world has gone off its rocker. First I get yanked out of bed and arrested for no earthly reason and now you tell me my best friend is going to kill me. What am I supposed to do now? Thank you for saving my life? Holy shit..."

"He wants to kill you because you're the only one who knows the truth. You're a walking time bomb," Mike said.

"Now tell me what I want to know."

"What people do is none of my business, Mike."

"I have ten minutes," Mike reminded him . "Last night I told Kevin about our talk. I told him we discussed your relationship with him. He knew you didn't betray any confidences but I think, for the first time, it occurred to him that one day you might. The closer you and I got, the more of a possibility that became. Kevin couldn't take that chance, so you had to die."

"I don't understand any of this. What truth did I know? What the fuck is happening?" Mike gripped Brad by the shoulders and shook him roughly.

"Was Stephen Burke fucking Kevin?"

Brad lowered his eyes as if the shame were his. "Yes."

Mike dropped his hands. "You thought Kevin's mother found out and that's why she killed Steve and a girl who was in the wrong place at the wrong time."

"Isn't that what happened?"

"Stay right here," Mike said, touching Brad's cheek. "Don't move from this room. I'll tell them to get you breakfast and anything else you want."

"Tell me what's going on," Brad begged.

"Later. Right now you stay put and if they try to toss you out of here confess to anything you can think of but don't leave this room."

Ten minutes to the second Andrew Brandt left his office. "Are they still in there?" he asked the cop on duty.

"Manning left, sir, but the boy's inside."

"Left?" Brandt shouted.

"Where did he go?"

"I don't know, sir." The cop looked worried.

"He told me to get the kid some breakfast and keep him locked up for the rest of the day."

"Since when are you taking orders from a gossip columnist and take that gum out of your mouth when you talk to me."

"Yes, sir. I thought...'

"Don't think. It might interfere with your chewing. Now open that door." Brandt walked into the holding room to confront a man child with a heavy growth of beard who looked on the verge of tears.

20

"I want a room."

Moe Jacobs squinted in the dim light. "Is that you, Mr. Manning?"

"I thought you only recognized faces on dollar bills."

"You look like shit."

"I made an effort to match the surroundings."

"You really want a room?"

"You heard right."

Moe reached under his counter and came up with a key hanging from a metal tab. "I don't like this," the clerk whined.

"No one asked you." Mike took the key and handed Moe a piece of paper. "Call this number and ask for the name I've written under it. Keep trying till you get him. When you do, tell him who you are and that you know he checked into the Chatham Arms with Stuart Symington. Say you want to see him and discuss a deal."

Moe looked scared. "Suppose he's not interested."

"Convince him. When he gets here," Mike looked at the metal tab, "send him to number two-twenty-eight."

"How will I know him?"

"He'll dazzle you with his beauty. And get me a pot of black coffee and a pack of cigarettes."

"We ain't got room service." Mike laid a fifty-dollar bill on the counter.

"Initiate it."

He didn't know how long he had been sitting in the dark room, listening to frantic whispers, nervous giggles and doors in constant motion. Thanks to the blackout shades it was always half-past midnight at the Chatham Arms. The coffee pot was empty and the few drops remaining in his cup had the consistency of cold mud. He had five cigarettes left. The rest, some long and some smoked down to the filter, filled a tin ashtray shaped in the relief of a reclining nude. He heard someone moving in the hall and knew instinctively it wasn't a buyer or a seller. He saw the door knob turn hesitantly.

"It's not locked," he called. Kevin Lakewood entered the room. He looked perfect. That was the word for Kevin Lakewood. Not handsome or pretty or beautiful…but perfect. From his lush brown curls to his small nose and square jaw down to his tailored jeans and leather loafers, Kevin Lakewood looked perfect.

"I knew it was you," Kevin said, closing the door and leaning his back against it.

"How clever."

"Can I explain…"

"Explain?" Mike laughed wildly. "You are either a comedian or certifiably insane."

"He used me," Kevin said.

"Are you talking about your late stepfather? Poor, poor, little Kevin. I bet you seduced that bastard ten minutes after you learned you could do more with it than pee. Or did you have him before Milly? Let me see…you were only twelve but all male and, I suspect, a yard long."

"Please, Mike. Just let me tell it from the beginning." Kevin took a step forward.

"No. Let me tell it and stand right where you are. You can fill in the blanks along the way."

"May I have a cigarette?" Kevin asked politely.

Mike shook his head and smiled. "No, you may not." He took one from the pack, lit it and blew smoke into the stale air. "The Christmas before last you were in Palm Beach with Stephen Burke. Symington was there showing off his new chicken. Did

Symington kill Robert Cimino?"

"He was feeding him a little bit of this and a little bit of that. I guess he gave him too much of one or the other." Kevin sounded like a stranger. The voice of a boy had been replaced with the hard, curt tones of a belligerent man.

"So we've stopped pretending," Mike said and Kevin answered with a nod of his head.

"The boy died and Symington called the only other prick he knew he could depend on. Stephen Burke. Steve, with your help I'm sure, moved the body and told Symington to scram. There was a flap in Palm Beach and a young detective was assigned the case in New York. Symington knew the cop from a long time ago…and very briefly. He didn't lean on the cop. Symington didn't have the nerve or the intelligence. He told you and Steve he knew the cop on the case and the two of you told him to put the pressure on the investigating officer."

"I didn't know Ken Farley was your friend," Kevin said quickly.

"You knew the officer in question killed himself."

"But I didn't know he was your lover until my mother told me about it."

"So when I told you my tale of woe you already knew all about it."

Mike paused but Kevin didn't answer.

"You are the consummate actor…besides all your other assets, of course. Now we're back in New York and everyone is happy. If a young man was foolish enough to take his own life rather than walk away from a murder…well, that was his hard luck. Then the dealing and double-dealing began. Steve began to lean on Symington. Nothing heavy at first. As I remember Steve he would have played it like a medieval inquisitor. One sadistic step at a time. First he made Symington get Susan a job. Then he had him buying her clothes and picking up little bills here and there. Am I right so far?"

"Steve told me she was his daughter and I didn't believe him. I thought she was one of his girls."

"When did you decide he was telling the truth?"

"When he had Symington introducing her to our crowd. Steve treated her like a princess but never laid a hand on her. I knew then."

"Why did Steve want the girl on the social scene?"

"I think it was her doing. She had some crazy idea about becoming a model or an actress. That's why she wanted the job at the agency."

"And Steve didn't tell anyone she was his daughter because his background was pure shit and so was his reputation. The newly-awakened father didn't want that rubbing off on his little girl. Right?" Kevin nodded.

"I think it went something like that."

"So Steve had a daughter and a steady supply of ready cash. He needed you like he needed a bigger dick. So Kevin goes out with the garbage and runs to Brad Turner for consolation. Tell me, did you think Steve would be jealous?"

"I thought he would notice," Kevin answered.

"And you thought wrong. Did you really believe that fucker was in love with you?"

"I loved him," Kevin said.

"Loved him? He was your mother's husband. Did that thought ever occur to either of you?" Mike shook his head in disbelief. "How much were you paying him for his love?"

"I didn't have any money of my own."

"But he took your lunch money whenever he could get his hands on it. You dumb shit...you were Steve's ace in the hole. When he got ready to leave Milly you were the trump card he would use to walk away with every penny of your mother's fortune. When his daughter came along he decided it was time to leave and set up housekeeping. That's what happened, isn't it?"

"He said he wanted to wake up to the first day of the new year in his new life. He wanted half my mother's money." Kevin spoke rapidly, his eyes moving as if the scene were being enacted on an imaginary screen. "He told Susan to pack and come to the apartment. He was going to tell my mother everything. I said I would give him all the money I could pull together and he laughed at me. The bastard laughed at me like I was his lackey."

"Did your mother know any of this?

"Nothing. When Susan arrived it was going to be a surprise. A big shock."

"Why didn't you tell your mother who Susan was?"

"At first because I didn't believe Steve. Later because I knew Steve didn't want anyone to know and I was afraid…"

"He would tell Milly her little boy was the star fucker of Ryder Prep. His knowledge being first hand, I might add."

"I was young and I thought he liked me," Kevin cried.

"You weren't that young and a year ago you were twenty-one, so spare me the tears." Mike put his cigarette out in the crowded ashtray.

"Milly was out when Susan arrived, bag and baggage, but you were home. You knew where the gun was…"

"He laughed at me. They both laughed at me. He called me a cocksucker. In front of that piece of trash he called me that." Kevin delivered the line so passionately Mike almost believed the tears were real.

"You shot them both. When your mother came home you told her…"

"The truth," Kevin shouted. "I told her the truth."

"Bullshit. You told her your version of the truth. You said Steve had seduced you and was running off with his girlfriend. He wanted money. Milly felt responsible for bringing Steve into your life. After your story she must have felt like the madam in a male whorehouse with her son as the main attraction. With a little help from you she decided to take the blame for the murders knowing there was a good chance of getting away with it. You set the scene but you overcompensated. Steve was packed to go and you unpacked, forgetting to leave even a pair of socks on display in your haste. You told Joe Stern to make Susan's luggage disappear, then you wrote the time table of events for him and hinted that his cooperation would make him a rich man.

"You made him believe that Steve was up to his old tricks and you wanted to spare your mother embarrassment. When he learned the truth it was too late. He had gotten rid of Susan's luggage and was up to his ass in conspiracy. He had no choice but to give the police the timetable you made up.

"When I started asking Symington questions about Susan Kennedy he turned to jelly and, true to form, called you. He was worried about Palm Beach and his own neck. He thought Milly had killed Steve and the girl and was happy to see Steve dead and off his back. I put a kink in his pretty dream when I mentioned Robert Cimino in the same breath with Steve's murder. By accident, I should add. I didn't know what I was talking about at the time. Symington knew about you and Steve and who the girl really was. You couldn't trust him to keep his mouth shut...I mean there were no cops left to blackmail. If the D.A. started shaking Symington down, especially on the witness stand, you didn't know what he might say and where it would end."

Mike paused long enough to light another cigarette. "You told me yourself that Brad mentioned the Chatham Arms to you. He didn't know it had a name but must have given you the location. You couldn't meet Symington in public so you took him here. With Symington's predilections it was the perfect place to get rid of him...or so you thought."

"Symington would have gone down the black hole of Calcutta if he thought there was a pretty boy waiting for him in the pit," Kevin injected.

"But he would have had it scrubbed and decorated first. Milly looked like the wrath of God that next morning. She suspected something, didn't she? Your mother knew Symington didn't come here with a hustler so you made up that story about Steve and Symington and the girl. It was such a good story you talked Milly into saying she knew about the trio from day one. After the distorted version of your relationship with Steve you fed her she would have believed anything so long as it didn't implicate her son. You had infested her with enough guilt to confess to a crime you committed but another murder would have been more than even a mother could tolerate. She believed you because the alternative was unbearable. "Is there no end to your ingenuity?"

"How much of this have you told the police?" Kevin asked.

"None. It's a Mike Manning exclusive."

A glimmer of hope lit up Kevin's eyes. "You're not going to tell them, are you?"

"No, I'm not," Mike smiled. "If I do they'll arrest you and our friend Sam Saxman will get a string of psychiatrists to tell the court exactly what you are. A psychopath. One of those rare individuals who exist without a conscience. A liar who's convincing because he actually believes the stories he fabricates. An egomaniac who thinks he's a million miles above the world, sitting on the right hand of God. They'll put you in some posh sanctuary for a few years and then another string of psychiatrists will declare you cured and send you home to take your rightful place in society."

"Don't let them lock me up, Mike."

"I won't. But let's save that till I'm finished. I told you that I was going to call Joe Stern and the next day he disappeared. I told you I talked to Symington and the next day he was dead. I told you about my discussion with Brad...did you enjoy the ride to Sands Point this morning?"

"It was rushed and rather fruitless." Kevin was almost laughing. He appeared completely at ease and acted like a schoolboy rehashing a prank with a friend. "You're not going to tell anyone, are you Mike?"

"I said I wasn't. But tell me, how was Brad going to get his?"

"I just went to talk to him," Kevin answered.

Mike nodded knowingly. "You went to tell him how important it was that no one ever learn about you and your stepfather. You would tell him that because of it, your mother killed Steve and a girl who happened to get in the way and should it become common knowledge, it would kill your mother. The scene would end with tears and a seduction, complete with blazing fire and expensive pot for good measure. And all the while you would be studying the terrain and plotting because you couldn't trust Brad any more than you could trust Symington…or anyone who happened to be a mere mortal.

"You had used this hotel once and twice would be a bit much, even for you. But it's very lonely in Sands Point and Brad jogs every day. A hit and run accident would be just your cup of tea. If not today, then tomorrow or next week…but I didn't know your frame of mind and wasn't taking any chances so I got Brad out the minute I realized who was behind this unholy nightmare. If I can believe you, all I did was deprive the boy of the best fuck of his young life…and probably his last."

"I went to talk to him," Kevin repeated, "and I came here to talk to you. Look," he opened his arms wide as if inviting Mike to search him, "I'm not armed."

Again, Mike let out a hysterical laugh. "Not armed? Just how stupid do you think I am? You carry a lethal weapon wherever you go. Your own self. The perfection that is Kevin Lakewood. The perfection your twisted mind thinks no one can resist. You flaunt it like the Whore of Babylon, taking and taking until you're bored, but God help anyone who gets bored with you. Rejection is the one thing your inflated ego refuses to accept. You came here unarmed because you think you're invulnerable. Milly told me she wanted to get help for you ten years ago. Christ, why didn't she do it?"

"I'm asking you for help, Mike," Kevin answered hopefully. "Let's get out of here and go someplace…"

"Like my apartment?"

"That would be perfect," Kevin said excitedly. "Let me tell you my side of the story. It's not what you think. They all deserved to die, Mike. They were lechers."

"Was Ken Farley a lecher?"

"That was an accident," Kevin began anxiously. "I didn't plan that. But I made you forget him, didn't I, Mike? Didn't I?"

"Almost. Unfortunately for you...almost." Mike slowly pulled the revolver out of his jacket pocket.

"No...you wouldn't...you said..."

"I said I wasn't going to tell the police and I'm not. This is strictly between us."

"You love me, Mike. I know you do. Put the gun down... please." Kevin's hand touched the fly of his jeans. "Remember... remember how you liked to watch me undress." His hand moved casually over the mound of his crotch. "We can do it here...now. That's what this place is all about. Then we can talk and I'll tell you..."

The first shot went through Kevin Lakewood's moving hand and shattered his penis. He opened his mouth to scream but only a gasp erupted from his throat along with a trickle of blood. The second shot tore his belly open. His brown eyes stared at Mike as he doubled over and fell to the floor. Mike looked at the body which now lay at his feet and reaching down he began to stroke the mass of soft curls he would never touch again.

"You're right...we do have to accept the bad for the ultimate good."

"Murder, for any reason, is never acceptable."

"And what difference did it make. It left Kenny dead and that was all that mattered."

As if coming from a great distance, Mike heard the sounds of the Chatham Arms being evacuated. The report had prompted a learned response to the hotel's inhabitants...flight. Then silence until footsteps...thumping, determined...brought Andrew Brandt bursting into the room. He paused before the body of Kevin Lakewood.

"The pretty boy."

"Not so pretty now." Mike's voice reflected the serenity of his demeanor. He sat, legs outstretched and hands, one still holding the gun, resting placidly on his lap. "It took you long enough to get here."

"Considering what I had to go on I don't think I did that bad." Brandt looked down at the body. "Late...but not too bad."

"You talked to Brad Turner?"

"He told us what you got out of him. Then we went to see your friend, Milly Burke, and got the rest from her before...we had to take her to a hospital."

Mike couldn't muster up the sympathy to say, "Poor Milly."

"From there we went everyplace we could think of, from your apartment to Sands Point. I was beginning to believe you ran away with the pretty boy. Finally we got a call from Moe, the clerk downstairs, and he told us you were here with the kid. He said he was worried. After five hours he gets worried," Brandt moaned.

Brandt took a step toward Mike and carefully removed the revolver from Mike's hand. "How convenient, a service revolver."

"Not for him it wasn't," Mike said, pointing.

Brandt took out his handkerchief and carefully wiped the gun's handle. "You helped me trap him and he tried to escape. I shot him."

"I don't want anyone taking the rap for my moment of glory."

"Stop giving the police department orders, Manning." Brandt hefted Ken Farley's service revolver. "And get the fuck out of here. Go downstairs and call the precinct. Then go find a typewriter...you might win a Pulitzer prize for this one."

MIKE MANNING'S NEW YORK

April 1...ELIZABETH TAYLOR arrived in the Big Apple along with spring looking slim, svelte and gorgeous. Over lunch at Le Perigord Liz confided that she would *not* be getting married this year...MILDRED HAMILTON LAKEWOOD BURKE, recuperating from the tragic events in her life in a Swiss clinic, called to say she's getting better every day and misses all her friends in New York. We miss you, too, Milly…Tom CRUISE told me at the Ginger Man that he's ready to take on adult roles. All interested adult roles should contact Tommy, not this column…Socialite BRADLEY TURNER, now toiling for producer Jonathan Prince, is happily mounting several of Prince's hit shows for the Strawhat Circuit. When Bradley isn't busy mounting he can be seen around town with a variety of partners. Brad thinks variety is the spice of life…That Hollywood star who told everyone who would listen that a Beverly Hills shrink had cured him of his gay inclinations is in desperate need of a booster shot…Inspector ANDREW BRANDT is a shoo-in for Commissioner when the mayor appoints our town's next Top Cop and it couldn't go to a more deserving member of New York's Finest…Mrs. Stuart Symington, mother of the late STUART SYMINGTON, has donated a cool million to the AIDS Foundation in memory of her son who did not die of that disease…For those who asked, the pretty girl on my arm at Four Seasons was Ms. THERESA ALLEN who is unattached and looking…The CHATHAM ARMS HOTEL will be the first flea bag to bite the dust in the wake of the Times Square renovation plans. Amen…To those who responded to my call for real estate losers in the Sun Belt I promise that help is on the way…I know a guy who hit the numbers for a bundle, TWICE, by playing the street addresses of rich folk. If you lose your shirt contact your banker and not this column… Yours truly is off to Wimbledon to report on the Grand Prix of tennis matches and anything else that catches my eye. I'll be betting heavily on America's Jack Montgomery to walk away with the big prize…

THE END

ABOUT THE AUTHOR

When word processors began to replace typewriters on Madison Avenue, Lardo began moonlighting as a budding novelist. His first effort, CHINA HOUSE, was published by Alyson of Boston and did well enough for Alyson to publish his next novel, THE PRINCE AND THE PRETENDER. A third for Alyson, THE MASK OF NARCISSUS, introduced Mike Manning, investigative reporter, and was the most popular in the Alyson series.

A play, ALL ABOUT STEVE, was published by Dialogus and had several readings in New York.

After three novels, Lardo turned from part time to full time novelist and left his native New York City to live permanently in his beach house in Amagansett. This resulted in his first 'Hampton' mystery, THE HAMPTON AFFAIR, published by Putnam. It was well received by both reviewers and readers, sparking his second 'Hampton' mystery, THE HAMPTON CONNECTION.

At this time Lardo's editor at Putnam noted a similarity between Lardo's droll humor and acerbic wit and that of the late best selling author Lawrence Sanders. Looking for a writer to continue Sander's popular Archy McNally series, Putnam contracted Lardo as Sanders' successor. McNALLY's DILEMMA, Lardo's first in the series, was an instant best seller and Lardo and Archy were off and running. Five more McNally's followed: McNALLY's FOLLY, McNALLY's CHANCE, McNALLY's ALIBI, McNALLY's DARE and McNALLY'S BLUFF. All were NY Times Best Sellers.

What's next for Vincent Lardo? Another McNally? Another Hampton mystery? A Mike Manning revival? A return to the stage? Stay tuned and be the first to know.

The author acknowledges the trademark status and trademark owners of the following wordmarks mentioned in this work of fiction:

Bergdorf Goodman: Bergdorf Goodman

Calvin Klein: Calvin Klein

Chevy: General Motors

Henri Bendel: Henri Bendel Inc.

Impala: General Motors

Mickey Mouse: Disney Enterprises, Inc.

Seconal: Eli Lily and Company

Sports Illustrated: Time Inc. A Time Warner Company

Tiffany: Tiffany (NJ) LLC

Xerox: Xerox Corporation

Lightning Source UK Ltd.
Milton Keynes UK
UKOW02f2155210915

259000UK00001B/13/P